Praise

"Perspective is everything. Nowhere is this more evident than in *America Acirema* where Cesi Davidson examines what it means to be in America, but not of it. Malcolm X once said 'I'm not going to sit at your table and watch you eat, with nothing on my plate, and call myself a diner.' This concept undergirds Davidson's excellent collection of plays which explore the hope and despair of life in America as lived by those who experience it from the periphery. Each play is uncomfortable and uncompromising, animating our history and bringing texture to our shared past and evolving present. Perhaps the most impressive aspect of Davidson's writing is her ability to grapple with some of the most difficult social and cultural issues of our time while simultaneously infusing humor and light throughout these stories. She has created characters that are so real, you can almost believe they might be stopping by your house for Sunday dinner to discuss their passion and pathos, their joy and yearning — their love and pain."

Malcolm X quote: The Ballot or the Bullet, Speech in Cleveland, OH, April 3, 1964

Heather R. Parker, PhD, Professor of African American History
Creator of the Community Memory Project

The Community Memory Project is an oral history collection and archive that brings to light the suppressed stories of the hidden lives of African Americans and their communities in segregated Florida.

Saint Leo University Community Memory
Oral History Collection and Archive
https://slulibrary.saintleo.edu/communitymemoryarchive

"Cesi Davidson's quiet personal strength emerges in characters she writes that demand, 'Listen to me.'These short plays are long on fearlessness, and thoughtful surprises. They have large and luminous themes that are digestible enough for reflection. What Cesi Davidson gives us in *America Acirema* is a chance to observe some of the complexity of our unresolved communication. Nothing changes unless something changes including limited and stubborn perspectives. We need playwrights who are able move us emotionally with crafted entertaining stories while reminding us of our responsibilities to each other. I praise this sista who is helping to lead the way."

Camille Yarbrough
Award-winning Producer, Singer, Dancer, Actress, Poet, and Activist
Author—*Cornrows*

"*American Acirema* is a brilliant collection of plays by Cesi Davidson that examines life in twenty-first-century America. The preface to the collection references the ritualized celebration of the Thanksgiving feast with its adult and child tables as well as table scraps caught by rodents as a powerful allegory for life in America. Each of the twelve plays examines how the complexity of human relations is still undergird and permeated by these exclusionary practices that appear ritualized, almost natural. However, each play is also a story belonging to a particular place, an insight into our evolving hope and our evolving despair."

Rosario Swanson, PhD, Professor of Latin American Literature and Gender Studies at Emerson College.

"*America Acirema* by Cesi Davidson is most definitely a wake-up call. It is not for the faint of heart or thin-skinned. It is a keen observation, intelligent, and, at times, witty probe on the complexities of America's dark history of colonialism, slavery, and race relations. Dr. Davidson turns the tables on us to make us see the grave injustices of the systemic racism, sexism, and homophobia that permeate our culture. The plays are short, spirited stories presented in ingenious theatrical ways. They inspire critical thinking as well as playful interaction that form new perspectives on old problems. The rebirthing of America has always been forward then backward then forward again and backward again, hence the title. A hearty congratulations to Cesi Davidson on more brilliant and illuminating works!"

Whitney Hamilton
Director, Writer, Actor, Visual Artist
Producer Bjornquist Films-UNION

"In this collection of new short plays, Cesi Davidson unveils a powerful political dimension to her ever-expanding art. Her earlier work was fanciful, wildly imaginative, and often hilarious. All those qualities can still be found in *America Acirema*, but Davidson has bigger things on her mind now as she tackles head-on the problems at the root of a sick society—racism, sexism, class. Though always entertaining, these plays are also deeply disturbing and at times painful. Audiences and readers will squirm with discomfort as Davidson reveals in subtle and not-so-subtle ways the cruelty and ignorance of a society built on a foundation of racism. Davidson is angry, but she is far from hopeless. As her characters learn, the path to resolution of our difficult and complicated problems begins with brutal honesty and ends with understanding and love."

Zachary Sklar, Oscar-nominated screenwriter
(JFK, with Oliver Stone)
Author—*The Work: A Jigsaw Memoir*

America Acirema

Plays by Cesi Davidson

Articulation NY

Shandaken, New York

Articulation NY
P.O. Box 192
Shandaken, New York 12480
www.articulationny.com

America Acirema

This book is fiction. Names, characters, businesses, organizations, places, events, and incidents either are the product of the author's imagination or are used fictitiously. Any resemblance to actual persons, living or dead, events, or locales is entirely coincidental.

Library of Congress Control Number: 2023947462

ISBN: 979-8-9889431-0-5

First Edition, Second Printing, September 18, 2024

Front Cover Photograph: Copyright © 2022, Celeste Rita Baker

Adinkra graphic credit: © Can Stock Photo / cteconsulting

DWENNIMMEN-Humility together with Strength

Bear: courtesy Ayumi Nakao, created 2020

Back cover photo courtesy Tim Geaney

Book and cover design by Kathryn Wilham

For my fellow Americans
and those who want to know more about us

When Acirema set the table, it was with full intention. This was the place for those to be served and those to provide service. Typical of many Thanksgiving feasts, there were set places, expectations, unwritten requirements, and secret codes in plain sight. A framework for generations. The Adult Table. Full Banquet. Luxurious linen, hand woven by small children. Bone china made from Indigenous bones. The utensils: precious metals and gems made for hands genetically shaped for power, control, and selfish self-nourishment. All embossed with "In God We Trust."

Sitting at the Adult Table was by implicit or explicit invitation. There were place cards strategically placed around the rectangular table in order to forge alliances and to keep the conversation informative. When Acirema noticed empty seats at the Adult Table the observation caused a slight pause. Seats at the Adult Table were inherited by bloodline. Whether the chair was occupied or not, the seat still belonged to the entitled. Absence from the table didn't deny the entitled the benefits of inclusion. Outside the dining room there were those with their noses pressed against the windows, looking at the feast on the dining table, and longing to be fed. Dinner was served but not for them. Every course timed and presented with precision.

Distanced from the Adult Table was the Child Table. A small square table and small chairs, all uncomfortable for adult bodies. Set with baby spoons, sippy cups, and hard plastic compartment bowls dotted with a protein, a starch, and a green vegetable. A small portion of a beverage was provided but no dessert. Those without vision and influence didn't require or receive the same quality of meal as the sovereigns. Yet a hallucinogenic effect of inclusion was created by the proximity of the aromatic delicacies on the Adult Table. Acirema found the longing, the delusion, and the pitiful gazes amusing. The assumption of possible advancement to the Adult Table emboldened those seated at the Child Table to bicker for attention and selection. The selected few had their uncomfortable, undersized chairs relocated behind an Adult chair and were told to protect their partitioned bowls, their sippy cups, and their baby spoons vehemently. And be grateful.

There were those considered rodents. They ran back and forth in crazed frenzy scrambling for crumbs from either table. Occasionally, the sitting classes spilled sweet nothings and strategized around the chaos that ensued. When there were no crumbs from on high, those considered rodents reached a state of scarcity anxiety. They ate each other.

There isn't a single description of how Acirema transformed into America. Written history tells us sustainable change only occurs after an unrelenting revolt of the masses. Oral history passes down two stories of those considered rodents. In one story the Child Table is destroyed. It becomes clear that there are two groups: the haves and have-nots. In the other story, those considered rodents stop eating each other. They gnaw at everyone seated.

The final story is unfolding.

Cesi Davidson
June 2023

Contents

Shut the Door

Open & Shut Scenarios

Characters:
Male and Female People

Setting:
Open room with white walls. There is an open door in the middle of the wall upstage. Two folding chairs are a few feet apart and face the audience.

(Lights Rise)

(Enter man wearing a tie. Enter man wearing a baseball cap. They both look around and then sit on the chairs.)

CAP MAN: Door's open.

TIE MAN: Yes, I can see the door is open. Someone needs to shut the door.

CAP MAN: Yes, someone needs to do that. Don't you think you should shut the door?

TIE MAN: No.

CAP MAN: Where I come from the last person through the door has to shut it.

TIE MAN: I'm not from that neighborhood. I suggest you shut the door.

CAP MAN: Aren't you concerned about the door being opened?

TIE MAN: Yes I am. Are you concerned?

CAP MAN: I'm as concerned as you. No, I'm concerned more because in the first place, I was the one who brought it to your attention that the door had been opened.

TIE MAN: You didn't need to bring it to my attention. There's nothing you could bring to my attention. I will always have more attention for everything that needs attention than you simply because I am who I am. I knew the door was open.

CAP MAN: I knew the door was open first because I was the first person to come through the open door.

TIE MAN: Irrelevant. The door was still open when I got to it that's how I know the door was open…because I came through an open door in order to come inside.

CAP MAN: It's relevant because that means I had attention on the door before you.

TIE MAN: I could have come through the door first.

CAP MAN: Maybe you could have but you didn't.

TIE MAN: But I could have.

CAP MAN: And we will never know if you could have because you didn't and I did and it's done. (Examines the door) Maybe the door can shut by itself? It's not a heavy door. (Comes back to the chair and sits down)

TIE MAN: You were near the door, you could have shut it.

CAP MAN: Yes I could have but I didn't because you think you are too good to shut the door. You think it's beneath you.

TIE MAN: Yes, it is. I've shut enough doors in my life and I'm not going to start shutting doors again without being compensated.

CAP MAN: You think you should get paid to shut the door?

TIE MAN: That's right.

CAP MAN: Do you think…not that I care what you think…but do you think I should get paid to shut the door?

TIE MAN: No. If there were money involved, and there isn't maybe you could get a token amount, a stipend, an acknowledgment that you shut the door.

CAP MAN: Greedy and selfish.

TIE MAN: No…we should get paid according to…according to…

CAP MAN: How much would you get paid according to?

TIE MAN: A six-figure salary and stock in the door company.

CAP MAN: It's a good thing there's no money involved because if I knew after walking through the door that I wouldn't make the money you could make I would refuse to shut the door on principal. (Pacing) so if you got paid you would shut the door?

TIE MAN: Not necessarily. There would be a chance but I doubt it.

CAP MAN: Not for cash money?

TIE MAN: There would be a chance, but I doubt it. Maybe.

CAP MAN: You know…because shutting doors is beneath me… it's for men like you.

(Lights Out)

(End of Scene)

(Lights Rise)

(Enter Anna-Woman I. She looks around.)

POLLY: Anna…come on in…this place is great.

(Enter Anna-Woman II.)

ANNA: Polly… It's beautiful.

POLLY: I love it.

ANNA: I wouldn't change anything. Plain walls…could always do colorful accents…but honestly it doesn't need anything. Simple is best, don't you think?

POLLY: Totally.

ANNA: Did you notice the door design when you came in?

POLLY: I did. (Looking at the door) What do you…

ANNA: Country French.

POLLY: Oo, that makes sense. I think so…we forgot to shut the door.

ANNA: So we did…

POLLY: I'll do it.

ANNA: Let me take responsibility. I came in last.

POLLY: Let's do it together.

POLLY & ANNA: Pollyanna!

(They get up from the chairs and walk towards the door.)

(Lights Out)

(End of Scene)

(Lights Rise)

(Enter Man wearing "Father to Be" T-shirt. He looks around the room and then exits. He returns accompanying a pregnant woman.)

FATHER TO BE: It's okay honey. I'll help you come through the door. We'll take our time. No worries.

PREGNANT WOMAN: (Breathing heavily) Okay…okay…okay…

(Man changes the woman's body direction trial and error in order to manage the woman's body through the door opening.)

FATHER TO BE: Keep breathing. On your third inhale I'll get you through the door. Ready…In…Out…In…Out…In…

(Woman breathing. Woman enters through the door followed by the man.)

FATHER TO BE: There's two chairs honey. Where do you want to sit?

PREGNANT WOMAN: (Breathing heavily) Okay…okay…okay…

FATHER TO BE: This chair looks fine. (Guiding woman to a chair) Let me help you.

PREGNANT WOMAN: (Breathing heavily) Okay…okay…okay…

FATHER TO BE: I'll be right back. I'm going to shut the door.

PREGNANT WOMAN: It's time. (Breathing heavily) The baby is ready.

FATHER TO BE: All right honey, I'm going to shut the door and then I'll be right back.

PREGNANT WOMAN: (Grabbing the Father to be's hand) Stay with me. (Breathing heavily)

FATHER TO BE: (Managing pain) I won't let go of your hand honey but would you squeeze a little bit lighter. I promise I won't let go of your hand.

PREGNANT WOMAN: (Breathing heavily) Okay…okay…okay…

FATHER TO BE: I want you to breathe in and out and on the third inhalation we're going to move a little closer to the door so I can stretch my other arm and shut the door with my free hand.

PREGNANT WOMAN: (Breathing heavily) Okay…okay…okay…

FATHER TO BE: Breathe in and out, breathe in and out, breathe in…

(Lights Out)

(End of Scene)

(Lights Rise)

(Man and woman enter through the door, separate the chairs further and sit on them.)

MARGE: Harry, this is the day you will finally kill me.

HARRY: Don't be so dramatic Marge.

MARGE: I don't ask for much, a little consideration…toss a little kindness my way…you have no idea what it's like being married to spouse who cannot anticipate his partner's needs.

HARRY: Can we talk about this later?

MARGE: You don't want to talk about this, admit it.

HARRY: No Marge, I don't want to talk about it because it's nothing worth talking about.

MARGE: Nothing worth talking about?

HARRY: It's nothing.

MARGE: Nothing?

HARRY: Baby, don't cry. (Walking to Marge) I'm sorry. It means something to you so it means something to me. Look. (He walks towards the door) I'll shut the door. (Marge pounces on Harry sexually aggressive)

(Lights Out)

(End of Scene)

(Lights Rise)

(Girlfriend and Boyfriend walk through the door together affectionately. They notice the two chairs and then sit together on one chair.)

GIRLFRIEND: I wait just wondering… Wait hot stuff… We have all night… I was just wondering when you were going to…I mean…I know you love me…

BOYFRIEND: I love you too…

GIRLFRIEND: I've never felt so complete with a guy I've dated before…and we've been together for over a year now but… we've never talked about the door.

BOYFRIEND: Huh?

GIRLFRIEND: The door… When are you going to shut it?

BOYFRIEND: We don't need to talk about the door. We can keep being happy with the door opened. I love you. I'm not going anywhere.

GIRLFRIEND: I know… It's a girl thing… I admit it… I would just feel better if you could make a commitment, make a promise about when you might be ready to shut the door.

BOYFRIEND: (Getting up from chair) I'm not comfortable doing that?

GIRLFRIEND: Have you been bringing another girl through the door?

(Lights Out)

(End of Scene)

(Lights Rise)

(Loud screams outside of the door. Girl 1and Girl 2 push against each other in order to come through the door first.)

GIRL 1: Me.

GIRL 2: Me.

GIRL 1: Me.

GIRL 2: Me.

GIRL 1 & GIRL 2: Okay. (While playing the game) Rock, paper, scissors…Rock, paper, scissors, Rock, paper, scissors…

GIRL 2: Stop. Nobody wins.

GIRL 1: Okay.

(Girl 1and Girl 2 squeeze together in order to fit through the door. They enter through the door.)

GIRL 1 & GIRL 2: Ooh…. (Scream)

(Girl 1 and Girl 2 run around the room in one direction.)

GIRL 1: Stop (Pause) Go.

(Girl 1and Girl 2 run around the room in the other direction.)

GIRL 2: Stop (Pause) Go.

(Girl 1 and Girl 2 run and scream and fall on the floor exhausted.)

GIRL 1: I'm bored. (Looks at chairs) Vehicle races.

GIRL 2: I'm a motorcycle.

GIRL 1: I'm a sports car.

(Girl 1and Girl 2 push the chairs around the room while making vehicle sounds.)

GIRL 2: Wait (Pause) Hide and Seek.

GIRL 1: You hide.

GIRL 2: (While arranging the chairs for a hiding space) Count to ten.

GIRL 1: One, two, three, four…. Ready or not here I come.

(Girl 1 and Girl 2 tag each other.)

GIRL 2: Awe.

(Girl 1 and Girl 2 sit on the floor and look at the door.)

GIRL 1 & GIRL 2: Shut the door.

(Both girls run to the door and aggressively open and shut the door. The door falls down. They kick and rip the door apart.)

GIRL 1 & GIRL 2: We're in trouble…

(Lights Out)

(End of Scene)

(Lights Rise)

(A couple stands and walks together around the perimeter of the stage holding hands. They stop mid stage left and get containers of popcorn. They seat themselves center stage on folding chairs and eat the popcorn while patiently looking forward. Their characters have transformed into B-Boy and Zoe. Alisha, wife, wearing an apron enters from stage right and stands in a frozen position. Ralpy, husband, enters from stage left wearing a tie. They each stand in a "frozen" body position center stage in front of B-Boy and Zoe.)

B-BOY: When is the movie going to start Zoe?

ZOE: Should have started already… Oh; I always forget the heavenly remote. (She puts down her container of popcorn and picks up a remote control device from under the chair and gives it to B-BOY) The Maker provides small joys for visitors… Control of the remote control for starting the movie is one of the blessings of an afterlife.

B-BOY: Very cool. (Aims the remote at Alisha and Ralpy and presses the controls) Maybe, you need to change the batteries?

ZOE: We don't need batteries here. (Takes the remote and shakes it) Should be good now.

(B-Boy aims the remote, presses the controls, and Alisha and Ralpy begin moving in slow motion with moving lips and no voice.)

ZOE: There's voice activation for volume and speed. Just say, "Louder" and "Speed up."

(Alisha and Ralpy move very quickly talking in cartoon unintelligible words that are nearly screaming.)

RALPY: (Unintelligible) Shut the door Alisha.

ALISHA: (Unintelligible) You can shut the door Ralpy, I'm cooking.

ZOE: Just a little tweaking. Say, "Natural."

B-BOY: Natural.

RALPY: Shut the door Alisha.

ALISHA: You can shut the door Ralpy…I'm cooking.

RALPY: Can't a man read a paper in peace?

ALISHA: (Walks to the window and opens it and screams out) Tricka… Would you come downstairs and bring me a cup of sugar please? (She returns to cooking)

RALPY: Shut the door Alisha.

ALISHA: Ralpy…I'm not shutting the door, I just opened the window.

RALPY: Bang, zoom…I'm sending you to the moon Alisha.

(Slams his newspaper on the table, gets up, and shuts the door. He returns to reading the newspaper.)

B-BOY: This is funny. When I was alive, I wouldn't have watched movies like this.

ZOE: Part of the small joys here. The simplest entertainment is pure luxury.

ALISHA: (Walks to the window and shouts towards the upstairs) Tricka…I need that cup of sugar. (Returns to cooking) Open the door, will ya Ralpy?

RALPY: Open the door? I just shut the door.

ALISHA: Tricka's coming down with a cup of sugar. How will she come in if the door is shut?

RALPY: When she knocks on the door, I'll open it.

ALISHA: Tricka can't knock on a door while she's holding a cup of sugar.

RALPY: (Opens the door, then sits down to read the newspaper) The moon Alisha…that's where you're going…

(Alisha shuts the window.)

RALPY: Open the window Alisha.

B-BOY: (Pauses the action of the "movie" with the remote) Wow… what do you thinks gonna happen Zoe?

ZOE: I'm not sure. So many choices.

"Door shut. Window shut."

"Window shut. Door shut."

"Window open. Door shut."

"Door shut. Window open."

"Window open. Door open."

"Door open. Window open."

B-BOY: Stop. (Uses the remote to continue the action) I didn't want you to spoil the story.

(Alisha and Ralpy fight with each other using the window and door as weapons.)

RALPY: Door shut.

ALISHA: Window open. Door open.

RALPY: Window shut.

ALISHA: Wait… Do you hear something?

RALPY: (Looking around) I don't hear nothin.

ALISHA: (Closing window) Window shut.

(Ralpy opens the window and blocks Alisha from coming near it.)

ALISHA: There was a time when you treated me like your sweetheart…always concerned about what I needed first. You opened the window. You shut the window. You opened the door. You shut the door. Do you love me anymore Ralpy?

RALPY: Do I love you? Do I love you? (Goes to the window and shuts it. Goes to the door and moves it back and forth open/close/open/close.)

RALPY: It's all about you Alisha. Whatever...whatever you need...I've been a dope. Will you forgive me Alisha?

ALISHA: Of course I'll forgive you Ralpy.

RALPY: Baby...you're the greatest.

(The couple embrace.)

B-BOY: Window and door shut. Window and door open. That was great. Let's watch it again.

ZOE: (Taking the remote) Not enough time. Chloe will be here soon.

(Lights fade on Alisha and Ralpy as they move to opposite sides of the stage and sit.)

B-BOY: You said visitors have control of the remote in Movie Heaven.

ZOE: Only for the short film...not for the feature and for Chinwaytahebatu (Waving) There she is.

B-BOY: Chin...chin...

ZOE: Chin...way...ta...he...ba...tu Chinwaytahebatu...simple...

(Enter Chloe with popcorn.)

ZOE: Do you like our comfort food here?

B-BOY: Not enough butter. Too much salt.

ZOE: Chloe and I've talked about the popcorn seasoning. (Waving at Chloe) Come on Chloe, he's ready. We don't agree. If we have salt and melted butter self-serve that's one thing. But Chloe wants a buffet like spread with cheese toppings, herbs, specialty peppers, and bacon bits. The real kind. (Waving at Chloe)

CHLOE: I've got more to transport and I'm by myself.

(Lights rise on the shadows of African American boys and young men in the rear of the movie theatre.)

ZOE: Hey Fellas. Say hello to the new B-Boy, Eric.

B-BOY: Hey.

ZOE: That's Trayvon, Emmett, Michael, Sean, Amodou, Oscar… you all can meet and greet later. We need to get started.

B-BOY: I don't know them.

ZOE: You know them in a way that we know things here… It's something you'll grow to feel…a transition.

CHLOE: Hey. Sorry, I'm late.

ZOE: You can help…I introduced some of the fellas but I didn't explain enough about Chinwaytahebatu.

CHLOE: I'm an ancient history buff B-Boy.

B-BOY: My name is Eric.

ZOE: It's just how we do things here…we'll use your personal name after you transition.

They're each watching their own internal reels. They're not directly involved with you.

CHLOE: Did you tell him about the problems with translation?

ZOE: More or less…

CHLOE: It's an ancient earth word that comes from a time when civilized earth dwellers lived in shelters without doors. Dwellers in and out of shelters were focused on greetings. "Welcome" and "Thank you for entering this space." When the dweller left the shelter, "Thank you for sharing space with me" and Good journey to your next shared space." Doors weren't shut because they weren't any doors.

B-BOY: What about windows?

CHLOE: Interesting question B-Boy. I'll mention it at our next meeting.

ZOE: Ready for your feature film?

B-BOY: Is it funny?

ZOE & CHLOE: No.

B-BOY: I liked the first movie. I want to watch more funny stuff.

ZOE: I'm sorry. It's your life movie…your last breaths…

ZOE & CHLOE: We'll be loving you through these moments.

(Lights flicker center stage. Shadow of a body lying down on a street. B-Boy walks to the location of the shadow.)

B-BOY: I felt so cold. The sidewalk underneath me was like an icebox creeping up through my skin. And my hands… first I could feel myself…then I couldn't feel one part after another… Like one by one every part of me was turned off. My neck…my own voice turned off last. Other voices…all around me. Did anyone else hear them? Was it only for me?

CHLOE: Your consciousness was begging for mercy.

ZOE: Tell us what you hear B-Boy.

B-BOY: "Take the sucker down and get this done."

"Joe's got it under control…he can handle it."

"I'm gonna be late for my hair appointment."

"That poor man. He wasn't hurting nobody."

"Somebody stop him…he's gonna kill him."

"Isn't that Eric?"

"This is some shit!"

What kind of paperwork we'll need for this one?

Oh my God! Oh my God!

"I have to remember to pick up the cake from Sal's bakery."

"I wonder if there's any coffee left in the car."

"Can't you hear him?
Don't you see him? He can't breathe.
"Keep it moving folks."

CHLOE & ZOE: Your last words.

B-BOY: I can't breathe.

ZOE: Your last breath.

CHLOE: Can you hear your consciousness Eric?

ZOE: What is your consciousness saying?

CHLOE: Say it loud.

B-BOY: I don't want to die.

CHLOE & ZOE: You're dead. Find your transition. What do you want?

B-Boy: I want my family!

CHLOE & ZOE: Find your transition. Why do you want your family?

B-BOY/ERIC: I need love!

CHLOE: You felt a final moment of peace.

B-BOY/ERIC: Yes…after number…number eleven. My body felt warm again. All the pain stopped.

ZOE: We were with you Eric. Making sure there was love surrounding you into your death.

ERIC: Thank you for loving me.

CHLOE & ZOE: You came into the world alone and you left alone but you were surrounded with love on your way here.

ERIC: Who are you?

CHLOE: We're the everlasting hope.

ZOE: We reside between the needs of others.

CHLOE: We're the pauses between words.

ZOE: We're the uncluttered, uncomplicated thoughts that connect one earth dweller to another.

CHLOE & ZOE: We're afterlife movie librarians.

CHLOE: Eventually, there won't be any life movies to watch. Humanity will exit. Just be. Visitors will come here for the fun short films. Feature films will be passé.

ERIC: Why?

ZOE: We help to reconcile regret.

ERIC: Is this the real heaven?

CHLOE: It's on the way. It's a resting place for you and the brothers of early, unforeseen fatality.

ERIC: When do I get to leave here?

CHLOE & ZOE: When it's over, you'll all leave together.

CHLOE: Here, the brothers help us each other with reconciliations. When the brothers continue on its without anger and regret. Change will happen.

ERIC: When can we all leave?

ZOE: When it's all over...

CHLOE: When the genocide stops.

ERIC: When will that be?

(ALL PAUSE AND GAZE AT AUDIENCE.)

(Shadow of dead body disappears from center stage. The shadow becomes the illusion of a passageway.)

ZOE: When you can shut the doors behind you.

(Lights Out)

End of Play

PRETTY

True friends (family) stab you in the front
Oscar Wilde

Characters:

Travis O'Neill/Black T: Twenty-something very dark complexion African American man; Willa's son, fraternal twin of Timothy. Could be considered unusually plain and unattractive by some. Travis is dressed in work clothes (uniform type).

Timothy O'Neill/Timmy: Twenty-something very fair complexion African American man; Willa's son, fraternal twin of Travis. Could be considered unusually handsome. He is fashionably dressed in current designer "trendy" clothing.

Clive Mayfield (same actor): Twenty-something African American man; Willa's college sweetheart.

Willa O'Neill: Sixty-something very fair complexion African American woman who could be mistaken for white; mother of Travis and Timothy. She still has traces of Southern Virginia dialect in her speech. She wears a "full face" of makeup, slippers, and a housedress.

Young Willa (same actor): Twenty-something Willa O'Neill, college co-ed.

Abena Ojoku: Twenty-something West African woman, model/actress.

Announcer

Setting:

September. Present Day. Living room of a one-bedroom apartment in the East River Housing Projects, a public housing project in Harlem New York. There is a convertible sofa bed, a television, an end table, a lamp, a makeshift coffee table, a kitchen table, and three chairs. The bedroom is adjacent to the living room/kitchen. It's simple with a bed, the fourth kitchen chair, and a dresser. There is a photograph of Willa from her college days on the dresser.

SCENE ONE: FRIDAY MORNING

Setting: Travis sits at the kitchen table reading a textbook and writing. Willa sits on the sofa in the living room. She is brushing her hair. Enter Timothy.

(Lights Rise)

TIMOTHY: I'm taking twenty dollars. Where's your purse Willa?

TRAVIS: I gave you twenty yesterday.

TIMOTHY: Shut up Black T. I need more.

TRAVIS: Mom, don't give him any more money.

WILLA: You know where my purse is baby.

TIMOTHY: (Holding up a black purse) There's no wallet in here.

WILLA: My red bag. The knock off. No one can tell unless they get right up close to me and look at that little metal triangle…that it says Pruda not Prada. And no one is getting that close to me. I know how to work it. Could always figure out a way to look good with a little bit of money. But, remember baby, you said one of the first things you're gonna buy me after you get that TV contract is a real Prada bag.

TIMOTHY: Yeah.

WILLA: A real, genuine red leather, imported from Italy, Prada pocketbook.

TIMOTHY: Where's the red bag?

WILLA: Maybe I could go with you to pick it out… What is that place called Timmy?

TIMOTHY: Milan.

WILLA: Get on an airplane and fly to Me Land, Italy…just to go to the Prada store.

TRAVIS: There are Prada stores downtown Mom.

WILLA: You think too small Travis. Will you ever learn to think big like Timmy?

I want to pick out my red pocketbook myself from the Prada store in Italy so in church when the Mother's Club ladies ask me, "Where did you get that red bag Willa? Downtown?"

I'll say, "My son Timothy, the television star flew me all the way to Me Land, Italy, so I could pick out my own red pocketbook.

TIMOTHY: I don't see that red bag Willa. Go get it. I gotta go.

TRAVIS: Late for the job?

WILLA: Stop pestering your brother Travis. You know why he's not working on a regular job…he's auditioning…that's his work now. When he gets one of those contracts he'll be bringing home more money than you'll ever have.

TRAVIS: You're right Mom. I think very small. Paying the rent. Light bill. Cable bill. Phone bill.

WILLA: I don't want to hear about the bills. That's your job.

TIMOTHY: The red purse Willa?

WILLA: The last time I used that bag was church? Sunday? I was looking good. I used my good red bag…wore my red coat, red lace dress, red hat…

TRAVIS: Yes Mom. You love red. I wish you loved being out of the red with our bills at least with the rent.

WILLA: TRAVIS, I told you I don't want to hear about the bills!

TIMOTHY: (Picks up the red purse from the floor, removes a wallet and shows a ten dollar bill) There's only ten dollars in here.

WILLA: After church last Sunday… I stopped at the drugstore. They had Ponds, large-size jars on sale. You know how I love Ponds cold cream. Keeps my skin feeling so soft after the foundation comes off.

TIMOTHY: Give me a ten Black T.

TRAVIS: Fuck you.

TIMOTHY: Plan to do some fucking today. Give me a ten.

WILLA: Travis O'Neill, give your brother ten dollars. He needs it and you have it.

TRAVIS: I have enough for my unlimited metro card.

TIMOTHY: Get the cheaper card stupid.

TRAVIS: A cheaper card won't get me to work and school for the whole month. Why am I telling you? What do you know about work and school?

WILLA: It's only ten dollars. Take it out of the light bill money.

TRAVIS: Yesterday, when you told me to give him twenty I took it out of the light bill money so this makes us short again.

WILLA: Take it out of the cable money. Just pay for less channels this month.

TRAVIS: Mom, they don't do that. They cut the service when you don't pay the whole bill.

WILLA: You better not let our cable service get cut off. I need the cable.

TRAVIS: More than our apartment? More than food?

WILLA: I told you Travis…I don't want to hear about the bills. That's your responsibility to figure it out.

(Travis takes his wallet out of his pants and takes out a ten-dollar bill and gives it to Timothy.
Timothy snatches the wallet and takes out an additional bill. Then he throws the wallet on the floor.)

TIMOTHY: Lunch.

(Willa positions herself between Travis and Timothy.)

WILLA: No fighting in here.

(Exit Timothy to the bedroom. Travis picks up his books and places them in his backpack with his laptop. He picks up his wallet from the floor.)

TRAVIS: I'm going to work.

WILLA: (Taking a store circular out of her red handbag) I need you to pick up this new mascara at SVS. They have a special…buy one and get a second one fifty percent off. "Volume us"

TRAVIS: "Voluminous." It means it will make your lashes appear thicker and longer.

WILLA: Don't correct me. I can look at the picture and see what it does. Just get it for me. I need it. And I need the new *Essence* magazine.

TRAVIS: Yes. You need it more than food.

WILLA: Travis?

TRAVIS: Goodbye Mom. (Exits)

WILLA: Bring home wings. I want you to fry up some chicken wings for dinner.

(Enter Timothy from the bedroom walking towards the door following his brother.)

WILLA: Timmy, make my part straight for me. You're the best.

(Timothy gets a hand mirror and a comb and approaches his mother on the sofa. He makes a part in her hair while making seductive, suggestive movements.)

TIMOTHY: (Removes red lipstick from Willa's purse) Let me fix your lipstick for you before I leave. (Gives Willa a hand mirror)

WILLA: How do I look?

TIMOTHY: You know how you look.

WILLA: Yes...but I like to hear you say it.

TIMOTHY: Pretty. (Puts away the lipstick and picks up his manbag) Look through your new *Essence* magazine when you get it and find the new lip colors for the season. Tell Black T to pick up a new shade of red lipstick and some lip liner for you. You deserve some new makeup to freshen up your face.

WILLA: That sounds good... Timothy, you know I don't like to think about the bills. That's Travis's job. But I think he may be stretching the money as far as it can be stretched. And do you have to call him Black T?

TIMOTHY: I could call him "Nigger T" instead. Makes no difference to me.

WILLA: You remind him how dark he is.

TIMOTHY: What's the problem? He's blue black, jet black... black and ugly...so what?

WILLA: It's not his fault that he was born dark. Your father had a beautiful light, creamy complexion. You look so much like him. Two babies born at the same time, I never would have thought you'd look so different. They told me I was having twins, two eggs, but I never would have thought you'd look so different. Maybe God made Travis smart because you got all the looks. I don't mean that you're not smart... I mean that maybe God gave him extra smart because he likes school and always did good in school. Nobody knows why God does these things with births. (Pause) Maybe he wouldn't pester you so much if you didn't remind him of his unfortune.

TIMOTHY: You mean misfortune.

WILLA: Don't correct me like your brother. I meant to say misfortune.

TIMOTHY: If Black T is stretching money as far as he can and he can't work it out, he may need to quit school.

WILLA: Oh…I don't know about that. It's not costing any money. He has scholarships for his tuition and his books. It's all paid for.

TIMOTHY: He could be working more hours, bringing home more money…if he wasn't going to school.

WILLA: He's almost finished. He has a few more months.

TIMOTHY: And he could get back to it later if he wants to finish bad enough.

He left here complaining about giving me money I needed for handling my auditions because he wanted a metro card for work and school.

WILLA: He needs to finish school Timmy. Travis will never be pretty. He could never get a job modeling or be on television, making commercials or be a movie star making big money like you.

TIMOTHY: Exactly my point. I'm an artist. I have to be ready for opportunities. There's more cash upfront because I have to be available, networking, being seen and looking good. (Pause) I've got a call back for this new series being shot in LA.

WILLA: Los Angeles? I don't want you moving to Los Angeles.

TIMOTHY: It's a negotiation point when my contract is drafted with my agent. They want to go with a new face for the leading man. (Poses) That's me. (Pause) I need to look my best. I need more clothes. (Holds Willa's face in a suggestive way) You need more makeup. (Pause) Fresh face. Pretty…

TIMOTHY: (Kissing Willa) See if Black T brings home your mascara and your magazine. Willa…this is a family and there's no need for selfishness. Nigger T is selfish. (Exit)

(End of Scene)

(Lights Out)

SCENE TWO: FRIDAY EVENING, 6 PM.

Setting: Willa stands in front of the sofa in the living room. She is wearing a formal dress.

(Lights Rise)

[Sound Effect: Applause and cheers from a crowd.]

ANNOUNCER: The moment we've all been waiting for…

[Sound Effect: Louder cheers.]

ANNOUNCER: Drum roll please.

[Sound Effects: Drums, cheers, and marching band.]

ANNOUNCER: This year's Kenyon Community College Harvest Festival queen is…
Ms. Willa Jean O'Neill.

[Sound Effect: Band Music.]

WILLA: (Giving a pageant wave) Thank you. Thank you. I'm so honored.

(Enter Travis carrying a bag of groceries, *Essence* magazine, and a small pharmacy bag.)

TRAVIS: Are you all right Mom?

WILLA: Thank you. I'm so honored.

TRAVIS: Mom!

WILLA: (Stops waving) Did you get my new *Essence* magazine and my mascara?

TRAVIS: Yes, and I had your prescription refilled. Maybe we need to ask the doctor about increasing the strength.

(Hands his mother pills and a glass of water. He puts the medication bottle on the end table.)

WILLA: Don't try to push those pills on me. I'm only taking the pills for my headaches.

Sometimes the headaches take me too far away, places I don't want to go to any more.

(Travis hands Willa the magazine and the mascara. He unpacks the bag of groceries.)

WILLA: I need a new shade of red lipstick and lip liner to match. Timmy says I deserve it.

TRAVIS: I have your chicken wings. We have greens left over from Thursday, and I'll bake a few of these quick biscuits. I only have an hour before I have to leave for work.

WILLA: Make enough wings for your brother. He's always extra hungry after his auditions. He has a call back for a big show out in California, but he won't have to move to California. Timmy said moving is…is…association point.

TRAVIS: Timmy has had callbacks for the "big jobs" in LA for two years. Ever consider that he's lying to you Mom?

WILLA: Jealousy is uglier when it comes from a man who's ug—

TRAVIS: Ugly?

WILLA: I never called you ugly. Ug…un…unusual. Unusual.

TRAVIS: Let's not go there Mom. I have an hour to make your food and leave for work. I may not have a chance to eat myself.

(Travis prepares the hot oil to cook the chicken wings.)

WILLA: That's because you're always rushing. Rushing here, rushing there. Maybe you need just one thing to do.

TRAVIS: One thing?

WILLA: One thing like work? Just work.

(Hot grease burns Travis.)

TRAVIS: Damn it.

WILLA: Rushing…burned yourself because you're rushing. Put some ice on it.

TRAVIS: Freezer's broken No ice.

WILLA: Will your job give you more hours if you ask for more?

TRAVIS: And why would I ask for more hours?

WILLA: I was just wondering.

TRAVIS: Something my brother put in your head?

WILLA: I'm the head of this family. I don't need you or your brother to put ideas in my head. I can think for myself. I'm asking for my own information because I have to make decisions for the family.

TRAVIS: You told me you don't want to know about the bills.

WILLA: That's your job. (Pause) Decisions. Other decisions.

TRAVIS: My boss would take me on fulltime anytime. Not only that. I'd be promoted. A more hours, more money, promotion. I get to work on time. I mind my business. I go to my job to work and nothing else, and I do the best work possible. My boss respects me.

WILLA: Then why don't you tell him you want to work fulltime?

TRAVIS: You know why. I can't work more hours and finish school by next semester.

WILLA: You can go other mesters.

TRAVIS: Semester…I have one semester left.

(Willa throws the bottle of medication at Travis. The bottle opens and spills on the floor.)

WILLA: Stop correcting me!

TRAVIS: Medicaid won't refill your prescription again until next month.

(Travis searches the floor and picks up all of the pills. He picks up an envelope. He places both on the kitchen table.)

[Sound Effect: Harvest Queen song.]

ANNOUNCER: Ms. Willa Jean O'Neill is a fashion design student in our certificate program. Her other interests are cosmetology and people watching. Willa is native born to Virginia and her family hails from Hisham County.

[Sound Effect: Applause.]

TRAVIS: One thing to do? I'll never have one thing to do. I'm the cook, the housekeeper, the personal shopper, the…forget it. (Pause) Mom, I can't do this. I can't manage things if you don't do your part, if you don't cooperate.

WILLA: I'm the mother. I make the decisions for this family. Your brother is right…you're selfish. You're jealous… Timmy is the pretty one. He has it all. Some men are handsome. But Timmy is handsome and pretty. Smooth; clear skin, light eyes, soft curls, perfect smile, snow-white teeth, straight nose and a body any woman would want. (Pause) A good-looking, handsome, pretty man. Every woman's dream.

TRAVIS: So you mean I was just screwed from birth Mom.

WILLA: Don't talk that way to me. It was God's plan. Who knows why?

TRAVIS: Well, at least I know my place. (He picks up the medicine bottle and places it in a kitchen cabinet. Then he picks up the envelope, opens it, and reads it.) When did this notice come?

WILLA: What?

TRAVIS: This cut off notice from Con Ed Mom?

WILLA: You'll take care of it. You always do.

TRAVIS: When? How? With what? (Travis puts some food in a container and gets his backpack) I'm covering for a buddy who called out sick. I'm working a double. Your food is here Mom. Manage to serve yourself please. I'll see you in the morning. If my boss offers me a triple, I'll do it and ask my boss for an advance so I can pay the Con Ed. I'll call you. Remember your pills, two at 9 tonight, again in the morning. This is important Mom...I may not get home to remind you. (Exit)

(End of Scene)

(Lights Out)

SCENE THREE: MID-MORNING

Setting: Mayfield Family guesthouse, Hisham County, Virginia Circa 1950s. Willa and Clive are in the bedroom. Clive gets up from the bed clothed in his underwear, looks for his pants, and begins to get dressed.

(Lights Rise)

YOUNG WILLA: I'm not finished with you. What are you runnin off to?

CLIVE: Come on Willa. Get your fine yellow self outta the bed now. We gotta go. My parents are havin a lawn party. Invitin some important people from up north.

WILLA: I wanna go. I got a nice dress wit me. Just take me a few minutes to fix up my face.

CLIVE: Come on Willa. (Throwing dress at her) I told Jasper to pick you up. Go on to the kitchen. He'll fetch you at the back door.

WILLA: When am I gonna start comin to the parties? I swear, your family has more fancy…

CLIVE: Come on Willa. (Making final adjustments to clothing) Thanks. You were nice.

WILLA: Thanks?

CLIVE: Yeah Thanks. (Throwing money on the bed) Get yourself something nice.

WILLA: What are you doing Clive?

CLIVE: What do you think Willa? It's time to cut this loose now. I'm starting Beauchamp Institute soon. Lots to do to get ready. I think Pops is gonna spring for a new car. Have his baby boy riding in style up to the front door of his Alma Mata.

WILLA: I thought…

CLIVE: Willa, you know what this was. It's been good for you too. Girls on your side of the creek are some uninhibited… hell…good fuckin…this has been some damn good fuckin. And tell me…I'm the best Johnson you ever had. See that Willa. You forced me to brag.

WILLA: I just thought…

CLIVE: (Exiting) Just thought what?

WILLA: I just thought we would get married and I'd go with you to Beauchamp.

CLIVE: Willa Jean, if only your cunt was in your brain you'd be damn genius.

(Takes Willa's hand) We are not special. You are not a different *round da way piece of pussy.* High yellow, wavy hair, and nice tits don't get you a ticket to my show. Not even after being crowned a harvest queen. Pops gives money every year to Kenyon Community College. I asked him to put in a word for you... I thought it would be nice for you if you won. Raise your status a little with the folks on your side of town. And white folks around here would get a kick out of having a Negro Harvest Queen for a housekeeper.

(Willa gets out of the bed and picks up her dress.)

Pops keeps hintin around about Rosalie Wright. You know about the Wrights don't you? Big lumberyard, hires a half dozen or more colored men for yard workers. And old Nathan Wright has contracts for three colored churches going into construction in Northern Virginia. You seen Rosalie, right? You think she's pretty?

WILLA: I'm pregnant.

CLIVE: Well...I guess that changes things for you a little. I know it has to be mine. You're loyal. Always appreciated that about you. So what are your plans?

WILLA: Clive...I'm pregnant with your baby. I want us to have a family.

CLIVE: Willa, you need to figure out what you're gonna do. I don't recommend that you go to that back alley doctor on Elm Street. He probably isn't a medical doctor. You have people up north, don't you?

WILLA: New York City and Chicago but they don't want...

CLIVE: Whatever you want Willa. I'll give you enough money for a northern doctor to take care of your condition and for the bus ticket to either city, makes no difference to me. I'll give Jasper some money. He can bring it to your place tomorrow. (Looking in a mirror) Damn, I'm handsome and pretty. (While exiting) And Willa, Jasper will give you enough money for a one-way ticket. Thanks again. Goodbye Willa.

(Lights fade to black on Young Willa. Lights rise on Willa present day. She sits on a chair in the bedroom staring at the bed.)

(End of Scene)

(Lights Out)

SCENE FOUR: FRIDAY, AROUND MIDNIGHT PRESENT DAY

Setting: Present Day. Living room. Willa sits on the sofa. She wears clean, cheaply sexy lingerie and heeled slippers. Her makeup is refreshed. Enter Timmy.

(Lights Rise)

WILLA: You're late.

TIMMY: Late for what? Who am I? Your husband?

WILLA: I was worried. Travis made some chicken wings before he left. I prepared a nice plate for you.

TIMMY: (While packing items in a duffle bag) I ate already.

WILLA: Where did you eat?

TIMMY: Go to bed Willa.

WILLA: Aren't you coming to bed? It's so late.

TIMMY: Staying at a friend's house.

WILLA: Travis brought me that special mascara. How's my face?

TIMMY: (While grabbing and hugging Willa) Sorry Willa. You look fabulous. I like it. Gonna need a few dollars.

WILLA: Maybe in my jewelry box?

TIMMY: (Taking money from jewelry box) I think you should get your beauty sleep so you can wake up nice and refreshed for tomorrow.

WILLA: I'm not.

TIMMY: Did you forget? Tomorrow is the Founder Day at Blessed Jesus. You should go.

WILLA: Really, I don't.

TIMMY: Yes, you should go. Wear your red. Have all the church bitches…

WILLA: Don't call them that.

TIMMY: I mean you will look so good, and they will be so jealous.

WILLA: Yes, especially Evangelene. She envies me. She started wearing a red outfit to church just because the pastor was complementing me on how nice I looked in my red outfit.

TIMMY: Heifer.

WILLA: The celebrations are all day. I don't know if I can be away from home that long.

TIMMY: Go out. Have a good time. Where's Black T?

WILLA: He said he might have to work extra shifts. He may not be home until Sunday.

TIMMY: (Putting on outside clothing) Yeah. Right. Remember, dress your best, have a good time. You'll look better than all the bi…mother's club church ladies.

WILLA: Yes.

(End of Scene)

(Lights Out)

SCENE FIVE: SATURDAY, LATE AFTERNOON

Setting: Bedroom. Abena and Timmy are getting out of bed and getting dressed.

(Lights Rise)

ABENA: (Looking at photograph of Willa) Oh, this is so cute. Your mother?

TIMMY: Yeah.

ABENA: This photograph looks so old. I think it's so nice that when girls weren't pretty enough to be real models they could do pageants.

TIMMY: It wasn't a pageant. It was. Never mind. Not important.

ABENA: Where does your mother live?

TIMMY: (Pulling Abena close to him) So many questions for a woman who should be thinking about California sunshine.

ABENA: And smog.

TIMMY: And ocean-side cocktails with the A list set.

ABENA: I know. LA will be great. It's a great contract for me, and I'm so lucky that you have time between your jobs to crash with me.

TIMMY: Naw, I don't mind being your eye candy. I need a few more things.

ABENA: Why are you packing stuff? You can shop when we land. I ordered some duplicate credit cards for you so you wouldn't have to wait for me. You should see my schedule.

TIMMY: And I will be right there…in front…behind…on top… and under…you know what I'm saying to support you all the way. Just a few of my favorite things. Go ahead. Meet you at first class check in.

ABENA: Maybe you should take your boarding pass in case you are a little late.

TIMMY: I will not be late my darling but probably a good idea.

(Timmy continues to pack. Abena goes to the front door. Enter Willa.)

ABENA: (While extending hand) Hello…you must be Timothy's mother. I saw your pageant photograph. So cute. I would like…

TIMMY: See you at the airport. Bye.

ABENA: Goodbye Mrs. O'Neill.

(Exit Abena. Door closes.)

WILLA: Who was that Timmy?

TIMMY: A friend.

WILLA: She was in the bedroom?

TIMMY: Yeah. What of it?

WILLA: Why was she in the bedroom Timmy?

TIMMY: That's where the bed is Willa.

WILLA: You got the job Timmy? The confact? I mean contract? Which TV show is it? I have to tell the ladies at the church my son Timothy.

TIMMY: No Willa. I didn't get a contract. I got something better…a sugar mama. That jet-black goddess who just left here is my ride to LA and then some. Loves herself some high yellow Timothy. You know what they say, "The blacker the pussy berry, the more attractive the golden yellow dick." Funny isn't it? So right now I'm not trending in the industry. Can't find a job.

WILLA: But you said…

TIMMY: (While packing) What I didn't say is I'm too White to get the Black male roles and too Black to get the white male roles…and I can't speak Spanish. But Abena…the season is ripe for dark fruit so I'll ride her pussy until the season changes…cause it will. Complexion is a commodity like that. (Closing duffle bag) Got what I need. Your good son Travis will look after you Willa and your other son, the one you thought gave a shit about you is just following your countrified footsteps. The mother's a whore. The son's a whore. What was my sperm daddy's name? Clive? Yeah, so I got me a lady Clive, only there ain't gonna be any babies…

(Willa picks up a heavy skillet from the stove and hits Timmy. He falls to the floor.)

(End of Scene)

(Lights Out)

SCENE SIX: SATURDAY EVENING

Setting: Living Room. The apartment is dimly lit by candlelight. Willa is sitting on the sofa. She's looking at photographs and her college yearbook. Timmy is lying on the floor with duct tape on his mouth, tied up an odd combination of panty hose, ropes, and rags.

(Lights Rise)

(The door opens. Enter Travis. He tries the light switch.)

TRAVIS: Mom…Mom…are you okay?

WILLA: Yes…I'm sitting here looking at photographs with your brother.

TRAVIS: My boss gave me an advance. Why is Timmy tied up?

WILLA: I hit him. Wasn't sure what I wanted to do next. So I tied him up.

TRAVIS: (Bending down to examine Timmy) He's breathing.

WILLA: That's good. Probably has a big headache.

TRAVIS: You? Tied him up like that?

WILLA: I had to put together a few things to make the ties strong. Glad you're home early. I didn't want to have to knock him out again.

TRAVIS: I could only do two shifts. (Sitting next to Willa) My boss gave me an advance so I paid the light bill. But they couldn't promise me they could stop the disconnection because the team was sent out already.

WILLA: Candlelight is fine.

TRAVIS: The lights should come up soon. (Pause) Did you remember to take your medicine?

WILLA: Yes I did. And I went to Founder's Day at the church. I had a really nice day.

TRAVIS: Can you tell me?

WILLA: (Covering Travis's mouth) I need you to rouse Timmy up and throw him out of the house for me. It's okay…he has a place to go. There's a ticket in his jacket pocket. (Releasing her hand over Travis's mouth) I don't want him to miss his flight. He can't stay here anymore. Just cut the ties, and push him into the hallway with his bag.

(Travis removes the duct tape from Timothy's mouth.)

TIMMY: (Jargon cursing)

WILLA: Your flight leaves in an hour son.

(Travis pushes Timmy out of the door with his bag. Lights come on in the apartment.)

TRAVIS: Goodbye Timmy.

WILLA: I don't like that child. I love him but I don't like him. (Blows out candle) He was born normal but I made him into a monster. And I made you…(Picking up the chicken wings that fell from the skillet) Can you make more wings? I like the way you make wings.

TRAVIS: Sure Mom.

WILLA: Lies you tell yourself are the worse kind of lies. You have to keep feeding them to keep them alive. It's like feeding the weeds in a garden instead of the flowers. Before you know it, the weeds grown strong and take over the garden and it's hard to tell which plants are the weeds and which ones are the plants that could have been beautiful. I've been telling so many lies to myself. (Looking at the bedroom) Timmy shouldn't have called me Willa.

TRAVIS: No, he shouldn't have.

WILLA: He's not my husband and he shouldn't have slept in... (Sitting next to Travis on the sofa, taking a photograph out of the photograph box) Your grandfather, my father.

TRAVIS: He's Bl...

WILLA: Dark ebony brown. You look like his mirror head to toe. (Taking out another photograph) Your grandfather and grandmother; Gerald and Hillary O'Neill.

TRAVIS: My grandmother was a white woman?

WILLA: White. Not passing. Green eyes. Blonde hair.

TRAVIS: She's beautiful.

WILLA: And he's handsome. (Pulling out a third photograph) Me with your uncle and your two aunts.

TRAVIS: They all look like your father. You and your mother look like a different family. A white family.

WILLA: I don't want to talk anymore now. But I would appreciate it if you could still live here maybe until you finish school. I could start pulling up the years of weeds...I think there's a pretty garden left...

(End of Scene)

(Lights Out)

End of Play

WHIZZ

Emergency Procedures

Characters:

Old Southern African American Gentlemen

Dr. Jeff: Medical Director of Southern Stars General Hospital

Dr. Will: Attending Physician, Principal Investigator Research Division

Dr. Bobby: Attending Physician, Chief of Emergency Medicine

African American Southern Belle

Nurse Sally: Charge Nurse Emergency Medicine Department

Yankee Import

Dr. Rebecca Schwartz: Asian woman, first year medical resident

Setting:

Present day, the conference room of Southern Stars General Hospital, a large teaching hospital in Central Kentucky. Dr. Jeff, Dr. Will, and Dr. Bobby are having a meeting to prepare for their presentation at Central Kentucky's First International Conference for Innovations in Holistic Medicine. There is a presentation board in front of the conference table. The doctors are dressed in shirts, pants, ties, and white lab coats. Dr. Will wears a fishing cap. He practices his fishing throws. The doctors are smoking Cuban cigars and drinking beer.

(Lights Rise)

DR. JEFF: Gentlemen, I believe our work is in excellent form for Central Kentucky's First International Conference for Innovations in Holistic Medicine.

DR. WILL: Cheers.

DR. JEFF, DR. WILL & DR. BOBBY: (Clanging beer glasses) Cheers!

DR. WILL: I believe we should take a final look at our graphs.

(Dr. Will places several white pieces of construction paper used in elementary school art classes on the display chart. The charts have bar graphs drawn in crayon. He names and shows each chart.)

DR. WILL: Description of our patient sample with relevant demographics. Response to the treatment using age as a variable. Long-term effects of intense treatment. Measurements of rebound effects or revisits to the ER after initial identification in the ER and the first course of medication. Here's my extra special analysis of Bobby's ten-year fishing record.

DR. BOBBY: All right now…lets be serious.

NURSE SALLY: Dr. Jeff, that new resident, Rebecca Schwartz is here to see you.

DR. JEFF: I don't have an appointment with her Sally.

NURSE SALLY: I know but she's having some kind of northern hissy fit. I'm too busy to handle this one. I'm frying up the rest of the chicken for the department picnic.

DR. JEFF: Now keep that hot grease away from the resuscitation bags. And don't use my scalpels to cut up those chicken breasts. Smells good Sally. Why don't you bring some wings in here to the conference room and let us sample your new recipe?

NURSE SALLY: Now Dr. Jeff you know this is the same fried chicken recipe that has won me a blue ribbon every year for the past five years at the Central Virginia FRY OFF. And you know there's no sampling until after church service.

DR. JEFF: Can't ever pull the scrubs over your eyes Sally.

(Enter Dr. Rebecca Schwartz. She is dressed in professional clothing and wears a white lab coat. She is holding some documents on a clipboard. She waits for the doctor's attention.)

DR. WILL: I didn't order any Chinese food. Will, you order any Chinese food?

DR. JEFF: Try the Radiology Department Miss. They order a lot of foreign food.

DR. REBECCA SCHWARTZ: I'm the new resident, Dr. Rebecca Schwartz.

(All the men stop what they're doing and stare at the resident.)

DR. JEFF: Schwartz? Did you say Schwartz? Will, you were in charge of choosing the residents this year. What happened with this one?

DR. WILL: We actually never interviewed her. I told the HR department to hire her based on her credentials.

DR. JEFF: Credentials?

DR. WILL: She went to Yale Medical School, graduating at the top of her class, she completed a PhD in herbal medicine and she wrote an excellent essay on her interest in our holistic medicine residency.

DR. JEFF: She's not white.

DR. REBECCA SCHWARTZ: I'm in the room Dr. Jeff.

DR. JEFF: I know, I know…just give us a couple of minutes to sort this out Dr. Schwartz. Sally, bring me Dr. Schwartz's professional file please.

NURSE SALLY: I have to flip my chicken breasts.

DR. JEFF: Will, why didn't you try Duke or Johns Hopkins… before you recruited from Yankee territory.

DR. BOBBY: Couldn't you get a boy resident? I can take the boy residents fishing.

DR. WILL: We waited a little too long this year to make a selection, and all the good candidates had been chosen already. You know the boys always get picked first.

DR. JEFF: Why did we wait so long this year?

DR. WILL: We lost the applications in Sue Ann's House of Delight remember?

DR. JEFF: Oh yes, I remember delights, southern delights. That's right, couldn't be helped.

What are you Dr. Schwartz?

DR. REBECCA SCHWARTZ: What am I?

DR. JEFF: Chinese? Japanese? Korean? Fillipino?

DR. BOBBY: I don't think she's an A-RAB. Her eyes are too slanty to be an A-RAB.

DR. REBECCA SCHWARTZ: Is this questioning about my ethnicity really necessary? I find…

DR. JEFF: Sit down…sit down…Dr. Schwartz. May I call you Becky?

DR. REBECCA SCHWARTZ: Actually, I prefer to be called Dr. Schwartz.

DR. JEFF: Yes, yes Becky…we're all friendly here…just have a set down.

DR. BOBBY: Did you do any fishing up North with your Dad Becky?

DR. REBECCA SCHWARTZ: No, I don't eat fish…I'm a vegetarian.

DR. JEFF: Going to be a little hard to be a vegetarian here Becky. We have Sally's fried chicken every year at the department picnic. Now tell me about your name, Schwartz,

Are you Jewish?

DR. REBECCA SCHWARTZ: Yes, I'm Jewish.

DR. BOBBY: First one of you folks we ever had. I didn't know Chinese and Jewish could be in the same person. Can Chinese, A-RAB, and Jewish be in the same person?

DR. REBECCA SCHWARTZ: I was born in China. My parents adopted me at birth and raised me in the Jewish faith.

DR. WILL: Jeff, we need to finish our preparation for the presentation.

DR. BOBBY: There are all kinds of combinations of people in the north. I wonder if you can be born in China, raised in the U.S. as a Moslem and then go back to China as a Jew?

DR. JEFF: Let's take care of Becky. What did you need? Everybody being nice to you here? Did you get your discount tickets for the Piggly Wiggly Shack? I didn't see you in church so to tell you the truth I forgot about seeing you for a meet and greet here at the hospital.

DR. WILL: If you don't want your discount miniature golf tickets you can give them to me Becky.

DR. REBECCA SCHWARTZ: Everyone is nice to me here. I feel a little odd bringing up this irregularity.

DR. JEFF: That's your first mistake. If everyone is nice to you and you like your job then there are no irregularities.

DR. BOBBY: I know you Chinese, A-RAB, Jews probably don't eat pork so you can give those discount Piggly Wiggly tickets to me Becky.

DR. JEFF: What's been going on in that ER Bobby that could get our new resident so upset?

DR. BOBBY: I haven't been in the ER for weeks. I went on my trout fishing trip.

DR. REBECCA SCHWARTZ: I'm very happy and I'm looking forward to beginning my work with the holistic medicine initiatives. (Indicates a place on the clipboard document) It's just this…

DR. JEFF: That's Sally's initials. In this hospital the charge nurse in the ER approves the invoices.

DR. REBECCA SCHWARTZ: In the ER we only have one stethoscope. Ten residents have to share one stethoscope. I placed an order for individual stethoscopes so we don't have to sign out on the pantry room door chart to share the only one.

DR. JEFF: Don't you share equipment in the ERs in the hospitals up north?

DR. REBECCA SCHWARTZ: Yes Sir. But every doctor has a stethoscope.

DR. BOBBY: We don't have much need for stethoscopes in our emergency room.

DR. REBECCA SCHWARTZ: (Holding up a document) Nurse Sally voided my order and replaced it with this one.

DR. WILL: (Looking at the document) This is outrageous.

DR. JEFF: (Takes the invoice) Sally, you replaced Dr. Schwartz's order for stethoscopes with an invoice for two cases of Cheese Whizz.

NURSE SALLY: Yes doctor, we have eight cases on back order. They'll be delivered before your conference.

DR. JEFF: Problem solved. That was very astute of you to notice that the cheese whizz order was so low.

DR. REBECCA SCHWARTZ: Cheese Whizz? She's ordering Cheese Whizz for the ER?

DR. WILL: She's not familiar with the research.

DR. JEFF: Right. Usually Becky, we wouldn't include first year residents in a principal investigation before he or she completed three hundred clock hours in the ER. But you're here and we want you to feel at home with our hospital, so have a set down and listen. We're finishing up our conference preparation. Go on Will.

DR. WILL: We need to finish with the visuals. Let's look at the WIZZMATIC.

(Dr. Will places a piece of construction paper on the chart board. There are three happy faces drawn in crayon with three kinds of mouths on the chart.)

DR. JEFF: Looks good Will. I think the bold black crayons for the smiley faces stand.

DR. BOBBY: An improvement over the pastels we used to use in the ER.

DR. WILL: Becky, our protocol in the ER is to establish the emotional disposition of the patient within the first five minutes of admit unless the person is unconscious. We've reduced the scale to three choices in order to simplify the response.

(Points as he describes) You are familiar with the pain level scales, of course. The WHIZZMATIC follows the same principal. We use desire for cheese whizz as an indicator of the patient's emotional disposition. This first face indicates the highest emotional state of contentment…or "I have all the Cheese Whizz I want." This second face indicates distress or "I don't have enough Cheese Whizz." This third face indicates the most extreme level of discontent and unhappiness or "I don't have any Cheese Whizz." By using three indicators of emotional state we can move the patient into the appropriate section of the ER. Those patients who indicate the very sad face go directly to fast track. We work on the patient's emotional state as a prerequisite to any medical procedure in order to facilitate the most favorable outcomes.

DR. BOBBY: If the patient is able to tolerate solid foods, we give them cheese whizz by mouth to improve or stabilize the patient's emotional state.

DR. JEFF: I think they'll want to hear about our plans for future research. That's what will attract the big funders.

DR. WILL: Good point Jeff and easily done. We can just mention a few, don't want to give too much away before we've finished collecting our pilot study data.

DR. BOBBY: We titrate intravenous Cheese Whizz coupled with an electrolyte solution two to one. The positive effect of the cheese whizz has a rapid turn-around effect in changing a patient's report of a sad face to a smiling face on the WHIZZMATIC. Will, maybe we can start using some other crayola colors for the smiley faces. Maybe could use pastel colors? Everybody likes yellows, blues, pinks, greens and the nurses' could wear scrubs matching the WHIZZMATIC.

DR. JEFF: You can mention it to Sally. Just remember, the color of the nurses' uniforms is her jurisdiction.

DR. WILL: Those patients that exit the ER and move to a specialty ward are served taters and Cheese Whizz as soon as they are able to manage more hearty solid foods.

DR. BOBBY: Becky, maybe you could give us your opinion. I suggest we experiment with spaghetti and Cheese Whizz as a variation. Everyone loves spaghetti, and I think the muscle in the esophagus needed to swallow a whole cheesy noodle can be exceptional support for our stroke and dysphasia patients.

DR. JEFF: Now Becky, don't be shy. Speak up. You're a first-year resident, but we welcome the opinion of someone who is not intimately involved in the project.

DR. WILL: She looks to be in shock.

DR. BOBBY: Maybe we can consider those little mini bagels and Cheese Whizz.

DR. JEFF: Becky? Say something Becky.

DR. WILL: Let's give her a little oxygen.

DR. JEFF: Sally, will you bring us some oxygen and a resuscitation bag.

NURSE SALLY: OOPS, a little too much grease went the wrong way into the bag. Sorry about that. I'll scrub it with a little Brilla in a few minutes after I fry the chicken thighs and gizzards.

DR. REBECCA SCHWARTZ: Cheese Whizz. How did this happen to me? I'm stuck here with some good old boys who are pumping Cheese Whizz into coronary patients! Is this what I went to medical school for to be trapped in the boon docks with some quacks pretending to be serious researchers who get their medicine from the local mom and pop grocery store or the Piggly Wiggly or maybe they make their own Cheese Whizz in the church basement while they document their research with Crayola crayons like the ones I used in preschool. I have to pay my student loans. Who is going to give me a job after a Cheese Whizz residency? Who knows what they're going to do next? Intravenous lard? No. Liquefied fried chicken? No. Hot grease? No. Pork rinds? Maybe they'll put the ER behind some fried chicken cheese whizz drive-in to save time? Send the ambulance directly to the drive-up window. Hello, hello, we have a man who was in a fishing accident…multiple wounds from bait and tackle…we need cheese whizz stat…Cheese Whizz stat…Chesse Whizz, Cheese Whizz…cheese…chee (Collapses)

DR. BOBBY: I'll get the crash cart. (Exits)

NURSE SALLY: Chickens ready.

DR. JEFF: Not now Sally.

(Dr. Jeff begins to feed Dr. Rebecca Schwartz cheese whizz with a tablespoon until she has eaten a whole jar. Dr. Bobby pours a shot glass of Southern Comfort from a bottle. Dr. Will props Dr. Rebecca Schwartz's head up while Dr. Bobby pours Southern Comfort down her throat. The sequence of pouring Southern Comfort in a shot glass and then pouring it down Dr. Rebecca Schwartz's throat continues until she is revived.)

DR. JEFF: You passed out young lady.

DR. WILL: After you said some rather unkind things.

DR. BOBBY: Not worried about that. Old geysers like us are often misunderstood. I'm more concerned that she is a resident in our holistic medicine division and she has no understanding of the principles behind what we are doing here.

DR. JEFF: Yes, you're right. We should fire her.

DR. WILL: No one will hire after she's fired and of course she would be leaving without a recommendation.

DR. REBECCA SCHWARTZ: (Looks at the empty jar of Cheese Whizz) You gave me Cheese Whizz? Was it kosher?

DR. JEFF: Becky, what do you know about citric acid?

DR. REBECCA SCHWARTZ: Citric acid…molecular formula C6H8O7, the conjugate base is citrate.

DR. JEFF: And citrate?

DR. REBECCA SCHWARTZ: Occurs in the metabolism of all living things.

DR. JEFF: What is the primary ingredient of Cheese Whizz, resulting in that delicious tangy flavor?

DR. BOBBY: Come on Becky, you're going to have to work harder than that.

DR. REBECCA SCHWARTZ: Citric Acid?

DR. WILL: Citric acid coagulates into its base citrate form once in the human blood stream. Once in the blood stream oxidation of fats, proteins and carbohydrates spontaneously begins as the heart pumps cheese-whizz-infused blood directly into the brain creating a state of euphoria.

DR. BOBBY: Repeated MRI studies from patients in the ER show stimulation of the limbic system, including the hippocampus, which you know controls memory; and the amygdala, which controls fear and love.

DR. WILL: We know how emotions are linked to memory… Post treatment patients recall events related to eating cheese whizz with family and friends as far back as early childhood. Regardless of the follow-up medical procedures, all patients show favorable outcomes from the optimism that occurs from support for a positive emotional state generated immediately after entering the ER.

DR. REBECCA SCHWARTZ: I…I…I…

DR. WILL: Plain English Becky…Cheese Whizz makes people happy.

DR. JEFF: WILL tells us you wrote an outstanding admissions essay on the importance of holistic medicine in traditional medical institutions. But it seems you haven't internalized any basic philosophy and dedication to holistic medicine. Food derived sources of medicine and treatments that support the body generating its own healing process are at the core of holistic medicine. Your response is so disappointing.

DR. REBECCA SCHWARTZ: None of this makes sense to me. It's so non-standard.

DR. WILL: Medicine is an art and a science Becky. Medicine will never move forward unless we challenge standard practices, hold on to old fashioned philosophy of helping the body heal itself, and keeping the patient happy. Cheese Whizz and happiness go together.

DR. JEFF: Can you be open to new ideas Becky? Can you be a team player?

DR. REBECCA SCHWARTZ: Have you considered making a salve of cheese whizz for applications to external wounds, sort of like an intense citric acid effect similar to vitamin C?

DR. WILL: She's a keeper.

DR. JEFF: I want you to take a couple of days off Becky. Get yourself together. We'll reduce some of your hours in the ER so you can start some small independent investigation with the Cheese Whizz research just to get your feet wet.

DR. BOBBY: Shoot. I want you to take a week off Becky. I'll take you fishing. I never taught a girl to fish, but I believe a girl from the north that comes to the south that comes from the east as a foreigner and then becomes an American who eats cheese whizz can learn how to fish in the north, south, east, and west.

(The doctors shake Dr. Rebecca Schwartz's hand and pat her on the back, as she exists with Dr. Bobby.)

NURSE SALLY: I made some soy chicken with Cheese Whizz gravy for Dr. Schwartz. You want grits or taters with that soy chicken honey? (Exits)

DR. JEFF: She'll stop by on her way out Sally.

DR. BOBBY: You have to know how to bait a hook that's the secret to all fishing. Don't worry, I'll teach you all the techniques slowly. I'm very patient.

DR. REBECCA SCHWARTZ: Cheese Whizz…who will believe me…cheese whizz…

(Dr. Jeff and Dr. Will pour shot glasses and toast.)

DR. WILL: Should we tell her about the Southern Comfort chaser to the Cheese Whizz?

DR. JEFF: Naw. What for?

DR. BOBBY, DR. JEFF & DR. WILL: Cheers!

(Lights Out)

End of Play

Sambomammiejockey

Cohabitants

Characters:

Co-workers and business partners

Black man: James, Nigger James, Malcolm X, Principal Banks, Hank, Roni

White man: Sean, Willie Lynch, Everett Young, Mr. Monroe, Cole, Peter

Black woman: Narrator, Decon Penny, Dead Collector, Dianne Sargent, Angela Nardone

Setting:

Ground floor office in a commercial building. Harlem. Present Day.

NARRATOR: (Sung) America, America, God shed his grace on thee.

(Lights Rise)

SEAN: Finished. In time.

JAMES: (High Five) I wasn't worried Sean. You always handle your stuff.

SEAN: Don't you want to take a look at the designs before the meeting?

JAMES: Not really. I'm sure they're fine. I need to concentrate on summarizing the market survey. Make sure I tweak it to support whatever you pitch. Get Peter to help you.

SEAN: He wanted a few days off.

JAMES: Not the best time, he just started.

SEAN: Look, he's an excellent graphic designer and he does what I tell him. He actually had a problem with the design concept I wanted. But he followed through.

JAMES: Wants to keep his job.

SEAN: Yeah.

JAMES: So what's up with this guy?

SEAN: What do you mean?

JAMES: He's nerdy? What's he into?

SEAN: No idea, and I don't care. Not trying to be his friend. I want the work done.

JAMES: Cool. What are we paying him?

SEAN: Minimum.

JAMES: More cool. (Pause) Remember, my nephew's birthday is Saturday. Liz and Danny are expecting you.

SEAN: I didn't forget. Is your mom bringing collard greens?

JAMES: I doubt it. Liz and Danny don't eat soul food. They'll probably cater—I'd guess from somewhere with Northern Italian.

SEAN: I need to get back to dinner at your Mom's house. Her collard greens are so good, they can make a white man sing.

JAMES: Would you say that in front of my mother?

SEAN: Maybe. As long as I finished the complement with, "Praise the Lord, Sister Penny," I'm sure she wouldn't mind.

JAMES: Exactly why I'm not going over for dinner anytime soon…but you can. I love my Mom's cooking but I'm weary of her preaching. "Boy, when you gonna come back to church?" Can't eat in peace.

SEAN: I'll fill in as her "Holy Roly" white fake son. I can be "saved" through a meal if it makes Deacon Penny happy. Think I'll call her and ask if I can swing by Friday.

JAMES: Outta town. Some kind of preaching bus tour. She won't be at the party Saturday.

SEAN: Must be important if she's missing her grandson's birthday party. I bought Tony, the new iPhone.

JAMES: Are you crazy? His parents wouldn't buy that for him. Too expensive for a ten year old.

SEAN: He goes to the Benchmark School. I know those kids have iPhones.

JAMES: Maybe so, but his parents make sure he remembers the price tag for his education is affordable because his parents teach in the high school. His parents don't have money to burn, and Tony doesn't have a school expense account.

SEAN: James, I got a good deal.

JAMES: You're not hearing me. His parents will still have to buy a phone plan.

SEAN: You think I should get a gift card to put towards the phone plan?

JAMES: No! Okay, thanks. You went beyond…beyond. You work it out with Tony and his parents. I'm sure they'll appreciate… Well…thanks…

SEAN: Sure. (Pause) I think you should stay and deliver the pitch for this job.

JAMES: No way.

SEAN: You're always behind the scenes quiet. You should take credit for the creative vision. Let's push you as leading the team.

JAMES: I like staying in the background.

SEAN: Not for this one…

JAMES: It's the Bernard Brothers and cereal. So what.

SEAN: Come on…the Bernard Brothers… They're niggers.

JAMES: Excuse me?

SEAN: It'll look better if the nigger on the team pitches to the niggers. We'll close the deal right at the table.

JAMES: You called me a nigger.

SEAN: (Looking at a menu) What do you want for lunch? There's a new sushi place on 123rd.

JAMES: You don't get to call me a nigger.

SEAN: Seriously? Why are you—

JAMES: No you don't.

SEAN: Why are you overreacting?

JAMES: You crossed the line.

SEAN: We've known each other for ten years. We've worked together for five. I've sat in your mother's kitchen and eaten her collard greens and cornbread. I bought a new iPhone for your only nephew. We're friends.

JAMES: And with that, you're entitled to call me a nigger, a name I find offensive?

SEAN: Let's have lunch.

JAMES: Apologize.

SEAN: (Continuing to look at menus) Okay. Sure. I'm sorry.

JAMES: Means nothing to you.

SEAN: James, you asked me to apologize and I did. Move on.

JAMES: Means nothing to you.

SEAN: (Looking around the office) I have the menu for the new place somewhere. What was the name? Sexy Sushi. I can taste it in my mouth.

JAMES: I expect more from you Sean.

SEAN: Lay it out for me. I've heard you call out nigger when you're on the phone. You and Claude from the health food store call each other nigger…

JAMES: Those examples are different and you know it.

SEAN: What I know is you don't object to the word because you use the word.

JAMES: What I object to is you using the word.

SEAN: So you can dictate what words I use?

JAMES: Only that word…nigger.

SEAN: And does your rule extend over all spellings and pronunciations, "nigger," "nigga," nigghas."

JAMES: Cut it out.

SEAN: What about "niggardly"? You do know it means stingy and has nothing to do with "niggers," "niggas," and "nigghas."

NARRATOR: (Sung) O Beautiful, O Beautiful.

WILLIE LYNCH: Let's make a slave. What do we need? We need a nigger man and we use the same principle that we use in breaking a horse. We break the independence of their natural state and we make them dependent. Like this old black nigger. Get over here James.

NIGGER JAMES: Yes'um Boss.

WILLIE LYNCH: Like this nigger James. He's proof of the effectiveness of my methods. (Pause) Turn around James.

NIGGER JAMES: (Showing his scars) Yes'um.

WILLIE LYNCH: Obedience. Then we pitch the old nigger against the young nigger, and the dark skin nigger against the light skin nigger. We make him incapable of caring for his female and his offspring. They must love, trust, and respect only the white master. Then they can be useful for production in our business and for our pleasure.

NARRATOR: (Sung) O Beautiful, O Beautiful.

JAMES: I believe what you're telling me is that you deserve an honorary Black man card.

SEAN: Race is a social construction. It's all about class.

JAMES: What?

SEAN: It's all about checking boxes. White, Black, Hispanic. What kind of race is "Hispanic?" It's just a name politically constructed for government censuses. I'm not a Black man and I'm not trying to be.

JAMES: Don't worry. When you're pulled over to the side of the road by the police you won't have to prove you're a white man to get your share of white entitlement.

SEAN: I can get a ticket for speeding just like you.

JAMES: You and I both know that legal and illegal have "Black and White go to jail or not stamps." Unless of course you have one of those special one drop of Black blood DNA chips on your license.

SEAN: Think you know someone.

JAMES: Yeah, think you know someone.

NARRATOR: (Sung) O Beautiful, O Beautiful—

EVERETT YOUNG: Everett Young reporting live. Malcolm, you've been in a controversy with your leader in the Nation of Islam. Why is that?

MALCOLM X: I've been silenced from public speaking for ninety days because of some statements I made about the assassination of the president that were distorted by the press.

EVERETT YOUNG: What did you say Malcolm?

MALCOLM X: I said the same thing everyone else said, that the assassination of President Kennedy was the result of a climate of hate, only I said, "The chickens came home to roost." It means the same thing.

EVERETT YOUNG: Do you feel this country is making progress?

MALCOLM X: I would never say this country is making progress. If you stick a knife into me nine inches and pull it out three inches, is that progress? No. If you pull the knife all the way out, is that progress? No. Progress is healing the wound that the knife made. America won't even admit the wound is there.

NARRATOR: (Sung) O Beautiful, O Beautiful—

SEAN: The plain truth of it is that you have more in common with me than you do with the Bernard Brothers…rich hood rats.

JAMES: You need to…

SEAN: It's all about class. Admit who you are. Entitled with a Black face. Your summer vacations. The car you drive. Your gentrified penthouse condo. Your wine of the month club deliveries. We went to the same Ivy League School and that comes with privileges even if you get admitted with affirmative action and a scholarship.

JAMES: And which of us would that be?

SEAN: I'm the one still paying off student loans and trying to break out of my prewar walk up. I didn't qualify for the Black free ride train.

JAMES: And you know this because you hacked the financial aid office database.

SEAN: Let's not go there.

JAMES: We're already there.

SEAN: How else could you get through four years and come out living large in such a short period of time. I was eating off my friend's meal plans, working for minimum wage in the library, and still scraping pennies to keep peanut butter and jelly and white bread in my dorm room.

JAMES: What other white myths are you carrying around?

SEAN: Let's stop.

JAMES: Go on my "nigga." Speak.

SEAN: We're entitled because we went to the right schools, met the right people, and had a configuration of good luck to get us started with the business. You're more matched in my personal company than you are with those niggers from the projects starting a cereal company with some gangbanger money. No matter how much money the Bernard Brothers make and we help them make, they will still be low class. Green is go only for traffic signals.

JAMES: Let's get back to work. I want to see your work up for the cereal box.

SEAN: Right. (Taking out some drawings) Harlem is trendy. So we're golden without working too hard. Everyone wants local food. We just appeal to the changing demographic in Harlem—the new Harlem—all about diversity. Bring in the old with the new. We need to learn from the past. When Friendly Oats got rid of Aunt Jermima's bandana and gave her makeup and a curly perm their sales dropped. Everyone loves a sweet old Black mammie. (Continuing to show drawings) And we can play around with the ethnic mix with the West African immigrants. We use the same fabric print of the bandana and we create a hijab. Slick. We capture the Muslim market. I know. Brilliant. No one is trying to break those people out of the habit of only buying from each other. And we use the same print to make the Black jockey's shirt. We've captured the Blacks, Muslims, West Africans, and middle and upper whites all with minimum changes to our concept and continuity to the brand. Too much? I thought about putting a hair weave under the bandana. (Pause) We could also just test out my original idea, "Little Black Sambo." A beloved piece of American tradition captured on a box of granola cereal locally produced in the former Black Harlem for the new Harlem. Trendy, upscale, exclusive… What's not to like?

JAMES: I don't recognize you. Or maybe I didn't want to recognize you…what you believed…all this time… Where have I been?

SEAN: What part don't you like? I can make minor adjustments.

JAMES: My grandmother ironed and mended dress shirts for the guests at the only luxury hotel in Kapersberg, Virginia from the time she was twelve until the day she died at age ninety-two. You can't imagine how deeply loved I felt when I found out all of her ironing money had been carefully invested into a college fund for me. It was enough for all four years tuition and board.

SEAN: From ironing shirts?

JAMES: And by the way, that hotel was for whites only officially until 1967. And unofficially for whites only until 1976.

SEAN: You people…

JAMES: You mean us niggers?

SEAN: You said that. You people never consider that white people faced discrimination and hardship. Do you think someone gave my grandmother a break when she was fresh off the boat from Ireland? Whites were the majority in Harlem once. My apartment is a pass down family home.

NARRATOR: (Sung) O Beautiful, O Beautiful—

HANK: Are you on your phone Cole?

COLE: Keep it down. I'll be off in a minute.

HANK: Finish packing 256 so I can load it on the skid before the meeting.

COLE: In a minute Hank.

HANK: Russell warned you about using your phone when we're packing orders.

COLE: Russell ain't here. Done. I had to call in a payment for my electric bill. Fran wouldn't be interested in excuses if I got home and she was sitting in the dark.

HANK: You should ask them for a budget plan so you can pay the same amount every month.

COLE: A budget plan doesn't add more money into the budget. When we get a union and management is forced to give cost of living increases we won't—

HANK: You mean when we get a union and they send the plant overseas.

COLE: They can't do that. I told you, they have some kind of tax credits to keep the plant in New York.

HANK: Then what is the meeting about?

COLE: Probably upgrading the shipping. Only our department is meeting with old man Fred.

DIANNE SARGENT: Gentlemen, thanks for coming in. Mr. Schrieber wasn't able to meet with you as planned so he asked me to provide you with the options that are possible through the Human Resources department.

HANK: Options for what?

COLE: You firing us?

HANK: It's a lay off for some employees until the company completes restructuring.

COLE: Does restructuring come with a full paycheck?

DIANNE SARGENT: We need to all remain calm. We've put together some good options for you.

COLE: My wife is eight months pregnant. The option I want is my job and my full paycheck.

DIANNE SARGENT: I was hoping to talk to your department as a group because—

COLE: Why is shipping the only department here?

HANK: Let's take our envelopes and leave.

DIANNE SARGENT: I'm willing to meet with every employee individually to go over the specifics for your situation.

HANK: That means you still have your job Ms. Sargent.

COLE: Yeah Dianne. Do you still have a job?

DIANNE SARGENT: Yes, I'm remaining with the company.

COLE: What's in these envelopes? Is everyone from shipping getting the same offer?

DIANNE SARGENT: I was going to explain some of the restraints we had as a company.

COLE: Don't bother.

HANK: Let's get out of here.

COLE: (Opening his envelope) This says I'm not laid off, I'm being counseled into career options. I'll tell you where you can stick your career options. I've been working here since I graduated from high school. I have more years in than—

DIANNE SARGENT: And we thank you for your service. Unfortunately, the company will begin to outsource the shipping. We absorbed some employees who had transferrable skills into other departments.

COLE: What did they offer you Hank?

HANK: I don't want to…

COLE: (Rips open Hank's envelope) Like my Buddy Hank. He's being transferred to Quality.

HANK: (Taking the envelope from Cole) You shouldn't have done that.

DIANNE SARGENT: Call Human Resources for an appointment gentlemen. (Exits)

COLE: I got more years in. I should be going to Quality.

HANK: What do you want me to say Cole? That I'm sorry they're offering me a job?

COLE: We both know why they chose you over me.

HANK: Maybe it's payback for trying to organize.

COLE: (Showing his forearms) White man payback. Try not the right shade, brother.

HANK: (Reading notice) Did you read my notice when you took it? They're offering me an entry-level position in Quality. A salary that won't pay much over my mortgage. I suppose they think I can stop eating and paying my car note.

COLE: Those grants for keeping the company in New York… they're probably some affirmative action thing. They gotta keep some kinda quota of you guys.

HANK: Why are you doing this Cole? We both need jobs. None of this is right.

COLE: What ain't right is getting pushed out of a job because I'm white.

HANK: Those contracts to stay in New York, the outsourced shipping going to inmates in Peekshill Correctional. Ten cents an hour. The new enslavement.

COLE: Prison labor. I didn't know.

HANK: Want the shipping job those guys will have?

COLE: Hey, I didn't know… How did you know?

HANK: Doesn't matter, does it… I heard you…

COLE: I was steamed up.

HANK: Yeah.

COLE: Hey, cards tonight.

HANK: Not feeling like it. By the way, I'm not taking this offer. Maybe it's a job for you if you want it.

COLE: Why?

HANK: Because this (Holds up the envelope) is a message to me to move on. And I'm more afraid of staying here than I am of leaving.

NARRATOR: (Sung) O Beautiful, O Beautiful—

PRINCIPAL BANKS: Thank you for coming in Mr. Monroe. I wanted to talk to you about the PTA, but what's on your mind?

MR. MONROE: Yes, good to meet you. At the last PTA meeting there were rumors that there's going to be a rezoning of the district lines to include the General Patton housing complex.

PRINCIPAL BANKS: That's right. It's not a rumor.

MR. MONROE: That means low-income housing residents and the new condominium complex on Eighth Avenue—

PRINCIPAL BANKS: Frederick Douglas Boulevard.

MR. MONROE: —will all be zoned for this elementary school?

PRINCIPAL BANKS: That's correct.

MR. MONROE: What can we do about it?

PRINCIPAL BANKS: There's planning the administration will need to do. We'll keep the PTA informed.

MR. MONROE: That means larger class sizes, right?

PRINCIPAL BANKS: Yes.

MR. MONROE: And what's going to happen to the gifted and talented programs and the art's initiatives and—

PRINCIPAL BANKS: Actually, we're hoping the PTA will help us with the challenges of a reconfigured school with fund raising for what the central board is now calling non-essential programming. We have to plan for more English Language Learners and remedial reading.

MR. MONROE: And lower school standards...

PRINCIPAL BANKS: Mr. Monroe, all children deserve an appropriate education. All children are equal. You believe that of course.

MR. MONROE: I believe my son's education shouldn't be sacrificed for children who don't have his intelligence and skills.

PRINCIPAL BANKS: This book you donated for the silent auction...

MR. MONROE: A gently used edition of Little Black Sambo with Helen Bannerman's signature will raise—

PRINCIPAL BANKS: Some parents are offended by auctioning a book that for many represents a disgraceful period of American history.

MR. MONROE: That book was a family heirloom.

PRINCIPAL BANKS: I agree with them.

MR. MONROE: It was very generous of me to—

PRINCIPAL BANKS: I want to return the book. We can't accept this. And I hope my action won't discourage you from continuing to support the school's fund-raising efforts.

MR. MONROE: We're Americans and Little Black Sambo is part of America's literary history. For decades children have enjoyed the entertaining characters of Little Black Sambo and Little Black Mingo.

PRINCIPAL BANKS: You mean white children, don't you?

DEACON PENNY: Satan is alive and well. I said, Satan is alive and he is very well. And it's because of you, and you, and you, and you. Now I hear all of your inner voices talking. Deacon Penny, I come to church every Sunday. I read my Bible. I follow the Ten Commandments. I'm not the sinner. I'm not Satan's disciple. And I say, you are when you tolerate sinful fornication in the same city as your Christ Everlasting Life Church. Two men did not give birth to the baby Jesus. Two men did not create the holy family. Jesus and Mary creating a family for baby Jesus were not two men. Every day you turn your back on the Lord with your misguided acceptance of homosexual pagans. How do you keep Satan alive? The same way you keep the Holy Spirit alive. The way to the Lord is clear. You cannot say maybe. You cannot say I need to think about it. It's when you experiment with the words of the Lord, when you experiment with the guidance of the Holy Spirit that is when you feed and nourish Satan with a gourmet meal. And Satan is greedy. He's a glutton who will continue to eat your soul until there is no possibility for redemption. Shut it down. Shut down Pulsar.

[Loud Salsa music.]

DEAD COLLECTOR: Stanley Almodovar IV, Amanda Alvearo, Arturo Aracena-Montero, Rodolfo Ayalas, Alejandro Martinez

PETER: (Talking with a loud voice) Did you say Ronnie? It's hard to hear you over the music.

RONI: Roni…think macaroni…but no jokes please. Plenty of those since high school thanks.

PETER: It was his eyes. The kind of eyes that made me melt. His eyes were beautiful. They called me into his soul. I looked into his eyes and I went through his window. His eyes were kind. His eyes told me he was kind. I was fighting the truth I was feeling.

DEAD COLLECTOR: Martin Benitez Torres, Antonio Jackson, Darryl Brown, Jonathan V. Camu, Angel Vega

RONI: How ya doin gorgeous?

PETER: Gorgeous? My mother called me gorgeous when she dressed me up in a bow tie for my first grade class picture.

DEAD COLLECTOR: Simon Pablo Carrillo, Juan Martinez, Luis Martinez, Cory Jones, Tevin Mitchell

PETER: I'm not gay.

RONI: Nobody here is gay. We're all actors.

PETER: I'm waiting for someone.

RONI: Everyone is waiting for someone. I think you're waiting for me gorgeous. Like the music?

PETER: Love the music. Love Salsa.

RONI: Let's dance.

DEAD COLLECTOR: Franky Meyers, Dante Drayton, Mercedes Johnson, Juan Guerrero Santos

PETER: I watched the rhythm in his body as he grabbed my hand. I pulled away.

He stopped. He looked at me. This time I felt a little sadness in his eyes.

RONI: I get it. You have a problem with chocolate.

PETER: No, chocolate is nice. Chocolate…is beautiful. In my neighborhood in New York, uptown, there is chocolate on every street just about I mean…

RONI: And I mean my precious cherry vanilla…have you ever felt warm chocolate with a hint of peppermint and raspberries on your lips?

PETER: NO. I'm a friend with a couple of chocolates, that's it, only friends. Can we stop now?

RONI: It's me. It's the eyebrows right? Too arched? Too much? I told my stylist, "Don't experiment. Give me my regular brow wax."

PETER: You look beautiful.

RONI: Come on. I love this song.

PETER: I'll dance with you but I'm not gay. I like Salsa and I like to dance. Fine. We'll both pretend not to be gay. It'll be fun.

DEAD COLLECTOR: Paul Henry Jacob, Paul Hernandez, Juan Honorato, Javier Rosado, Jason Reyes, Chris Feliz, Xavier Serrano, Gilberto Josaphat, Tomas Shane, Leroy Fernandez Reyes, Luis Holder, Benny Wilson, Jerry Wright, Peter Cruz

RONI: Peter. Is that your real name?

PETER: Peter Cruz.

DEAD COLLECTOR: Edward Justice, Tony Disilva, Tommy Leinonen, Brenda Santos, Jean Perez, Antonio Murray, Kim Morrison, Jean Rodriguez, Luis Capo

PETER: You don't understand. I've been saved.

RONI: Me too. Gorgeous boy, you saved me from a same old…

PETER: I've never been…

RONI: I know. Most of us have our "never beens" until we do and then been there, done that, and ain't going back to the before.

DEAD COLLECTOR: Geraldo Ortiz Silvera, Eric Ramos, Joel Montana, Enrique Paniagua, Juan Velazquez, Yessica Sanotos

PETER: I can't.

RONI: I'm not going to stalk you, Peter, if that's your real name. If you're not interested, fine.

PETER: I'm interested. More than interested. That's the problem.

RONI: Not a problem gorgeous. You're free here. Be you.

ANGELA NARDONE: This is Angela Nardone and welcome to Morning Coffee with Friends. Earlier this morning beginning about two o'clock, police had a standoff against a gunman who single handedly began a rampage of shooting with semi-automatic weapons killing at least fifty and wounding more before killing himself at the Pulsar Nightclub on Caledonia Avenue. This popular lesbian, gay, bisexual, and transgender nightclub known for its weekly Latin night was filled to capacity. Chief of Police Sutton is calling the incident probably the deadliest mass shooting by a single shooter in United States history. The shooting has not been identified yet as either a hate crime or an act of terror. Police and firemen are still looking for survivors in the wreckage.

RONI: There are some things you can tell about a person by little things. My mother was so concerned that I grow up to be a gentleman. She sent me to dancing school, ballroom dance. Waltz, quickstep, fox trot… Mom said I would learn how to behave properly with young ladies. Growing up with an absent Dad, she was always thinking of ways to increase the male presence in my life. All boys' private school, scouting, worked for me…loved being around guys. Not exactly what Mom was thinking. Mom knew about love. Didn't work with my father but she wasn't bitter about how alcohol became my father's wife and lover before killing him. We all make choices she said. "Make good choices in your life Roni." Peter was my choice. A few hours and I knew. It was the subtle loving. The way he held my hand when we went to the dance floor together. His shyness and his denial of who he was that slowly drifted away. I came to the club for hook ups. I held his hand and knew I was past that. Peter was my good choice.

NARRATOR: (Sung) O Beautiful, O Beautiful—

SEAN: It's cereal. Granola. Made and packaged in a local community. And the point is we all want cereal.

JAMES: It is what it is. There doesn't have to be any gimmicks or tricks to entrap people in a changing Harlem demographic to buy something we all need and want.

SEAN: Maybe we could convince the Bernard Brothers to take a small percentage of the profits for the one of the local libraries…some literacy initiates for the test launch.

JAMES: I doubt if we'll have to convince them. They are anonymous donors for kid's programs in the neighborhood. They grew up here and they want to give back.

SEAN: B&B Granola wholesome, healthy, and local. That's all we need.

JAMES: Smart and simple.

SEAN: Everything should be that simple.

NARRATOR: (Sung) And crown thy good with brotherhood from sea to shining sea.

(Lights Out)

End of Play

Endnotes:

1. Adapted excerpts from a speech given by British slave owner Willie Lynch circa 1712 in Virginia. Original source unknown.
2. Adapted excerpts from film footage of Malcolm X interview circa December 1964. Original source unknown.
3. Adaptations of America the Beautiful circa 1910. Lyrics by Katharine Lee Bates. Music composed by Samuel A. Ward.

Note to the Director:

Time Course Episodes
Harlem Office 2016
Plantation-Virginia 1712
Factory-New York 2016
Harlem 2016
Florida 2016
Harlem Office 2016

HOLE

Hollow Spaces

Characters:

Becky Parker: African American woman (young adult & elder)

George Benjamin Davis: African American man (young adult & elder)

Announcer

Setting:

Circa 1960. Becky and George as young adults stand on opposite hilltops overlooking an open sea surrounding Fool's Island, a small island off the coast of North Carolina. They look forward as they describe their lives.

[Music Interlude: Southern Blues.]

SCENE I:

(Lights Rise)

GEORGE: The sun was warm, warm, warm. It beat down on my face till I be sweatin hard. The more I wipe it off, the more I sweat. My back be sweatin too. My school uniform shirt feel like a wet rag. It's okay. Once I gets by the sea I be fine. Folks say the sun on Fool's Island reach down like the devil break out of hell and when it hot it hot. Not like a hot you can measure, like a hot that just take you down, make you feel things, make you think things that drive your mind to not be right. The old folks say that's why they calls this place Fool's Island. The devil sun make you act like a fool. So you gots to watch yourself in the sun. In the high heat of the high sun, teachers keep the kids in the classroom, mother's keep the babies cozy in they day beds, bosses make the workers come into the field houses, and wives threaten their husbands to stay in the house. But I don't believe in this silliness. Only a fool on Fool's Island gonna believe the foolish local talk. And I ain't nobody's fool.

[Music Ends.]

BECKY: Ms. Morgan had an appointment. The doctor from Emory Creek is the closest doctor to Fool's Island. Folks say Fool's Island is halfway between North Carolina, South Carolina, and hell. The doctor come once a month to do annual checkups. By the end of one year, he would have seen all five hundred folks that live on this island. If you have some special problem you better have that problem on the time of the month when Doc Kennedy be here. So all us kids, you know…one school…one teacher we had the morning off. For us, it's like Christmas in June. We sorry Ms. Morgan is sick. But on an Island as small as Fool's Island, can't pretend you sick, cut school…can't get away with being bad…except unless you George and Becky. We the experts on being bad and not getting caught. (Looking at the opposite hilltop) George!

GEORGE: Becky!

BECKY: George!

GEORGE: Becky!

BECKY: George!

GEORGE: (Running towards Becky) I love you this wide.

BECKY: (Running towards George) I love you wider.

GEORGE: (Running towards Becky) I love you this high.

BECKY: (Running towards George) I love you higher.

GEORGE: (Running towards Becky) I love you bigger than the biggest big.

BECKY: (Stops running. Stands in front of George) I changed my mind. I don't love you no more. (Runs towards rocky shore)

GEORGE: You know I'll catch you. Stay away from the rocks.

BECKY: (Stopping at the edge of the cliff) George Benjamin Davis, you are the slowest slow. Come on. (Looking over the edge of the cliff) I won't climb down without you.

GEORGE: (Pulls Becky back away from the edge of the cliff. Sitting on the rocks with Becky) Your mama ever tell you stories about the life for life curse.

BECKY: Why you want to talk about somethin like that now?

GEORGE: Some sayin Ms. Morgan real sick, she could die, and when Doc Kennedy git here she may have to go to a hospital in one of the Carolina's.

BECKY: Don't make up stories.

GEORGE: I swear.

BECKY: And don't swear.

GEORGE: The elder's council met over our house after church last week. I overheard them sayin that they has to advertise in a big city Negro paper for a teacher, and they not sure how to get one interested in coming here.

BECKY: And they right. Ain't nobody but somebody born and raised here want to work here. What kinda work is here? Pig farmin, tobacco growin, and drinkin til you drink yourself to death.

GEORGE: You so negative girl. You know what's happenin to Black folks on the other side? In North Carolina? Folks is struggling to make ends meet and gettin beat down for tryin. And they want the same rights as white folks. There some students from North Carolina Agricultural and Technical College walked right into a Woolworth store in Greensboro and sat down at a Woolworth Store lunch counter.

BECKY: So.

GEORGE: They sat down in the whites only section.

BECKY: That's just stupid.

GEORGE: Equal rights Becky Parker. The way Dr. King speaks about all Negroes needin respect and privileges as citizens of the United States. My grandma Kate say, the sunshine so hot it make the island disappear during the day and white folks blinded to us and this place. But when it rain, and when it night, the devil sun can't do nothin to protect us so we has to be extra careful about drawing attention.

BECKY: Nobody wants what we got.

GEORGE: Girl, do you hear yourself talkin? We got land. We got rich, good land. And we have freedom to live the ways we want. We ain't sharecropping, workin somebody else's land.

BECKY: You got your mind buried in this red dirt George.

BECKY: Maybe, one day I'll ask Doc Kennedy if I can go to Emory Creek with him.

GEORGE: And do what?

BECKY: Explore, and have fun.

GEORGE: I love you Becky, but I want to shake you up sometimes. Seems like you don't want to think about the dangers that are out in the world.

BECKY: Always got to think safe George. Risk makes life interestin. Ready to climb down?

GEORGE: Hold my hand.

BECKY: I ain't never hold your hand before. I ain't holding your hand now. I knows these rocks just as good as you.

GEORGE: Today is different.

BECKY: You needs to stop. Don't get me wrong. I'm sorry bout Ms. Morgan but we have a whole morning off to have fun. We can be as bad as we want to be. Let's not lose the opportunity. (Climbing down the rocks)

GEORGE: (Following Becky) The sun felt hotter than I ever felt before. The rocks feel different today too.

BECKY: (Climbing down the rocks faster) You talkin like a Fool's Island fool.

GEORGE: Slow down Becky.

BECKY: That's why I don't love you anymore. You a sissy boy and I can't love a sissy boy.

GEORGE: (Pretending to fall down on a rock) Damn!

BECKY: (Climbing back up the rocks towards George) George, you all right?

BECKY: Well, I ain't everybody.

GEORGE: We don't have to have eight or nine kids. Five or six should be enough.

BECKY: George Benjamin Davis, just because you been my one and only sweetheart for my whole life, and just because I have a vagina.

GEORGE: Don't talk like that.

BECKY: I seen the books in Doc Kennedy's office. I have a vagina. I want to use it for sex!

GEORGE: That's sinful. Pastor John…

BECKY: Pastor John is married, and he feels up the vaginas of every woman he can get to pray with him in his private prayer room.

GEORGE: Lying is sinful.

BECKY: No lie. I seen it myself when…

GEORGE: I don't want to hear no more.

BECKY: I love you George, but I need a bigger world than this island can give. I may need you for a boyfriend and then a few boyfriends in the Carolina's after we graduate.

GEORGE: A few boyfriends?

BECKY: Maybe only North Carolina. I heard the men in South Carolina is crazy.

GEORGE: I can't believe you sayin these things to me.

BECKY: I'm messin wit you George Benjamin…you the sissiest…I mean sweetest boy I know. I needed some proof…of how much you loved me. Cause I do so love you, you foolish boy. I do so love you.

GEORGE: I love you Becky. (Pause) Let's climb down and get in the water. (Pause) You want a man who takes risks, right? Let's climb down. The tide is low. We can pull off our uniforms and get into the water. A little swim…in the safe part of the cove.

BECKY: What you say?

GEORGE: The sun is hot and we'll get dry in no time when we get out. We still have a few hours before we have to show up at school. Nobody (kiss) is lookin (kiss) for us (kiss).

BECKY: Who is this? Are you my George? Safety pin, safety net George.

GEORGE: I think you're tryin to tell me you want a man that excites you, isn't afraid of change…I can be that man Becky.

BECKY: I'm ready when you are. You lead.

(George and Becky walk down the steep rocks near the water's edge. At the edge, George takes off his pants.)

BECKY: Aren't you something George?

GEORGE: I can be the man you want me to be Becky.

BECKY: (Removing her uniform blouse) But no messin around. That was just talk about my vagina. I'm not that kind of girl.

GEORGE: I know. You aren't Carol.

BECKY: Carol?

GEORGE: Nothin—

BECKY: It's something, so spill it.

GEORGE: Everyone knows about Carol. Let's get in, gettin a little cold standin here in my drawers Becky.

BECKY: Carol. Why her name, right here, right now? Tell me.

GEORGE: Leave it alone please.

BECKY: Tell me.

GEORGE: I said her name because you were talkin about messin around. And I would never ask you to mess around because you're not that kind of girl.

BECKY: And what kind of girl am I?

GEORGE: You're special. You're precious. You're the kind of girl to build a life with.

BECKY: And what kind of girl is Carol?

GEORGE: We don't need to talk about Carol or anybody else. This is about us.

BECKY: What kind of girl is Carol? (Pause) What kind?

GEORGE: She's a whore. She's a pussy machine. Everybody knows it. You can smell her in heat coming down the street.

BECKY: Maybe Carol is a whore because everybody treats her like one. I think maybe your information about Carol is more than gossip George.

(Becky trips and falls into the water. The undercurrent pulls her out quickly from the shore.)

[Sound Effects: Splashes, screams, torrential ocean water.]

BECKY: It's pullin me out. It's pullin me out.

(George reaches out to Becky. He grabs her skirt, pulling off a piece of the fabric and making a hole. He jumps into the water. His leg is secured by tangled seaweed. He's not fast enough or strong enough to pull Becky into shore. She quickly disappears.)

GEORGE: (Loud to fading screams) Becky. Becky. Becky.

[Sound Effects: Spiritual music of India.]

ANNOUNCER:

Mahatma Gandhi- 1925

Non-violence is the answer.

"We have no secrets. Let us begin by being clear about General Smuts' new law: All Indians must now be fingerprinted, like criminals, men and women. No marriage, other than a Christian marriage, is considered valid. Under this Act, our wives and mothers are whores, and every man here is a bastard. And our policemen, passing an Indian dwelling — I will not call them homes — may enter and demand the card of any Indian woman whose dwelling it is. Understand, he does not have to stand at the door. He may enter. Whatever they do to us, we will attack no one, kill no one, but we will not give our fingerprints – not one of us. They will imprison us, and they will fine us. They will seize our possessions, but they cannot take away our self-respect if we do not give it to them. I am asking you to fight! To fight against their anger, not to provoke it. We will not strike a blow, but we will receive them. And through our pain we will make them see their injustice, and it will hurt — as all fighting hurts. But we cannot lose. We cannot. They may torture my body, break my bones, even kill me. Then, they will have my dead body – not my obedience. We are Hindu and Muslim, children of God, each one of us. Let us take a solemn oath, in His name, that come what may we will not submit to this law. I praise such courage. I need such courage because in this cause I, too, am prepared to die. But, my friend, there is no cause for which I am prepared to kill."[1]

[Musical Interlude: Medley of Negro Protest Songs.]

ANNOUNCER: Inspired by the philosophy of non-violent struggle of Mahatma Gandhi, Reverend Martin Luther King leads the struggle for Negro equality. It reaches its peak in the mid-1960s with more African Americans becoming committed to nonviolent protests throughout the South.

Southern Christian Leadership Conference

Student Nonviolent Coordinating Committee

Solidarity

Sit-in

Boycott

Demonstrate

Rally

Freedom Rides

March, March, March…

"I have a dream that one day on the red hills of Georgia the sons of former slaves and the sons of former slave owners will be able to sit down together at the table of brotherhood.

I have a dream. I have a dream. I have a dream."[2]

(Pause)

Negro girl found by fishermen off the coast of North Carolina. Authorities say, it's a miracle she survived. Her identity is unknown.

[Sound Effects: Ocean waves hitting against rocks.]

SCENE II-TWENTY YEARS LATER. CIRCA 1980

(Becky stands over the cove on Fool's Island looking at the ocean. Enter George.)

GEORGE: Not too many folks know about this spot on the island. See that hole between the large boulders? My grandfather used to say it was, "Behind God's Back."

BECKY: Or behind a fool's back.

GEORGE: What was that?

BECKY: I was just exploring. How you know about this place.

GEORGE: Born and raised here. I come here often…look out on the ocean, clear my head…

BECKY: It's peaceful in a haunting way.

GEORGE: How long are you staying on our island?

BECKY: Leaving tonight.

GEORGE: Tonight? Small island town as we are, I'm surprised I haven't heard any talk about a beautiful woman such as yourself.

BECKY: I'm married. My husband is working on a missionary project with Grace Baptist Church.

GEORGE: No offense Ma'am.

BECKY: None taken.

GEORGE: May I ask your name?

BECKY: (Staring) You may.

GEORGE: Your name is…

BECKY: I said you could ask. I didn't say I would answer.

GEORGE: My name is George. Pleased to meet you.

BECKY: Mrs. Russell.

GEORGE: Okay Mrs. Russell. We're an old fashioned small town like friendly-island here but that's okay. Something familiar about you, that's all.

BECKY: I have that kinda face. A face people think they know.

GEORGE: Maybe. I supposed we could have ever met.

BECKY: No.

GEORGE: I guess not. As old as I am, I've never left the island.

BECKY: Why?

GEORGE: Lost someone I cared about once, right out there. Always blamed myself. Before I met my wife, I just sank deeper and deeper into the hole that was in my heart.

BECKY: You have kids?

GEORGE: Not one. We wanted kids, and we tried. My wife went to one of the healers on the island.

BECKY: You don't have to—

GEORGE: Sorry. You remind… I felt I could talk. I come here, because this is where I lost my sweetheart. I try to forgive myself but I can't. I'm happy with my life, but I can't seem to move away from guilt. My wife, Susie, she's a good woman. We have plenty of nieces and nephews that we spoil…just like having our own. My farm supply store is on the other side of those ridges there. Do you have kids?

BECKY: Five boys and one baby girl. We're stayin at Miss. Amy's Bed & Breakfast.

GEORGE: That's a big family. You've been blessed.

BECKY: Yes, I've been blessed. And you too.

GEORGE: Ever loose someone dear to your heart?

BECKY: Yes. And I hope that wherever he is, that he's happy. (Pause) See those rocks. I believe I had a few of them in my head when I was young. Couldn't nobody tell me nothin. Everythin was about me. We all have to grow up but some mistakes in our youth, we just can't take back and erase. I had to learn. Folks shouldn't dwell on things they can't change. Lean from the past, and live without regret.

GEORGE: You right about that. I think about my nieces and nephews. They have more opportunities for magnificence and for destruction than I ever had.

BECKY: The world is changing, and it has to change some more. I remember so many times in my life when I fell deep down into despair. Love from kind people lifted me up. I know now that love is always the answer. You have to receive it, give it, and make sure it gets passed around.

GEORGE: Have you always been so wise?

BECKY: See those boulders over there? I had miniature ones in my head for a long time, until circumstances woke me up.

GEORGE: I've been very fortunate to meet you here today. Thank you for listening to me and for…

BECKY: It was nothin…

(Exit George. Becky takes out the piece of cloth she had saved when she became lost at sea.)

(Enter George. He looks at Becky and shows her the piece of cloth he saved when Becky became lost at sea.)

(Lights Out)

End of Play

Endnotes

1 Adapted from the 1925 speech on non-violence by Mahatma Gandhi.

2 Adapted from the 1963 "I have a dream" speech by Dr. Martin Luther King, Jr.

PEE

"Some people are other people to those they love."
Oscar Wilde

Characters:

Buster Spencer/Pops: African American man, senior citizen

George Spencer/G: African American, son, thirty something

William Spencer/Will: African American, son, thirty something

Nurse Johnny Booker: White, late middle aged woman

Setting:

Present day. Mid-morning. Inside a waiting room in an outpatient clinic. Buster and George sit on waiting room chairs with end tables next to each chair. On the end table closest to Buster are several plastic cups for collecting urine samples. Buster "plays" with them by making towers and then knocking them down. He also makes funny faces with the cups. He places cups on his nose, his head, in his mouth, etc. He tries to get George's attention. On the table next to George is a laptop and cell phone. George looks forward at the nurse's station (audience), annoyed and ignoring Buster. He goes back and forth between working on his laptop and putting it down. Nurse Booker works behind the counter. On the opposite end of the stage. Inside of an apartment/music studio. William is engaged in various activities related to composing music.

(Lights Rise)

GEORGE: Pops! (Pause) Pops!

BUSTER/POPS: Sitting right next to you. I can hear you. Not wearing a hearing aid yet. There's nothing wrong with my ears. You're not going to make me wear a hearing aid. Randy's son forced him to get a hearing aid. He was better off when he didn't have to listen to that non-stop nagging wife and those stair-step grand kids. Do you know what Irish twins are?

GEORGE: No Pops, I don't know.

BUSTER/POPS: I don't know either.

NURSE BOOKER: All right guys. Blood work is back from the lab. The doctor will call you Mr. Spencer if he has any concerns.

BUSTER/POPS: The doctor doesn't need to call me. You can call me Nurse Booker. My number is on the chart.

NURSE BOOKER: I did look at your labs Mr. Spencer. They're beautiful. Cholesterol level, liver function, kidney function, glucose…

BUSTER/POPS: (Growling like a lion and adjusting his pants) That's what I'm talking about.

NURSE BOOKER: If I didn't have your chart, I'd say you were half your age, and very healthy.

BUSTER/POPS: (Growling) Like a young lion…ready to stalk his prey.

GEORGE: Pops, you're embarrassing us.

BUSTER/POPS: I'm not embarrassed. Are you embarrassed Nurse Booker?

NURSE BOOKER: No Sir.

GEORGE: Besides, it's the lionesses that typically do the hunting for a pride.

BUSTER/POPS: Ruin everything for me George. (Pause) I was talking about Randy. His son forced him to move in with his "tongue and temper" wife and his screaming, spoiled grand kids. Can you understand why he didn't want a hearing aid?

NURSE BOOKER: Waiting on that urine sample Mr. Spencer. Half a cup will be fine.

BUSTER/POPS: Take me home.

GEORGE: Pee in one of those cups instead of playing games, and I'll take you home.

(Lights fade on clinic. Lights rise on William and George as teenagers in the family apartment. William and George stand with their backs to the audience as they urinate on the apartment wall. William is dressed in Las Vegas style chorus line boa, headdress, and heels.)

GEORGE: I don't want to do that song. Why do we always have to sing one of those lame show tunes?

WILLIAM: Then do some beats while I hum.

GEORGE: Cool. I'll start. (Makes hip hop beatboxing noises)

WILLIAM: (Hums, sings, and makes vocals to his rendition of "New York, New York")

(George and William urinate on the wall to the music. Enter Pops. George and William stop urinating and zip their pants.)

GEORGE & WILLIAM: Hi Pops.

POPS: Are those your mother's Las Vegas show girl clothes?

GEORGE & WILLIAM: Yes Pops.

POPS: And whose idea was it to dress up in Las Vegas showgirl clothes?

WILLIAM: Mine Pops.

POPS: And urinating on the wall I painted yesterday? Whose idea was that?

WILLIAM: It's like a Jackson Pollack painting now Pops, with all these pee lines.

POPS: Jackson Pollack. You learned about him in school.

WILLIAM: Yes Pops.

POPS: That's what I get for giving you boys an expensive education. (Sits down) Clean the wall with bleach and water. And don't do it again.

WILLIAM & GEORGE: Yes Pops.

POPS: You like those clothes William?

WILLIAM: They're great. I like the colors, and…

POPS: Only wear them in the house. And don't tell anybody about them.

WILLIAM: Thanks Pops.

POPS: You're not interested in these clothes George?

GEORGE: Naw.

POPS: Why were you peeing on the wall?

GEORGE: Cause Will was doing it. I was playing army, and using my gun. It was fun.

POPS: Have they given you boys that talk about safe sex yet in school?

GEORGE & WILLIAM: No Pops.

POPS: Okay…George, make sure you remember it. William…I'll think of a better talk for you. But remember, show girl clothes only in the house. With the shades down.

BUSTER/POPS: Las Vegas. Show girls. I only dated showgirls. Beautiful girls. Long legs. Always liked those long legs. The ones that could tap dance were the best. The ones that could tap dance, swing dance, and can-can kick… That was your mother.

(Lights fade on apartment. Lights rise on clinic.)

BUSTER/POPS: You know what they say about fruit and tree, Nurse Booker.

NURSE BOOKER: I do.

BUSTER/POPS: Handsome, athletic, and viral. My son inherits it all from me.

NURSE BOOKER: It takes an egg and a sperm Mr. Spencer.

BUSTER/POPS: It's mostly the sperm. That makes the man. My son was quarterback starting freshman year in high school. Sent him to a big, fancy, Catholic school. Football scholarship. Could have finished Notre Dame on a football scholarship.

GEORGE: Cut it out, please Pops.

BUSTER/POPS: What do you think he does with that talent?

GEORGE: Forms his own successful IT company.

BUSTER/POPS: Goes one year, and drops out of school. Most valuable player. Guaranteed four-year ride, or NFL recruitment.

GEORGE: Yes Dad, waste of talent.

BUSTER/POPS: You're not happy son. I think it's because you regret the legacy you could have had.

GEORGE: How much longer do you need? I have to get out of here. I need to get you home.

BUSTER/POPS: I can take the bus. I still have my senior discount card. (Searches his pants and coat pocket) Left my wallet on the kitchen counter. I need to borrow a few dollars to get home...exact fare for the bus...and some money for donuts. There's that nice bakery on Third...

GEORGE: You keep showing me reasons why you can't live alone anymore. You're away from home, without money, without ID, and the bakery that was on Third is now a dry cleaners.

BUSTER/POPS: That's small stuff son. Nurse Booker, would you loan me money for bus fare if I need it.

NURSE BOOKER: Of course, Sir.

BUSTER/POPS: Maybe she would drive me home. What kind of ride do you have sweetheart?

GEORGE: Pops, you can't talk to a woman you don't know like that in a workplace. That could be considered sexual harassment.

BUSTER/POPS: William, do you need to make something out of nothing? She might give me money. She might drive me home. And she is a sweetheart. So I said it aloud. And she isn't a stranger. This is the same clinic you drag me to every month to look for medical problems I don't have. (Looking at Nurse Booker) Is there a problem Nurse Booker?

NURSE BOOKER: No Sir. But I'd just like to get that urine sample to the lab for processing before I go on break.

BUSTER/POPS: See. If I said, "I wonder what Nurse Booker looks like under those scrubs." And "I would love to have a few squeezes of that nice, shapely buttock," or "I think if she doesn't do it already, she should shave her pubic hair in the shape of a heart. I could smear mascarpone cheese all over it, and eat it off…" That would be sexual harassment.

GEORGE: Pops!

BUSTER/POPS: But, only if she heard me.

GEORGE: I have better things to do than listen to your dirty old man fantasies.

BUSTER/POPS: Yes, I know you do George.

GEORGE: I apologize. I didn't mean it.

BUSTER/POPS: Yes, you did.

GEORGE: I apologize. I didn't mean it in a bad way.

BUSTER/POPS: George Washington Carver Spencer, you always mean what you say. But look what you're doing? Stop trying to make me old and keep me old. I don't want you to take care of me. Get yourself a wife and kids. I'm not living with you, but we can visit. And you're not dropping those kids off for me to watch.

GEORGE: You want to be a grandfather or not?

BUSTER/POPS: I want to be a virtual reality grandfather. I'll have all the photographs to show off. I'll go to the kid's games. Because your boys will be athletes…your girls too. And I want to go to all of the Grandparents' Days at their schools. And I'll send them a few dollars in birthday cards once a year. And they'll send me "I love you Grand Pops" cards on Father's Day.

GEORGE: Seems kind of selfish actually.

BUSTER/POPS: Selfish? I raised my kids. Now, you raise some. I don't expect any grandkids from William.

GEORGE: I don't think William wants kids.

BUSTER/POPS: Probably for the best. How would he get a kid? Surrogate mother? Adopted? You have a couple of kids the regular way. Get married and get your wife pregnant. What's the hold up anyway? What's the name?

GEORGE: The family doesn't like me. And it's Buttercup.

BUSTER/POPS: Cute name. Am I ever going to know the real name?

GEORGE: No.

BUSTER/POPS: Am I ever going to meet this person?

GEORGE: No.

BUSTER/POPS: Ugly? Unemployed? Uneducated? Skank?

GEORGE: No. Swimsuit model in Miami, in demand, making a great salary.

BUSTER/POPS: Then what's the problem?

GEORGE: The problem is you won't pee in the damn cup.

NURSE BOOKER: Sh……… Your father needs to feel relaxed. Come back tomorrow. Or, be patient. He'll go eventually. The clinic closes at six.

GEORGE: My flight leaves at six.

(Lights fade on clinic. Lights rise on William and George as teenagers in the family apartment.)

WILLIAM: (Counting water filled balloons) Six, seven, eight, nine, ten.

GEORGE: That's enough. Five each.

WILLIAM: Maybe we shouldn't have put black shoe polish in this balloon (Pointing to one of the balloons) What if it falls on someone's clothes? Pop's will be really pissed off.

GEORGE: Naw. Just the right amount of wrong makes this right.

WILLIAM: What time is it?

GEORGE: (Looking at clock) Six.

GEORGE & WILLIAM: (Pushing the balloons out of the window) Dad's coming.

BUSTER/POPS: (Covered with shoe polish) Damn! What is this?

(Lights out on apartment. Lights up on the outpatient clinic.)

BUSTER/POPS: Damn. I gave you and your brother too much freedom after your mother left. Trying to make up for… Maybe I should have tore your butts up like the other Dad's in the neighborhood.

GEORGE: Naw. That's wasn't you. You always tried to reason with us. And we respected you. We had that Jewish guilt without being Jewish. Always felt bad when we disappointed you.

BUSTER/POPS: Then why did you give up football?

GEORGE: That couldn't be helped. (Pause) How much longer Dad?

BUSTER/POPS: I passed all of my water before I left the house. I don't have to go.

GEORGE: You should have held it until we got to the clinic.

BUSTER/POPS: No, I shouldn't have. When you have to pass water, you have to pass water.

GEORGE: What about some more to drink?

BUSTER/POPS: No. I've had enough.

GEORGE: I can get you more ginger ale from the soda machine.

BUSTER/POPS: You don't think four cans of ginger ale is enough?

GEORGE: Apparently, not enough to make you go.

BUSTER/POPS: I have something I can try. (He takes a metal flask out of his coat pocket)

GEORGE: (Snatches the flask and smells it) Vodka! You can't drink that in here.

BUSTER/POPS: It's medicinal.

GEORGE: You can't drink alcohol before they test your urine.

BUSTER/POPS: Doesn't matter George. I'm not sick.

GEORGE: It does matter. You need to be more serious about your check-ups.

BUSTER/POPS: I need to relax, then I could pee some more. (Takes out a pack of wrappers and a lighter, then stands up to exit)

GEORGE: What are you going to do?

BUSTER/POPS: What does it look like I'm doing? It's only a little weed. I'll just be a few minutes. I'll smoke on the side of the building.

GEORGE: (He snatches all the items) Where did you get these?

BUSTER/POPS: Really George? You're asking how I got weed? I'm healthy and a little weed helps get the edge off from the stress caused by my children.

(Both men sit down. Buster returns to his activities playing with the urine collection cups.)

GEORGE: Pops, you're healthy now, and we want you to stay that way. Men of your age need more frequent tests and check-ups. Think of it like an old car that needs attention even when it's running.

BUSTER/POPS: I get it. I'm the old car. You're the newer model.

GEORGE: I didn't mean it that way.

BUSTER/POPS: Yes, you did George.

GEORGE: I did, but I didn't in a mean way. Pops, I have to make appointments for you around my work schedule. What about a little more appreciation and more cooperation?

BUSTER/POPS: George! If I wanted to go for check-ups, I could go myself.

GEORGE: And you wouldn't go…so I bring you.

BUSTER/POPS: And what is the point? Same thing, every time. They do the tests. They find nothing wrong. They bill my insurance company for hundreds of dollars to test a quarter ounce of pee. A waste of my time, and a waste of money.

GEORGE: You're not paying for it.

BUSTER/POPS: Somebody is paying for it…and I don't mean the insurance company. That's the problem with you kids… you think the paying is only about money…I'm always paying something. Now, I'm paying with aggravation. Sitting here. This office. These tests. Reminding me I'm old, I'm healthy, and that my friend's aren't. I was popular. I had my pick of friends. Now, all of my friends are dead…all of them. The only ones left, drool, can't walk alone, and talk nonsense).

(Lights fade on clinic. Lights rise on William and George as teenagers in their bedroom in the family apartment. George sits on one of the twin beds. William stands, holding a stack of magazines.)

WILLIAM: You could have your pick.

GEORGE: What are you talking about Will?

WILLIAM: You could have your pick. You know all the girls run after the jocks, not just the cheerleaders. You could taste pussy everyday if you wanted to. (Pause) Then I found these. (Throws erotic gay men's magazines on the floor) You don't like pussy do you?

(George throws a punch. The punch escalates into full scale fighting. George is winning. Enter Pops.)

BUSTER/POPS: (Pulling George off William) Break it up you two. Play fighting again?

GEORGE & WILLIAM: (Kicking magazines under the bed) Yes Pops.

BUSTER/POPS: Haven't I told no play fighting in the house. Play fighting always turns into real fighting.

GEORGE & WILLIAM: Yes Pops.

BUSTER/POPS: George, you should be ashamed of yourself. You know William is (Pause) "soft."

WILLIAM: Pops?

POPS: It's okay William. George is the big brother, but he needs to protect you.

GEORGE: Yes Pops.

WILLIAM: Pops, George is the one…

POPS: We've never talked about this as a family. I'm not one to talk about the obvious. But, I've known you had a sugar coating for a long time. At first, I thought you were just reacting to your mother leaving you boys…and me…but then I saw all the signs.

WILLIAM: Signs?

POPS: I have one son who plays football, and one son who plays dress up. Don't make me say anything else. I love both of you for who you are. There's room in the world for young men like you William, but people are full of hate and prejudice so we have to protect you.

GEORGE: Yes Pops. It'll never happen again. (Moving his arms over to hug William) Our family business.

WILLIAM: Pops, you've got it all wrong. I'm not the one…

POPS: That's enough William. Everything is fine. Remember, shades down. (Pause) Did I give you boys that talk about safe sex yet?

WILLIAM & GEORGE: Yes Pops.

POPS: There's a box in my night drawer. Keep some in your wallet. No…we're gonna have to make some special considerations for William. I hope I don't kick myself later for saying this. (Pause) I know you boys are gonna have sex, no matter what I say about it because you're my sons. So, if you're gonna have sex, be discrete…only in our house. In our house. In your room. Be careful. I don't want to know about it.

WILLIAM & GEORGE: Yes Pops.

POPS: And William…I'll get you some books…some magazines.

WILLIAM: I already have some Pops.

(Exit Pops)

WILLIAM: Why didn't you just tell him?

GEORGE: (Pause) I can't.

WILLIAM: (Comforting George) So, I've got a little brother who loves dick. Doesn't matter G. I'm always here for you. But you owe me big time.

(Lights change in the apartment to festive, party lights. Festive music. George and William play sex tag. They take turns using the bedroom for sexual escapades. Expressed in movements. Lights fade on bedroom apartment, and then rise on clinic.)

GEORGE: I'll be back Pops. I need to make a call. Keep trying to pee...please... I'm not the boss of you...but I want to finish this appointment before I leave town. Your check-up isn't complete without all the lab results. (He exits with his cell phone)

(Lights rise, bright on William. Telephone rings. He picks up the phone while continuing his composing. Lights continue on George. Lights dim on Pops.)

WILLIAM/WILL: How's it going G?

GEORGE: It's not Bro. Still at the doctor's office.

WILLIAM: What? Wasn't the appointment at 10:00? It's noon. Problems? He's sick?

GEORGE: Perfectly healthy except we don't have all the lab results. He won't pee. If he pees they promised to get the sample processed and the results today. Then I can fly out of here with a clear head. Going to Miami. Gonna spend a few weeks with Buttercup.

WILLIAM: Won't pee? That's strange. He's never had a problem when I bring him for his appointments.

GEORGE: And Will, he's complaining about being healthy and not having friends.

WILLIAM: He's playing with you G, trying to get your attention maybe.

GEORGE: The only thing he's playing with is the urine cups.

WILLIAM: Playing with the urine cups? He's bored. Take him home. Gotta go G. Gotta a gig composing music for this performance artist.

GEORGE: Wait, I don't know what to do. I can't think of anything to make him go. He said he peed before we left the house.

WILLIAM: You should have had him hold it.

GEORGE: Will! You're not helping me.

WILLIAM: Okay. Give him some ginger ale.

GEORGE: I did. He drank four cans.

WILLIAM: And that didn't make him pee? Pops is healthier than we are. Bring him home.

GEORGE: Listen up. We need the lab results to make sure he doesn't have diseases. Men his age can have medical changes at any time…

WILLIAM: George…we're not talking about Mom. Men and women have different bodies and different issues when they get old.

(Lights out on conversation. Lights up on Pops sitting on one of the beds in the apartment bedroom. William and George are in the room listening to him.)

BUSTER/POPS: It was never about you boys. Do you know that?

GEORGE: You never really talked about Mom. You always talked around her, like she was a visitor. Not a part of the family.

WILLIAM: Pops, I was only three, I don't remember Mom to be honest.

GEORGE: You've always been MOMPOP. I never missed anything. Some kids had a mother and a father that hated each other. You always showed us love Pops.

BUSTER/POPS: Then let me say this for me. Aloud. So I can let it go. You know your mother was a showgirl, but you don't know that when I met her, she was a chorus line dancer on her way to the top, a solo dancer, with a whole production designed around her. She was beautiful, long legs, perfect posture, charisma, grabbed attention whenever she walked down the street. Didn't hurt that she was a six foot two chocolate sister with long wavy hair. I was struck , defeated by her everything. I met her every night after her gig. William, you came, and then two years later you George. Happened, and happened again. I suppose for a hot minute, your Mom thought she wanted what people would suppose she would want: a husband, and kids. And she played house with me until you were born George. Then she stopped lying to herself, and left. I did my best to make her happy, but it was an impossibility from the beginning. I haven't thought about her in a long time. Why am I thinking about this now? I want you to have love in your life. But that love isn't going to happen if you aren't the person you are meant to be. Your Mom, wasn't meant to be a mother except to bring the two of you into the world.

WILLIAM: Pops.

BUSTER/POPS: Your mother loved me, but she wasn't in love with me. I know the difference now.

GEORGE: Why are we talking about this now Pops?

BUSTER/POPS: You're two fine young men. You should know the truth. Sons, two people make a relationship. I blamed your mother for everything. We had fun. It was easy. But it wasn't love. Your mother would give me a hand job…

WILLIAM & GEORGE: Pops!

BUSTER/POPS: She would give me a hand job, and I would feel a little something. But when I was honest with myself, I realized, I could do a better hand job myself. I didn't like the way she did it. I was pretending. She would do her thing, and then I would go into the bathroom, and as quietly as I could, I'd jerk off.

WILLIAM & GEORGE: Pops!

BUSTER/POPS: I wasn't a monster. I'd never hurt her feelings purposely. Then I started thinking about our sex, all the way sex, intercourse…

WILLIAM & GEORGE: Okay Pops.

BUSTER/POPS: I realized, there wasn't sexual attraction. Your mother was physically one of the most beautiful women I ever laid my eyes on, but there was nothing between us sexually. (Pause) Oh man. Do I feel better! Just getting that out. How do you boys feel? Good?

WILLIAM & GEORGE: Good. Yeah. Right.

GEORGE: Are you finished Pops?

BUSTER/POPS: William, that's why there was never a question in my mind about your…you know…when I realized…you were a little light in your loafers.

WILLIAM: Pops…

GEORGE: Yes Pops. And you know, I love William just the way he is too. Right William?

WILLIAM: Pops…

BUSTER/POPS: That's good. Good. We're good. Don't pretend to be someone else to get love.

GEORGE: Sometimes people get trapped into pretending Pops.

BUSTER/POPS: Look. I love you boys for who you are. I've got my soft, sweet son (Grabbing William), taking after your mother, and my hard, manly son, taking after me. It's all good. We're family. (Pause) Have I given you that talk about sex yet?

WILLIAM & GEORGE: Yes Pops.

BUSTER/POPS: How are you making out William?

WILLIAM: Good Pops, I…

POPS: I don't need any details… (Pause) I know I don't have to worry about you George, stud, like your father.

(Exit Pops)

GEORGE: If he knew the truth, it would hurt him. It would hurt me.

(Lights out on apartment. Lights rise on present day conversation between George at the hospital and William in his apartment on the phone.)

GEORGE: Tell me something to help him pee in a cup.

(Pause)

Will?

(Pause)

Will?

WILLIAM: Have him go to the bathroom and run the water from the faucet.

GEORGE: Tried it. There's only one bathroom here. After Pops was in the bathroom playing with the water for thirty minutes the nurse told me he was preventing bathroom use for other patients.

WILLIAM: Give him your phone. Play some water relaxation sounds.

GEORGE: No. And did you know he smokes weed?

WILLIAM: I don't see a problem…

GEORGE: And he keeps a flask with vodka in his coat pocket.

WILLIAM: Pretty cool, right? I gave it to him last Christmas.

GEORGE: What are you trying to do to Pops?

WILLIAM: Those things are not serious G. Pops should live the way he wants to live. His life, remember? (Pause) Want to try a last resort?

GEORGE: Anything to get me outta here.

WILLIAM: Go into the bathroom with him, whip out your dick, and start peeing. He'll start peeing, catch some pee in a cup mid-stream. Be careful not to hit the walls.

GEORGE: I'm not peeing in the bathroom with my father!

WILLIAM: Hey, we learned how to pee standing up by watching Pops, not by going into the bathroom with Mom.

(George hangs up the phone. Enter Nurse Booker.)

NURSE BOOKER: How are you doing with helping your father relax?

GEORGE: Not good. Not good at all.

(Exit Nurse Booker.)

GEORGE: Pops, do you want me to go into the bathroom with you? Maybe I can help?

BUSTER/POPS: Help?

GEORGE: I could help you pee.

BUSTER/POPS: Do you think at my age that I've forgotten how to pee?

GEORGE: I could help you…maybe hold your…or hold the cup…

(Enter Nurse Booker.)

NURSE BOOKER: I'm going on break soon Mr. Spencer. (Handing him a new urine specimen cup) Try to fill half of the cup for me.

(Exit Pops with the specimen cup.)

NURSE BOOKER: Have you been taking care of yourself?

GEORGE: Why do you ask?

NURSE BOOKER: Because, sometimes the caregivers forget to take care of themselves. Maybe that could be you? (Pause) Your father is a remarkably fit and healthy man. The only thing I believe he needs to have a complete life, is to be happy, and to see his sons happy. Don't worry so much. Let me take your blood pressure while we wait for Buster.

GEORGE: You know his nickname is Buster?

NURSE BOOKER: (Taking George's blood pressure) I've gotten to know your father during his office visits. He's a fine gentleman. He talks about you and William all the time. I feel as though I know you.

BUSTER/POPS: (Screams from off stage) I need help.

GEORGE: Coming Pops.

BUSTER/POPS: Not you. Nurse Booker.

NURSE BOOKER: I'll be right there Mr. Spencer. (To George) And George, you have dangerously high blood pressure. I'm giving you a list of immediate dietary precautions, and I'll make an appointment for you too.

(Exit Nurse Booker.)

BUSTER/POPS: (From offstage) [Sounds of orgasm]

(Enter Pops, escorted by Nurse Booker.)

NURSE BOOKER: Nice and relaxed aren't you, Mr. Spencer?

BUSTER/POPS: (Nods his head, and smiles) Yes Nurse Booker.

NURSE BOOKER: Your father should be ready with a urine sample in no time.

GEORGE: Thank you Nurse Booker.

(Nurse Booker exits. Pops sits with a constant smile.)

GEORGE: I'll be back in a minute Pops.

(Lights out on Clinic. Lights up on conversation between George and William.)

WILLIAM: Hey G. How's it going with Pops?

GEORGE: Mixed and mashed up.

WILLIAM: Well, did he pee?

GEORGE: No. But the Nurse thinks he's going to go soon.

WILLIAM: Cool.

GEORGE: But it's cutting too close to my flight time. I need you to come down here and stay with Pops.

WILLIAM: I'm in the middle of a composition. I'm into this new…

GEORGE: I need you to handle Pops.

WILLIAM: When are you going to let Pops handle himself? And when are we going to be truthful with him. He's probably figured out…

GEORGE: Not the time, and not the time… And something is strange. The nurse here. She's nice. She's helpful. But I could swear, when she went to help Pops in the bathroom that he was having an orgasm. And she knew Pop's nickname was Buster. No one knew that except his friends.

WILLIAM: Got me. Now I'm just curious. Be there in a few.

(Lights out on George and Williams conversation. Lights up on Pops and George siting in the clinic.)

GEORGE: Pops, I have to get to the airport. William is going to come sit with you until you're finished here.

BUSTER/POPS: I want to talk to you alone for a few minutes.

GEORGE: Why are you going to lay something heavy on me just before I'm getting ready to leave? I knew it. You're sick. What is it? Oh no? Cancer? Prostrate? Lung? Colon? You'll be dead in a month.

BUSTER/POPS: I'm in love.

GEORGE: Love?

BUSTER/POPS: I'm in love. Deep, real, compassionate love. The kind that comes once in a lifetime. The kind a man wants to hold on to forever. More than sex, it's completion.

GEORGE: That's good Pops. I'm happy for you.

BUSTER/POPS: You don't understand. It's a different kind of situation.

GEORGE: Let's start with a name.

POPS: Johnny.

GEORGE: Hold that thought Pops. Let me check on Will.

(Exit George. Lights up on William and George in a conversation.)

WILLIAM: I'm on my way.

GEORGE: Pops is Gay.

WILLIAM: What?

GEORGE: He's in love with some dude named Johnny. He was afraid to tell me.

WILLIAM: Our old man still has some juice. I'm happy for him.

GEORGE: This doesn't make sense.

WILLIAM: Whether it makes sense or not. This is a good time to be truthful yourself. Tell him about Buttercup. If Pops is gay, he'll be more than understanding.

(Lights out on conversation between George and William. Lights up on Pops and George.)

GEORGE: Thank you for telling me about Johnny Pops. I want to tell you about Buttercup.

POPS: You're going to get married?

GEORGE: We've been living together. We feel married already.

BUSTER/POPS: Okay. Okay. Children can do better in a family where there's a good marriage if you can do it.

GEORGE: I think so too Pops.

BUSTER/POPS: I don't see any problem then.

GEORGE: Buttercup is a guy.

(Enter William)

WILLIAM: Did you tell him?

BUSTER/POPS: Your brother told me his girl is a guy. He likes men. Did you know that?

WILLIAM: Yes Pops.

BUSTER/POPS: So both of my sons are gay?

WILLIAM: Not me. I like women.

BUSTER/POPS: You don't like men?

WILLIAM: I really don't like men.

GEORGE: I like men.

WILLIAM: I like men for friends, not for sex.

GEORGE: I like men for sex. William likes women for sex.

BUSTER/POPS: You both like sex.

WILLIAM & GEORGE: Yes Pops.

BUSTER/POPS: George you like women. And William, you like men.

WILLIAM & GEORGE: No Pops.

BUSTER/POPS: William Clayton Spencer, do you like kids?

WILLIAM: I don't like kids. I had a vasectomy. George likes kids.

BUSTER/POPS: Well, at least you know what you like. I don't know if I like kids anymore.

WILLIAM: George is gay, like you.

BUSTER/POPS: I'm not gay.

WILLIAM: It's okay Pops. George told me about Johnny.

BUSTER/POPS: Buttercup?

GEORGE: I'm in love with Buttercup. We met playing football. Butter was his name on the field. He ran smooth…like butter. I added cup, because a buttercup is a sweet, delicate flower. That was the part of him that he was hiding from the world.

BUSTER/POPS: Like you were hiding from me. Does he love and respect you? Does he have the same dreams?

GEORGE: Yes Pops.

BUSTER/POPS: Then I love him. And my love for you could never change, son.

WILLIAM: Why did you take so long to tell us you were gay?

POPS: (Calling out) Johnny. Johnny. Could you come out here? Johnny Lynn Booker!

NURSE BOOKER: (Enters holding motor cycle helmets) Nice to officially meet you both. Want a ride home on my Harley Buster? Or maybe we can go to my place?

BUSTER/POPS: (Looking down at his soiled pants) I'll need to change my pants?

(Lights Out)

End of Play

Adagio

Slow Finish

Characters:

Madame Ruben: Wheelchair bound aging former Russian ballerina

Natasha (Tasha): Young Black woman

Setting:

A simple kitchen in a basement apartment in West Harlem. The audience can see a ballet barre on one wall, a small rectangular-shaped kitchen table, two chairs, a large calendar on the wall, the apartment door (leading to the corridor), and the apartment window (faces 145th Street).

(Lights Rise)

(The scene opens with Madame Ruben looking out of the window. Natasha can be seen running down the street and to the front door of the apartment. Madame Ruben is waiting with the door open.)

MADAME RUBEN: (Screaming out of the apartment window) Natasha! (Pause) Natasha! (Pause) You're late. (Pause) Late. Late. Always Late.

NATASHA: (Enters, throwing her backpack on the floor and catching her breath) Hello Madame.

The coach wanted me to do some extra laps and then I wanted to stretch out and change before I got here. We have a track meet coming up in a few weeks—regional championships.

MADAME RUBEN: How do you expect—

NATASHA: Do we always have to start every class with a fight?

MADAME RUBEN: In my day, if you were late to the dance floor, you wouldn't expect to return to the dance floor. You were already replaced with another dancer by the Director.

NATASHA: Oh, yeah, is that the same Director that only let you wear your good Pointe shoes for the special performances?

MADAME RUBEN: Yes, yes, you mock me, but we were lucky we had shoes. There was no such thing as going downtown to buy shoes. We waited for months for new shoes.

NATASHA: (Pulls off sweat clothes, takes Pointe shoes out of backpack. Gives a series of kisses to Madame Ruben) I'm surprised you had shoes.

MADAME RUBEN: Stop it. Stop it.

NATASHA: You know you love my kisses, especially the wet ones.

MADAME RUBEN: Yes I love it, but it is bad luck if you don't kiss both sides.

(Natasha gives one last kiss on the other cheek, sits down, and then begins to put on her Pointe shoes.)

MADAME RUBEN: (Extending her arm to block the shoes) No. We will begin on the flats today. But first, come eat.

NATASHA: You have my patty cakes?

MADAME RUBEN: Why must you call them patty cakes? latkes, potato latkes. Do you think you can go into a kosher restaurant and ask for patty cakes?

NATASHA: You know I'm just messin with you.

MADAME RUBEN: And I have the real applesauce, not the moots.

NATASHA: Moots? You mean Motts.

MADAME RUBEN: Moots, Motts, supermarket applesauce. Homemade latkes deserve homemade applesauce. All morning I'm grating potato because my darling girl Natasha insists on latkes even when it's not a holiday.

NATASHA: (Sits down and eats) They're just so good.

MADAME RUBEN: Eat, eat, but slow down. I have plenty in the freezer. In my day—

MADAME RUBEN & NATASHA: We only ate latkes for Hanukah!

MADAME RUBEN: OK—Enough. (Removes the plate with the potato pancakes)

More after rehearsal. I don't understand how you can eat so much and never gained a pound.

NATASHA: I never gain weight when I eat a lot. I've always been that way. My Grandma says I'm built for speed.

MADAME RUBEN: (Patting Natasha on the legs) I don't know about that, but for dance, this body is good. Let me see your feet before you put on the shoes.

(Natasha still sitting, lifts one foot at a time for examination.)

MADAME RUBEN: Wait. Look.

(Natasha continues to hold up one foot at a time, playing with her movements, while Madame Ruben wheels over to the calendar.)

MADAME RUBEN: Look Natasha, I have put an X for each day that goes by before the audition. You see six days left. Not that much time.

NATASHA: I'm ready.

MADAME RUBEN (She wheels back to where Natasha is sitting and begins to examine her feet again) Do not be arrogant! You must be humble Natasha. (Touching every crevice of her feet) You prepare but you can never be prepared enough. Natasha…many dancers have fine feet but yours are special, you have the tempo in your feet. I have never seen such precision with tempo, with adagio…that I have seen with you. The training I give you is good but you have something natural that God gave you. Be grateful for this gift Natasha. In your career, many will be jealous; many will envy and resent you for your gifts.

(Natasha has finished putting on her shoes and walks towards the ballet barre.)

MADAME RUBEN: But your hair, what will we do about your hair for the audition?

NATASHA: What do you mean?

(Madame Ruben touches Natasha's hair. Natasha pulls away.)

MADAME RUBEN: Look at my photograph. (Takes the photograph of herself in a ballet pose that has been sitting on the table and shows Natasha) You need a bun Natasha; your hair must be smooth, tight, neat, and pulled back in a bun.

NATASHA: Madame, you know we don't have the same kind of hair!

MADAME RUBEN: What about a wig?

NATASHA: A wig? I'm gonna have one of my girls corn row my hair real tight and then twist the ends into a bun. It'll be fine.

MADAME RUBEN: OK, I guess that will have to do.

(Natasha has gotten up from the table and she has begun to stretch at the ballet barre. Madame Ruben is "pacing" with her wheel chair. She stops and stares at Natasha while she stretches.)

Natasha, I know these people. I know what is in their heart, in their head. If they look at your face, that ugliness will come out. If they look at your feet they will see talent, they will see magic.

NATASHA: Just say it! Just say it.

MADAME RUBEN: We want them to see your feet. We want them to forget that you're colored.

NATASHA: You mean Black. Remember, you have to say Black or African American.

MADAME RUBEN: Natasha, you have to dance with perfect adagio so they will see, so they will feel the tempo that comes through your body, your gift.

NATASHA: Whatever.

(Madame Ruben stops "pacing" and comes to a military like stance in front of the ballet barre.)

MADAME RUBEN: Let's begin. (She presses the tape player on an old boom box. An Adagio selection from Mozart begins) Move away from the barre. Preparation from fifth position. Lift in attitude, Croisé. Promenade efface, extend into arabesque.

(Natasha executes the movements with precision and grace.)

Now. Preparation for pirouette en dehors from fourth. I want to see a series of doubles and triples then follow with pirouette en dedans.

NATASHA: Madame, can we take a little break?

MADAME RUBEN: There is no time for a break Natasha. Now…I want to see développé front, side, back then around to arabesque.

(Natasha executes the movements precisely but she obviously is tired.)

MADAME RUBEN: Quickly Natasha, other side.

NATASHA: Just a little break and water Madame.

MADAME RUBEN: Natasha. Do it.

(Natasha complies and performs the movements.)

MADAME RUBEN: Show me passé, arabesque.

(Natasha complies.)

MADAME RUBEN: NOW HOLD, HOLD, HOLD, HOLD IN POSITION NATASHA!

(Natasha holds but then falls.)

MADAME RUBEN: (Wheeling over to Natasha) I told you to hold!

NATASHA: I'm just a little tired Madame.

MADAME RUBEN: (Slaps Natasha) (Pause) What have I done?

(Natasha pushes herself towards the wall with the ballet barre and stares at Madame Ruben tearfully.)

MADAME RUBEN: My darling Natasha, I'm so sorry. Please Tasha, don't leave. I don't know what happened.

(Natasha gathers her things and faces the door, motionless.)

MADAME RUBEN: In my old life when a teacher slapped me it was because of love. The teacher loved and respected the art. She wanted to get my attention so that I would be true to the movement, true to the art. The teacher knew I was talented…it was a form of affection because she was giving me attention. It just happened.

NATASHA: On 145th Street and Riverside Drive, a backhand across the face doesn't mean love.

MADAME RUBEN: Let's continue. We haven't practiced for your Pas de Deux!

NATASHA: I'm outta here. (Opens the door. Stops. Turns around) Don't you get it? I don't want to be a ballerina. I'm a runner.

MADAME RUBEN: You don't want to be a ballerina?

NATASHA: No, I don't. My grandma told me that if I ever had the opportunity to learn ballet I should learn it.

MADAME RUBEN: Not a ballerina? Foolish girl, you waste my time, all the practice, rehearsal, and preparation for the audition. Why have you wasted my time Natasha?

NATASHA: You people are all the same. It has to be about what you want for me not about what I want for myself. Did you ever ask yourself why I am always late for my classes with you? Yeah, sometimes the coach keeps us late. But I can only use my metro card during school hours. And my grandma doesn't have cash to give me for bus fare so I run. I run from school to your house. And I run fast because I can and because I have to. There is a whole lot of HOOD between school and your apartment that I shouldn't be walkin through. (Pause) Do you know how I run? I push through my feet. I separate my legs from my torso. I find the spring in my steps like I am doing chasse across a wood floor. I find the rhythm in my body. (Pause) I came here because my grandma told me it would be good for me. Then I saw that the ballet helped my speed running and my spring for jumping hurdles. I found the secret in my body. I found the adagio in my body. (Pause) There's a very small moment between when you kick one leg and then the other leg for running and jumping that is adagio. It is a slow rhythm that restores the energy just before you kick or jump again.

I can run the 100-meter hurdles with my secret adagio in 10.73 seconds.

MADAME RUBEN: Is that good?

NATASHA: It's damn good. I have the record for my team and for our division. (Pause)

I like to run, but running will give me an opportunity for a scholarship. (Pause)

I want to go to school to be a physical therapist. I want to help people like you and my grandma have good working bodies longer.

MADAME RUBEN: I didn't know.

NATASHA: You didn't know because you never asked.

(Natasha sits down on one of the kitchen chairs. She starts to get dressed. Madame Ruben turns towards the table and picks up her photograph. She looks at the photograph then she places it next to Natasha.)

MADAME RUBEN: My full name is Natalia Rubenstein. I had an important audition once. It was with a small but very important company in my home city, Kraznodar. My audition was almost flawless, my barre, floor work, partnering... When we finished the director kissed my hand—"beautiful feet," he said. We had numbers on our leotards. There were so many of us. The choreographer came in. We all recognized him. He looked at the final roster of accepted dancers. Number sixty four he called out, Rubenstein, step out. I walked forward. He threw the roster on the floor, "I don't choreograph for Jews," he announced. I left the floor quietly. Later I would find out the many ways numbers can be used to separate people.

(She held up her wrist and pulled back her sweater revealing a concentration camp number identification.)

NATASHA: I didn't know.

MADAME RUBEN: You didn't know because you never asked.

NATASHA: I'm sor—

MADAME RUBEN: I'm sorry. It was wrong for me to use you to fulfill my dreams.

NATASHA: Adagio, it's magic.

(She walks over to the boom box and starts the music again. Then she takes the wheelchair and moves it about the floor in sync with the music. Natasha and Madame Ruben dance together.)

(The music starts to skip. Natasha stops and walks over to the boom box. She turns off the music. She puts her dance shoes in her backpack.)

NATASHA: I should go now before it gets dark.

MADAME RUBEN: Wait Tasha. (Gets some money from a canister on the table and hands it to Natasha) Just a little money so you can take the bus here for your classes.

NATASHA: I can still study with you?

MADAME RUBEN: If you are going to jump hurdles, we need to work on your jumps: Toure Jete, Tour en L'air, Pas de Chat…

NATASHA: Why don't you watch me run at the championship at Madison Square Garden?

MADAME RUBEN: Is it handicap assessable?

NATASHA: Sure is. You can come with my grandma. She has a walker.

(Lights Out)

End of Play

Beullah Rising

Rising in Place

Characters:

Dr. Gretta Von Beullah (Beullah): White middle-aged instructor of Woman's Studies at Florence Nightingale High School

Beullah's attire resembles a pre-civil war plantation slave including bandana, apron, and rough cotton top and skirt.

Kim Townsend (Judith): African American high school senior

Judith is dressed in the attire of a Southern belle including a hoop skirt, petticoat, and adornments.

Setting:

Lecture hall stage resembling a southern belle's bedroom in a plantation mansion.[1]

(Lights Rise)

JUDITH: (Deep southern accent throughout all discourse) Beullah. Beullah. Come here at once. You hear me?

BEULLAH: (Southern plantation slave dialect throughout all discourse) Yesum Missy Judit?

JUDITH: What took you so long Beullah?

BEULLAH: Well Miss, your Mama, Mistress Julie…

JUDITH: You sassin me Beullah? I ought to tan your…

BEULLAH: No Missy Judit, I's jis wanna tell ya dat Mistress Julie been havin me doin some of Esther's chores cause she been sent over to da neighbor man for help his wife deliver her—

JUDITH: Did I ask you about Esther?

BEULLAH: Nosum Missy.

JUDITH: Missy Judith!

BEULLAH: Yesum Missy Judit.

JUDITH: I want to know why I have to call your name more than one time?

BEULLAH: Yesum Missy Judit.

JUDITH: Who's my Mamie?

BEULLAH: I's yo Mamie, Missy Judit.

JUDITH: Then, if you're my Mamie, you have to do what I tell you gal, I don't care what my Mama tells you.

BEULLAH: Yesum Missy Judit.

JUDITH: Because if you don't come when I call you, and you don't do what I say, you may get a beat by my Mama, but you are sure to get a beat by me.

BEULLAH: Yesum Missy Judit.

JUDITH: Now we're gonna try it again. Get out of my sight, and when I call your name, I want you to run as fast as you can.

(Exit Beullah)

JUDITH: Beullah.

(Beullah enters running quickly knocking over things in her path.)

JUDITH: Now pick up those things and there better not be anything broken.

(Beullah picks up the scattered items.)

And when are you ever going to say my name correctly?

BEULLAH: I can say it. Missy Judit.

JUDITH: Oh it pains my ears sometimes to hear the way you crackers talk.

BEULLAH: I's jis be quiet like now.

JUDITH: Beullah, you're so ignorant. I'm just commenting. (Pause) Come over here gal.

(Beullah approaches Judith.)

JUDITH: Now look at my lips. Watch me. Not too close.

(Beullah moves away slightly.)

JUDITH: My name is Judith. th…th…th… Put your tongue between your teeth and blow th…

BEULLAH: th…

JUDITH: Now say my name correctly…Judith.

BEULLAH: Yesum Missy Judit.

JUDITH: I don't know why I bother. Your lips are too thin, your tongue is so little it can barely move, and your brain is probably the size of a kidney bean. (Pause) Charity, charity, charity. I have to remember Christian charity even to you white blue-eyed devils. You're an ignorant heathen, and I suppose you're doing the best you can. Mama says that's why it's our Christian duty to give you meaningful work and prevent you from living like the uncivilized animal you are.

BEULLAH: Yesum.

JUDITH: Work? Did you finish all the chores my Mama told you to do around here.

BEULLAH: Yesum.

JUDITH: Did you scrub the upstairs and downstairs floors?

BEULLAH: Yesum.

JUDITH: Did you change all the bed linen?

BEULLAH: Yesum.

JUDITH: Did you wash the windows in the guest rooms?

BEULLAH: Yesum.

JUDITH: Did you polish my grandmother's silverware?

BEULLAH: Yesum.

JUDITH: Did you put my petticoats on the clothesline to catch the fresh breeze?

BEULLAH: Yesum.

JUDITH: No you didn't you lying cracker. (Takes a collection of petticoats from a nearby closet and throws them at Beullah) You didn't hang these.

(Beullah picks up the petticoats.)

JUDITH: I tore these and they need mending first.

BEULLAH: Yesum.

(Beullah begins to exit.)

JUDITH: Where are you going Beullah?

BEULLAH: I's goin ta fetch de sewin baskit so I's cans mend dese here petticoats likes ya tells me.

JUDITH: I don't mean now. I'm not finished talking to you. Don't you ever walk away from me before I finished talking to you, you hear?

BEULLAH: Yesum. I's sorry Missy Judit.

JUDITH: What to do? What to do?

BEULLAH: You kin…

JUDITH: I'm not talking to you, you mindless fool. I'm talking to myself. I'm hungry and I'm bored. BEULLAH, I want to eat and then play games.

BEULLAH: I's jis bout ta fetch yo noon tray Missy Judit Mistress Julie tells me ta…

JUDITH: I don't care what my Mama said, I want candy, cookies, and pie for lunch.

BEULLAH: But Missy Judit…

JUDITH: Beullah, what did I say about sassin me. You're my mamie and you have to take care of me like I say. (Pause) I want sugar gum drops, and vanilla cookies, and sweet potato pie for lunch.

BEULLAH: Lawd, Lawd, Is gonna git a beat for sure.

JUDITH: Go get my sweets.

BEULLAH: Yesum Missy Judit.

(Judith sits on the bed and arranges her dolls and stuffed animals. Beullah gets the treats and places them on the bed. Judith eats them quickly and also pretend feeds them to her dolls and stuffed animals.)

JUDITH: How many gentleman callers do my mama and papa have coming by this afternoon for tea? (Pause) Beullah? Beullah?

BEULLAH: Yesum.

JUDITH: I'm talking to you now gal.

BEULLAH: Yesum.

JUDITH: Well, what's the answer dumb bunny?

BEULLAH: Please don't gets mad wit me Missy Judit.

JUDITH: What did you do?

BEULLAH: Is jis done what Mistress Julie tells me ta do.

JUDITH: And what was that you nit wit?

BEULLAH: Mistress Julie tells me dat ifin you don't eats your noon day meal I's ta tell Esther ta send word dat de gentlemen callers is not ta come taday.

JUDITH: You told on me?

BEULLAH: Mistress Julie be sayin dat you is too tiny n she wants ya ta eat. She don't care what she have ta do ta get yous ta eat.

JUDITH: Hum… Go get my meal tray.

BEULLAH: Yesum.

(Exit Beullah. Judith sits at a vanity and arranges her hair and makeup. Enter Beullah with the food tray.)

JUDITH: Now you sit over yonder and eat that food.

(Beullah remains in place without movement.)

JUDITH: I said, you eat it.

BEULLAH: Aw…no Missy Judit, I's not possed ta eat from your food tray only ifin de food left over come down ta de back porch for hog scrapes. I et sum corn biscuit n sum brown gravy bout… two days back.

JUDITH: You're hungry?

BEULLAH: Yesum.

JUDITH: Are you saying my Papie isn't giving you enough food.

BEULLAH: Nosum. I's know I's git de food a white gal like me is deservin. (Pause) But I's still hungry.

JUDITH: Then you sit down and eat it.

(Beullah sits down on the closest chair.)

JUDITH: Not on my chair! Sit on the floor and you be careful not to soil my pretty pink carpet.

BEULLAH: Yesum Missy Judit.

(Beullah devours food quickly. Judith watches and then interrupts her before the food is finished.)

JUDITH: That's enough. You're eating like my Papie is nearly starving you to death. Now put the rest of that food in the trash. (Pause) Something wrong Beullah?

BEULLAH: Nosum Missy Judit.

JUDITH: Now eat some of those treats left on my bed. Make sure you leave one of those cookies for my teddy bear.

BEULLAH: Yesum.

(Beullah picks up treats from the bed and eats them. Judith interrupts her before she has finished eating all of the treats.)

JUDITH: You are such greedy white gal. Toss the rest of that food away except for my teddy bear's cookie.

(Beullah walks towards the trash containing the discarded food. Judith takes a handkerchief out of her vanity drawer and extends it to Beullah.)

JUDITH: No. I want you to put those treats in my silk and lace hankie. This one is from Paris. My Papie brought it home for me. (Pause) Now I want to play. You know any songs Beullah. I want to hear you sing. What songs do you know?

BEULLAH: I knows field songs Missy Judit. Like one's we white folks sings when we's picking cotton and tabacca.

JUDITH: Are they funny?

BEULLAH: I's don't knows Missy Judit.

JUDITH: I want to hear one.

BEULLAH: (Sings) "Precious Lawd, take my hand, lead me on…"

JUDITH: That song reminds me of church. Sing something else.

BEULLAH: (Sings) "Oh freedom, oh freedom, oh freedom…"

JUDITH: That's enough you pickaninny. I'll sing. But first I want you to take off that bandana so you can wave it in the air while you pick up your feet high up into the air like a stepping dance. This is going to be fun!

(Beullah takes off her bandana.)

JUDITH: Is that hair? Straight, and thin…and…you don't have no naps. Your hair's not nappy! Put that bandana back on. With that chalky skin I didn't think you could be any uglier. Never mind. I'll clap while you step.

JUDITH: (Judith props her stuffed animals and dolls up on the bed) Start your big stepping.
(Sung) "Look away, look away, look away, Dixieland."
(Spoken) Higher. (Sung) "I wish I was in the land of cotton."
(Spoken) Faster. (Sung) "Look away, look away, look away."[2]

(Beullah collapses on the floor out of breath.)

JUDITH: You take the fun out of everything Beullah. You're too old. I may have to ask my Papie to get me a new Cracker Mamie, one that has some common sense and can play with me. You're just useless. (Leaves the bed and sits on her vanity chair)

Get on over here and fan me, and get the big fan. I'm perspiring so after all my singing and my laughing at you.

(Beullah gets a fan and proceeds to fan Judith as she catches her breath.)

A little powder and then I'm perfect. Now you run and tell Esther you made a mistake, that I finished my meal tray and I'm ready for gentlemen callers.

BEULLAH: I cants do dat Missy Judit.

JUDITH: Oh yes you can and you will. (Picks up the handkerchief wrapped around the treats) This is the hankie you stole from my vanity.

BEULLAH: Oh no Missy Judit. I did no such ting.

JUDITH: (Indicates the food in the trash) And you remember the food you tossed away. I'll tell my Mama that you gave me sweets to eat so you could hide this food and take it to your quarters.

BEULLAH: Missy Judit, I did no such ting. I's done whats you tell me to do. I's told you Mistress Julie want for you ta eat dat food you self.

JUDITH: But you were eating my food.

BEULLAH: Yesum. But you tells me ta et it.

JUDITH: You shouldn't have eaten it. You knew it for me.

BEULLAH: Nosum.

JUDITH: I'm thinking I will ask my Papie to take you out of the house and send you back to the fields.

JUDITH: Peas don't do dat Missy. I's do betta. Whats ever you say. I's do it better.

JUDITH: The field is where you belong Beullah. You ain't fit for keeping house or being my mamie. I have no time to train you to be a good cracker. The overseer's whip will make sure you do right. And I know you devils can pick your legs high when you want to and spread them so the mens…

BEULLAH: Peas Missy Judit. I mean no harm ta nobody. I's jis tryin ta live one day ta da noder wit no trouble. But seems, I cants do nuf ta peas ya even when I's do my bestest. Have some mercy Missy. I's …

Voice Over: Dr. Gretchen Von Beullah call the office immediately please.

DR. GRETCHEN VON BEULLAH: (Picks up the intercom) Yes. One student enrolled in the Female Stereotypes in Cinema course, Kim Townsend. She's a senior. That's terrible. Is there no one else? This course is so important. (Pause) I understand. I'll let Kim know. (Hangs up the intercom telephone) Kim, it seems your course is ending almost as fast as it begun. A course on Female Stereotypes in Cinema isn't a priority. You need to go to the guidance department. You'll be advised into another elective course. I'm taking over Senora Morales's remedial reading classes.

She's beginning an extended medical leave and sadly Florence Nightingale High School isn't getting more staff.

(Judith takes off her hoop skirt and top revealing contemporary clothes underneath.)

KIM: I want this course. This was way better than a lecture class. I thought we were going to just read books and write papers.

DR. BEULLAH: Was there ever anytime when your character felt compassion for Beullah?

KIM: It was the food. I wanted to let her eat the food, especially when I saw how hungry she was. But I couldn't do that because as much as I felt sorry for her, I had power over her that I didn't want to give that up. Giving her food would be a sign of weakness.

DR. BEULLAH: Why not share?

KIM: Sharing is with equals. Judith didn't believe Beullah was an equal. She didn't believe she was a woman. She was an animal, like a pet or a workhorse to entertain and serve.

DR. BEULLAH: Did you feel sorry for her?

KIM: I felt sorry for Judith. She had power over herself. Her way. Her control. Who would ever want to give that up? Think of the pain she'll feel when that changes.

DR. BEULLAH: What would cause it to change?

KIM: Beullah will wake up. (Pause) It's about Shuckin and Jivin. That's what Beullah knows. Her place. What to do to stay alive. Beullah does it well. Do good or do bad, there's no difference. She's Judith's domesticated animal. I feel sorry for Judith.

DR. BEULLAH: Judith owns everything.

KIM: For now. She's like a queen with a seat on the thrown. Her family built the kingdom on the backs of Beullah and her people. And Judith inherited it. Born in. Privilege. That's the way of the world. Some have it. Some don't. Why do I feel sorry for Judith? When you're on top, someone is always behind you to take you down. Beullah will rise up from her persecuted sleep. Like a junkyard dog, chained up, starved who turns on the master. She'll be crazy angry Black. (Walking around the room throwing items from the role playing on the floor) It may happen when she is so hungry, she can barely put one foot in front of the other. She may be so exhausted from washing petticoats. It may be a misstep or a hesitant look followed by the threat of a beat down. Beullah has been watching. She's been Shuckin n' Jiving until she knows more about Judith than Judith knows about herself. She's sick and tired of being sick and tired. Being treated unfairly. Is that too much to ask?

DR. BEULLAH: (Blocking Kim from moving) Move. Move back.

KIM: I have a right to be here.

DR. BEULLAH: (Blocking Kim) What do you see?

KIM: Everybody running.

DR. BEULLAH: What do you smell?

KIM: Gasoline. Fire. Smoke. Screaming. Crying. I can't see my friends.

DR. BEULLAH: Look through the smoke. What do you see?

KIM: I can't see my friends. There's Chris. They beat her to the ground. Chris, get up. I'm coming. (Pause) I stop. My head hurts. I feel the back of my head. (Looking at her hand) I'm bleeding. I'm dizzy. I fall on the pavement.

DR. BEULLAH: Tell me about the pavement.

KIM: Bodies on the ground. Chris, I'm coming. Don't move. Play dead. Everyone is scared. They keep coming. Sirens. I hear gunshots.

DR. BEULLAH: What do you feel?

KIM: They don't care. Beating, pushing.

BEULLAH: See Chris.

KIM: They surround her. They pull her and drag her by her hair. "Stop it." "Leave her alone." (Pause) I think of church. "After you die, you will truly live." They want to kill us all.

DR. BEULLAH: Chris?

JUDITH: I don't want to see her anymore.

DR. BEULLAH: Is she dead?

KIM: Leave us alone.

DR. BEULLAH: Is she dead?

KIM: I don't know.

BEULLAH: You know. (Pause) Is she dead?

KIM: (Pushing and hitting Beullah) Yes.

BEULLAH: (While being hit by Kim) Chris is dead. We can't bring her back. It's was wrong. It was criminal. It was inhumane. You couldn't save her. You saved yourself.

KIM: This has to end.

DR. BEULLAH: (Holding Judith) Yes. (Pause) In this moment, you're safe. In this moment, I can protect you. Forgive me.

(Lights Out)

End of Play

Endnotes:

[1] Although the play takes place in the present day, the opening setting of the play gives the illusion of the pre-civil war American South, and the audience is unaware of any dynamic of the characters other than that of the master and slave.

[2] Dixie (circa 1850) credited to Daniel Decatur Emmett

brother & sister Chronicles

Characters:

Robert/Rory: Adult brother

Lucinda/Lucy: Adult sister

AND: Conjunction[1]

Setting:

The dream realm. Rem sleep.

(Lights Rise)

The dream realm. Arrays of objects are placed across the stage in a linear arrangement. AND, dressed completely in unisex black clothing stands in the middle of the stage in front of the objects holding two folding chairs. AND places the folding chairs one at time center stage making sure they are precisely touching. Lucinda lies sleeping stage left (Rem sleep) Robert lies sleeping stage right (Rem sleep) Exit AND.

LUCINDA/LUCY: I smell pizza.

(Enter AND carrying ten boxes of pizza.
Enter Lucy into the dream realm. Looks at AND.
Looks at the folding chairs.)

LUCINDA/LUCY: Really AND? (Separates the folding chairs. Folds one of the chairs and places it in the audience. She sits on the unfolded chair) I was having a private moment. I wished this would happen, but I didn't actually want this to happen.

AND: *Places a piggy bank under Lucy's chair, then moves to get the folding chair.*

---

1 AND- in grammar used as a function word to indicate connection. All of the character's communication is non-verbal. All of the non-verbal communication is indicated in italics.

(Lucy confronts AND. There is back and forth pacing. AND is blocked from getting the chair. AND returns to center stage.)

LUCY: (Reaching under the chair picking up the piggy bank and coins) Oink Oink! How did you get here? Look at this money outside of your tummy.

[Sound Effect: Sound of money jingling.]

ROBERT/RORY: I smell money! Does money have a smell? I must be dreaming. (Enters the dream realm. Notices Lucy) LUCINDA ESTOSHIA ZULA MAE HENDERSON.

AND: *Takes Rory's hand and tries to move him and the chair next to Lucy.*

RORY: (Resisting) You haven't been around for years AND. I don't need you now. What's done is done.

LUCY: That's right. Officially removed.

LUCY: (Speaking to AND) I want Rory out of my dream.

RORY: This is my dream, "Big Head." You get out.

LUCY: I was here first, "Stink Pants."

(Lucy and Rory stand up facing each other during the insults.)

AND: *Places a chain around the chairs.*

RORY: Freak.

LUCY: Clown.

RORY: Wussy.

LUCY: (Pushes Rory with every word) You…never…take… responsibility…for… anything…I…was here…first…

RORY: (Raises his hand to push Lucy back) You're getting on my last nerve.

LUCY: (Running into the audience) Dad said you better never put your hands on me.

RORY: Dad's not here anymore.

LUCY: No, he's not.

(Rory and Lucy struggle to unchain the chairs. After several tries, they sit on the chairs facing opposite each other.)

RORY: You…

LUCY: I don't want to hear it.

RORY: You…

LUCY: Don't talk to me.

AND: *Gives Rory and Lucy yo yos.*

RORY & LUCY: My super imperial master class yo yo.

RORY & LUCY: Cool…

LUCY: Remember any tricks?

RORY: Yeah.

(Lucy and Rory play with the yo yo's. They take turns showing each other what they can do.)

LUCY: Remember this one? (Demonstrates) I can help you. (Reaches towards Rory then pulls back) I'm not showing you anything.

RORY: So. I don't want to play with you.

LUCY: You didn't do your homework. You're not supposed to be outside playing. I'm telling Mom.

RORY: I did my homework at school.

LUCY: Homework…school…

RORY: Mom's not here anymore.

LUCY: Mom's not here anymore.

RORY: What's happening? Are we kids again?

LUCY: We don't look like kids.

RORY: Lucy, you have the same big head. Now, you have a big head and a big body.

LUCY: (Screaming) Mom! Rory's picking on me. He's called me big head. And he's a liar. He didn't do his homework. He…

RORY: (Covering Lucy's mouth) Shut up or when Dad comes home from work… (Releasing Lucy).

(All pause)

RORY: When Dad got home from work, he was tired but he always remembered to bring us treats.

LUCY: "Don't tell your mother I gave you sugar. She'll say I spoiled your dinner."

RORY: "You know sugar makes those kids hyper. They won't want to go to sleep."

LUCY: Events of the day. My favorite time with Dad after dinner. "LUCINDA ESTOSHIA ZULA MAE, were you kind to someone today?"

RORY: Dad's jokes before dinner. Ridiculous. Never funny. We pretended we never heard it before. We laughed every time.

LUCY: It's the good ridiculous things that make a family feel like a family.

RORY: "ROBERT EGBERT ZOFELLA MARTIN, Name one thing a Black man should never forget if he wants to survive in America."

LUCY: Why do you think he never asked me what a Black woman should never forget?

RORY: Maybe he thought Mom talked to you about those things.

LUCY: Mom never did.

RORY: What did you and Mom talk about in private?

LUCY: Honestly, I only remember the talks about not getting pregnant.

RORY: Did you ever?

LUCY: What?

RORY: Get pregnant…never mind.

LUCY: Mom and I didn't have to talk too much. I just watched her. Everything. I wanted to be around her. Be like her. Only a GED diploma. She still is the smartest woman I ever knew.

RORY: I remember Mom ruled the house. How many times did you hear him say, "Did you ask your mother? Then that's the answer."

LUCY: Mom and Dad…I hope I feel some kinda love like they had one day.

RORY: Have you…

LUCY: Stop trying to make me feel comfortable around you. I don't. I'm not saying anything about myself and don't tell me anything about yourself.

(Exit Rory and Lucy to their respective Rem sleep.)

AND: *Walks around the Rem sleep areas with a brown grocery bag.*

LUCY: What's in the bag AND?

RORY: So aromatic. They're calling me.

AND: *Lures Rory and Lucy to return to their chairs by enticing them with the grocery bag. When they are seated, And releases the bag to them.* (Rory and Lucy take turns reaching into the bag)

RORY: Heidi Ho Ho's.

LUCY: Doggie Devils.

RORY & LUCY: Fruit pies.

RORY & LUCY: Cherry. (Sighs of anticipation) Thanks AND.

RORY: (Pulling out a snack pack of lunch-size raisin boxes) What's this doing in here?

LUCY: You know we hate raisins. (Throwing the box at AND)

RORY: You should just eat a few. Mom wants us to have healthy snacks too.

LUCY: I'm all mixed up. Why am I…

AND: *Enters carrying a large black bag.*

LUCY: What is AND waiting for?

RORY: Figure out your dream. What is AND doing?

LUCY: My dream's been hijacked. I have nothing to do with this.

RORY: Say you're sorry for throwing the raisins and maybe we'll get that bag.

LUCY: How do you know we want the bag?

RORY: Because in this dream, good things come in bags.

LUCY: Yeah. (Pause) Sorry AND.

AND: *Slowly revealing a giant snack box.*

(Lucy and Rory rip open the box and grab at their favorite snacks. They eat all of the snacks ferociously and leave a mess.)

RORY: Now I know I'm grown up in this dream, because my stomach is killing me.

LUCY: I feel terrible. Do you think AND knew we would eat all those snacks?

RORY: Try to take over the dream and make the pains go away.

LUCY: How would I do that?

RORY: Maybe you just wish it.

LUCY: Ah… Pain, pain, go away. Don't come back another day.

(Rory and Lucy sit up normally as though nothing had happened.)

RORY: Damn. That was incredible. Maybe, we're like super heroes. I'm gonna try flying. (Jumps up and down. Runs and stops)

AND: *Laughs silently.*

LUCY: I told you. AND hijacked my dream. We need to ride out the dream until it's time to wake up. I have some place to be in the morning.

RORY: I have some place to be too.

AND: *Brings some beat up tires and places them in front of Rory and Lucy.*

(Rory and Lucy pick up and examine the tires)

RORY: It's your birthday. I have to go get the pizza.

LUCY: Get enough for everybody in my sixth grade class.

RORY: Mom and Dad ordered delivery. They went to work.

LUCY: Pete, the delivery guy is out sick. Angelo can't bring the pies.

RORY: (Picks up the tires and creates a bicycle with a basket) Don't cry Lucy. I'll take care of it.

AND: *Gives out paper plates.*

LUCY: Everybody. Pizza, pizza, pizza…

(Rory arranges the pizza boxes to carry in the bike basket. Rides bike around audience with the pizza boxes.)

AND: *Helps give out the pizza to the audience.*

LUCY: There's enough for everyone to have two pieces. Thank you Rory. You're a good brother.

RORY: I'm a good brother.

LUCY: I dreamed a good brother. That's it.

AND: *Throws two ropes in front of Rory and Lucy.*

LUCY: I want to try out for the team. Will you help me?

RORY: You want my help?

LUCY: I want your help. Mom has to work. She doesn't have time to practice with me.

RORY: Get one of your friends.

LUCY: They'll make fun of me. Everyone knows how to jump. Please Rory.

AND: *Gives one end of each rope to an audience member.*

RORY: You better not tell any of my friends that I taught you how to jump.

LUCY: I won't. I promise.

(Rory looks for an audience volunteer. Rory and the audience member turn the Double Dutch ropes.)

RORY: Come in from the side. (Pause) Stand close to the ropes. (Pause) When each rope hits the ground, we'll count: Ready, Set, Go. (Pause) Ready, Set, Go. (Pause) Ready, Set, Go. Come on Lucy.

LUCY: I'm afraid. The ropes are gonna hit me.

RORY: Every time a rope hits the ground, jump.

LUCY: I can't.

RORY: Dad said, "No such thing as can't do in the Henderson family." You get nothing for not trying. (Pause) Aim for the middle of the rope. This is your dream. You can be Double Dutch champion of the world.

LUCY: Yeah. (Jumping, doing amazing tricks)

RORY: On three you stop. (Pause) One…Two…Three…

(Ropes drop.)

RORY: My turn.

LUCY: (Turning the rope for Rory) How did you learn to Double Dutch?

RORY: (Jumping amazing Double Dutch) Watching Susie.

LUCY: Susie King.

RORY: The one and only Susie Q.

LUCY: She wasn't that great. She wasn't on the team.

RORY: But so many parts of her could bounce…

LUCY: Too much information.

RORY: I taught you a few things when we were growing up. I'd forgotten all about them.

LUCY: I get it. You're scheming with AND. Want forgiveness Rory. I don't have it in me. Just because we had some fun when we were kids, you don't get a pass for…

RORY: I didn't ask to be here. I was dreaming about Susie. Then I heard money. I'm trying to buy my apartment. I thought I would get some ideas about financing in this dream, so I didn't wake myself up. I didn't know the dream would take me here. AND was a surprise. (Pause) We can't pretend our lives haven't been mixed together. We're family. You can't erase what was, and what is…

LUCY: I can erase what won't be. What won't be is "brother and sister." When you're adults, family is a choice. I don't choose to be around you ever again. You haven't been family to me in long time Rory.

RORY: One-way street, right. Our relationship. You call it. You define it. You make the rules.

LUCY: I can choose to live my life the way I want. And what I want is for you to stay away from me forever.

RORY: If you think having a brother is only about what I give and what I get then I don't want to be a part of that madness.

LUCY: I think having a brother shouldn't hurt.

RORY: Having a sister shouldn't hurt either.

(Rory picks up the yo yo and plays. Lucy bangs her head, claps her hands, and does other startling movements.)

RORY: What are you doing?

LUCY: Waking myself up to get away from you.

RORY: You look foolish.

LUCY: You have a better idea?

RORY: Obviously AND has some plan here to force us to reconcile. (Looking at AND) Isn't that right AND?

AND: *Indicates that is the plan with an up and down head nod.*

RORY: As you are making perfectly clear…relationships are a choice. You don't want me. Now, I'm very clear…I don't want anything to do with you. What I realize is that if I'm entrapped in this zone until my body naturally wakes up I guess, I'm going to have fun.

(Picks up the bicycle tires.)

LUCY: Where are you going?

RORY: Into town. Exploring. On this high-speed super deluxe ten speed bike that Mom and Dad could never afford to buy me.

LUCY: Can I come?

RORY: Why?

LUCY: I want to see the neighborhood. I haven't been back since Mom and Dad died.

RORY: Come on.

LUCY: (Sitting on the seat) I'm not riding on the handlebars.

RORY: You never did.

AND: *Follows the bike as Rory and Lucy go around the audience. AND carries a bag.*

RORY: Maybe we can make the bike fly.

LUCY: Don't try it.

RORY: If I can dream it, I can do it.

LUCY: Seems some things can be controlled in this dream and some can't.

(The bike flies.)

RORY: Oh my God. This is amazing.

LUCY: Land the bike. I'm feeling nauseous.

RORY: Don't spit up on me.

LUCY: Everything is the same. "B B Barbecue," the baseball field, the handball court, Hazel's Beauty Shop, Jimmy's Hardware.

RORY: The haunted house.

LUCY: Lets fly down and take a look.

RORY: Yeah.

(Bike lands on the ground.)

AND: *Gives Rory and Lucy a carton of eggs.*

RORY & LUCY: Let's do this.

RORY & LUCY: (Throwing eggs on the house) Egg fight!

LUCY: (There are no more eggs) Let's get out of here.

RORY: The bike's not lifting off.

LUCY: Hurry, before someone comes.

RORY: It's not happening.

LUCY: We have to make a run for it.

RORY: There's Townsend's Pool.

LUCY: There's a lock on the gate.

RORY: That never stopped us before.

(They go through the gate and put their feet in the water. AND gets on the lifeguard chair. Rory and Lucy look at each other and then jump into the water together.)

RORY: Let's smoke…cigarettes.

LUCY: Why?

RORY: Because we can. When we were kids, we didn't dare. But we're in a dream.

LUCY: Right. AND? (Gesturing AND to give them cigarettes)

AND: *Reluctant magic gesture.*

(Rory and Lucy smoke and then cough.)

LUCY: We didn't miss anything.

RORY: I never picked up the habit either.

LUCY: You know, you're the only reason I learned how to swim. I was so scared. In high school and still couldn't swim.

RORY: It wasn't me. It was Dad. He taught me that fear wasn't a choice. I just passed that wisdom on.

LUCY: You used to be a good brother.

RORY: Is that how you measure me Lucy? A scorecard of plus and minus. I do this for you, I get a plus. I don't meet your expectation, I get a minus. Look at us now. I'm a negative number in your mind. How do you measure yourself? Have you been a good sister?

LUCY: Mom and Dad kept everything so simple. Stick together. Take care of each other. I could be annoying. I could be selfish. I never harmed you. I never let my own failures become your burden.

RORY: It's easy to be a brother and sister when there are no mistakes, no problems, when you don't have to ask whom the other person is.

AND: *Takes a set of car keys and throws it on the ground in front of Rory and Lucy. She puts a bag of marijuana next to the keys.*

(Through the dialogue that follows, Rory and Lucy look at the objects, not at each other.)

RORY: Cherry red convertible mustang. Four new tires with sport rims.

LUCY: Can I borrow your car?

RORY: Trunk with hidden compartment.

LUCY: You taught me to be a great driver. I'm going to the corner store and I'll be right back. About fifteen minutes.

RORY: No LUCY. I need to clean out my car.

LUCY: RORY is so selfish. I'm coming right back. (Loud to fade as backing away from Rory) I'm coming right back. I'm coming right back. I'm coming right back…(Stands in front of AND)

(Light cue: Flashing police lights)

[Sound Effect: Police car siren.]

RORY: Pull over.

(All pause)

RORY: License and registration.

LUCY: I'm sixteen, Officer. I have a permit. This is my brother's car. I live right over…

RORY: Step out of the vehicle.

LUCY: I don't have the registration. The car belongs to my Dad…I mean my brother…my family… Can I call my Mom and Dad?

RORY: Put your hands on the hood.

LUCY: I know I shouldn't have taken the car. I wasn't going to be long. If we go to my house, my brother will tell you everything. Can I call him?

RORY: Spread your legs.

LUCY: You're touching me…Stop touching me…

RORY: Put your hands behind your head.

LUCY: Stop touching me…

RORY: (Loud to fade) Stop resisting. Stop resisting. Stop resisting…

(LUCY, RORY, AND all pause. Hands up, then hands down. All pause.)

LUCY: Found… One bag. Over the legal limit.

LUCY & RORY: Convicted. Sentenced. Nothing can be done. Mom and Dad…broken hearts. They die. One then the other.

RORY: It wasn't my stash. It was Dad's. Once in a while he sold some stuff to make ends meet. I helped out. They always kept your life beautiful. You never knew how tight the money was.

LUCY: Hard to believe Dad…

RORY: When you put a person in a perfect glass box and the glass shatters, everyone gets hurt. There are few perfect people. There are few perfect boxes.

LUCY: Blamed you. Why didn't you tell me?

RORY: You never considered your own choice. I told you not to take the car.

LUCY: I took the car. (Pause) I've been so angry with you. I erased all of who we were, brother and sister, because I blamed you for my record and the whole domino effect from there. Couldn't get a job. No one wants to trust a felon. You saved me so many times when we were kids. Now I was alone.

RORY: So many wrongs. But you shouldn't have taken the car.

LUCY: Yeah.

AND: *Steps between Rory and Lucy and holds their hands.*

(Rory and Lucy turn opposite each other, leave the dream realm and return to bed. AND places folding chairs in the audience. AND sits on one chair. Lucy stands center stage. Rory walks at a fast past around the audience. AND directs Rory to sit on the folding chair. Lucy walks forward, center stage slowly.)

RORY: (Stands, cheering) That's my sister. (Improvised enthusiasm)

(Audience is encouraged to clap. Rory, AND, Lucy move towards each other.)

LUCY: I was hoping you'd come. I wanted to look out and see family. You're the only family I have.

RORY: I don't know what made me come but couldn't stay away.

LUCY: My brother.

RORY: My sister.

(Lights Out)

End of Play

Endnotes:

Writer's notes:

A. Props (in order of appearance in the story)

1. Ten pizza boxes
2. Piggy Bank and coins
3. Two Yo Yo's

4. Paper grocery bag with contents-boxed fruit pie pastries, Doggie Devils (Devil Dogs), Heidi Ho Hos (Ho Ho's), raisins
5. Large assorted snack pack of chips
6. Paper plates
7. Double Dutch rope
8. Container of eggs
9. Paper plates
10. Car keys
11. Bag of marijuana

B. Some sections of the play will encourage audience participation. Interested audience members should sit in the seating closest to the actors. The play is written for an intimate theatre experience (in the round, galley, etc.).

Eric and Terisa Deconstructed

Characters:

DR. ERIC SMITH: Middle age African American man

TERISA MARIA SMITH: Adolescent, mixed-race female Eric and Katherine's daughter
Fourteen-year-old girl
Seventeen-year-old girl
Twenty-one-year-old woman

MS. CLARISE/CLARISE: Middle age African American woman

KATHERINE (KAT) SMITH: White, thirty-something woman, Eric's former wife and Terisa's mother

UNCLE JEFFREY/TOLSTOY: White, twenty-something man, Kat's brother, Eric's brother in law, Terisa's uncle/Life size teddy bear:

Time:

Circa 2007-2013
Act One: Fall 2007
Act Two: Spring 2007
Scene One—Evening
Scene Two—Night
Scene Three—Deep Night
Act Three: Spring 2009-2013
Scene One—June 2009
Scene Two—Late August 2009
Scene Three—June 2013

Setting:

Living room of Eric and Terisa's home in a groomed middle-class area of the Bronx. The front door of the house opens into the living room and the adjacent kitchen. As the play begins, Eric is dressed in "formal" casual attire sitting on the sofa and arranging women's fashion magazines on the coffee table. He's surrounded with stacks of student papers, journal articles, and various writing tools. Eric browses through the magazines as he arranges them. Enter Terisa bouncing a basketball. She's wearing an oversized basketball jersey, basketball shorts, and sneakers.

ACT ONE: FALL 2007

(Lights Rise)

TERISA: Ready to hit the court Eric?

(Terisa tosses the basketball. Eric catches it.)

ERIC: Terisa, I told you not to call me by my first name. I'm your father; I'm not your buddy. It's disrespectful.

TERISA: Can you indulge me a little while Eric? I'm experimenting.

ERIC: What kind of experimenting is that Terisa?

TERISA: Like the *Hurt Girls.*

ERIC: More information please.

TERISA: There's so many of them now like they have their own table in the cafeteria near the dairy case because they all drink reduced fat milk, and they have like a club because they all go to therapy at the same outpatient clinic, the adolescent program, because they're not in crisis so they don't have to go to the twenty-four-seven residentials because like they have these ongoing unresolved emotional conflicts with their parents… Eric, did you save the pizza? (Looking in the refrigerator) So like when it's on-going conflict like, "I hate my Mom" or "I hate my Dad," it's different then like you want to hide in a closet or run away. It's like your adolescent development is like stuck… Eric do we have any hot dogs? And they call their parents by their first names so they can like break down the barriers of feeling like they're oppressed by the power and control status of their parents. Eric, I hate these soy dogs, they're processed vegan food. We can eat grass fed organic meat from cows that were happy before they were slaughtered. When they call their parents by their first names there's like an illusion of equality that begins the path of healing the relationship. If the "*Hurt Girls*" get well I wonder if we'll start calling them the "*Well Girls*"? But everybody should be well. There shouldn't be a practice of calling one group of girls well…that would be discrimination. I'm calling Gino's Pizza Palace.

(Terisa picks up the telephone. Eric hangs up the telephone.)

TERISA: The *Hurt Girls* embrace their name…*Hurt Girls.* I fully support them. Why should they hide their journey to recovery?

ERIC: You want to call me Eric because girls in your school in therapy are calling their parents by their first names and you… Too much information Terisa. Help me out here. You feel hurt like the *Hurt Girls*?

TERISA: I like the way your name sounds. I'm experimenting to see if the whole familiar identification of the adult person in the home helps with building trust. Actually the *Hurt Girls* invited me to comradeship at their cafeteria table. As a whole I think they are sensitive perhaps empathic perhaps compassionate perhaps psychic no maybe not psychic everyone assumed I had some hurt issues of my own because of our family baggage but I'm not sharing our personal drama especially with other girls who are already over the top emotional waterfalls so I assumed they asked me to join their table when I didn't make the cut…to the Mixed Race table.

ERIC: Cafeteria table assigned by race?

TERISA: It's accepted protocol in the cafeteria caste system. The Mixed Race Table is one of the elitist groupings. I don't believe in any segregation by race…that's primitive… barbaric…besides everyone knows it's all about the DNA not the complexion. I heard that Stanley Wolenski wanted to find out Mr. Breslow's pedigree because he's makes subtle comments in class that could be construed as borderline racist, so he took a Q-tip sample of his saliva from his tossed coffee cup and sent it to his father's lab for like rush analysis. You know his father is Dr. Peter Wolenski, the Dr. Wolenski who works for the, well I don't know where he works exactly but he came back with this analysis that Mr. Breslow was almost eighty percent African. Can you believe it? Eighty percent African! This man who has negative things to say about people of color that is so underneath the wire of his being fingered as racist and he is himself a person of color… I'd like to know about his karma. I applied to the Mixed Race Table just to see if I would get in, but I didn't make the cut.

ERIC: I can't manage this one right now Terisa. (Pause) You are mixed race. Why didn't they accept you?

TERISA: They revised their entry criteria this year. Being the offspring of a mixture of two lineages is considered passé. You have to have at least three verifiables. Kids who have one Black parent and one White parent are considered ordinary. What's that smell? (Holding up her arms and smelling her armpits) It's me… Stank! I'll clean up before we eat pizza.

ERIC: The hair in your armpits looks long.

TERISA: I'm not shaving my armpits anymore.

ERIC: Shouldn't you?

TERISA: Do you?

(Pause)

ERIC: There are some ladies in the church that say I'm not paying enough attention to your grooming and your clothing.

TERISA: Let me guess…the *Bait and Hook Ladies*?

ERIC: What are you talking about Terisa?

TERISA: That's what we call the single church ladies looking for a husband. They want to catch the few single men in the church with treats on a hook and then reel them into a marriage.

ERIC: That's not a nice way to talk about the ladies in the church.

TERISA: Only some ladies. Besides, I'm not the only one who calls them bait and hook. ERIC, where do you hang out on open school night?

ERIC: I do what I'm supposed to do. I visit each of your teachers, ask them how you're doing, and then sign for your report card.

TERISA: Is that it?

ERIC: Is there something else Terisa?

TERISA: Eric, I'm in all Advanced Placement classes, I'm in the honor society, and I'm on the dean's list every semester. Do you get any new information when you see my teachers?

ERIC: Actually, I don't.

TERISA: You're doing it wrong. Don't feel bad. Most parents are victims of the meaningless ritual of Parent Teacher Night.

ERIC: I'm afraid to ask what I should be doing.

TERISA: You should have my report card mailed home and hang out in the cafeteria with the mother's association. They would so totally accept you since you're like my mother and my father. They bring in homemade dishes to munch on while they gossip except for the corporate types who order something catered and have it delivered but I can tell what's homemade and what's not because of the presentation. Homemade food may not have the foo foo presentation but it has serious unique taste quality. That's why I feel so sorry for Benita. She is like one of the nicest girls. I really like her but she can't have too many carbs because her mother who is like this size two supermodel type has Benita on this crazy really really really low carb diet thingy and so I eat her lunch so she doesn't have to tell her mother she threw the food away because I don't mind low carbs you know ERIC like how I always make a sandwich for breakfast and two for lunch and like cause I'm her friend and I can like feel her suffering so I give her a sandwich and when Mrs. Mancuso, Alexa's mom, sends in left over eggplant rollatini it is so nasty good it's crazy. I describe the sensations of the taste to Benita so she can eat vicariously through me. All the girls on the basketball team like so love it and like you know Eric everybody can't make eggplant rollatini it takes crazy skill…where is the pizza man? Some people think that just because a person can make eggplant parmesan that the same person can make eggplant rollatini are they crazy or what Eric? One is flat layers and one is rolled layers did you ever try to eat eggplant rollatini when the rolls are not rolled tight it's impossible to eat with full enjoyment. Maybe we can munch on the frozen pizza until the pizza man comes?

ERIC: I told you we aren't eating pizza.

TERISA: I heard that Mrs. Mancuso's eggplant rollatini is really from the frozen food section of some overpriced gourmet food store in Little Italy that's what Connie Di Palma said I said like no way and then I said to myself Terisa you are like so crazy like all Italians should know how to cook good Italian food like all Black people should know how to cook good fried chicken…see that's how prejudice starts from food assumptions but who cares who cooked the food if it tastes good. (Grabs a soda) Just a few ounces of steroid Eric.

(Eric grabs the can of soda just after Terisa has finished drinking all of it. She belches.)

TERISA: Excuse me…There's a few vitamins in soda…they make me belch.

You have to so get to know Mrs. Byrd; she's with the cafeteria mother's group. She's so crazy. We call her JB, short for Jay Bird. In and out of rehab a few short stints for petty theft she's the largest alumna contributor. Mrs. Mancuso told Mrs. Panagrahi, that's Benita's mom, that JB contributed big bucks to the new interior design of the faculty lounge they have slot machines in them and JB sponsored the faculty retreat this year to St. Lucia. I know because last year when the faculty went to Saint Bart's somehow, and I know how some way nudie pictures were attached to the year-end auditors report that went to the school board. They're not going to St. Bart's again. If you hung out in the cafeteria Eric you would know all the insider information. The ladies in the church are boring and religious.

ERIC: I send you to the Sacred Heart of Jesus Preparatory School so you can be religious.

TERISA: Maybe some of the parents are religious but almost everyone in school I know is atheist or agnostic…I always confuse those words. I'm going to look them up. I left Tolstoy on top of the dictionary. (Gets Tolstoy and the dictionary) My favorite book…my favorite Teddy.

ERIC: Some ladies in the church group say I let you dress like a ragamuffin.

TERISA: Ragamuffin…rather archaic term don't you think Eric? I want to find out the origins of that word. Sounds like a word straight out of Charles Dickens's "A Christmas Carol."

ERIC: TERISA, the origin of the word aren't important now.

TERISA: Yes, it is Eric. If they're going to call me a name then I should at least know the full context of the word's etymology. They could be misusing the word. And then it's like name calling and you don't understand the meaning of the words you're using. That's so crazy. Or maybe they're using the word correctly and the word means something that resonates with me. Like maybe it means "crossdressing" and then maybe I would say crazy because okay so I'm not a crossdresser, but you're not insulting me. Because if I was a crossdresser then it would be like I understand the female and the male like interpretation of clothes so well that I can like put outfits together to wear that are like really really really crazy on myself so you look at me and you have to ask like, "Is that a boy or a girl? That's a complement Eric. I so love learning new words. My mind is so popping right now ERIC because Julissa, you know, Melissa's step sister, she was like talking yesterday after biology lab that she wished somebody like anybody on the street could just look at her and think… Whoa…that's a person like no gender…like only a person…a human person…and I was like and Kimmy was like…dude…that's so stupid. You need to know who you're dealing with unless like you're a fish and it's not mating season and all the fish are like in the same situation like "Hey we need to stay together in a school of fish and avoid the predators. Solidarity…." So I asked her okay so if you needed a sanitary napkin would you ask a "person" or would you ask a girl…you're not gonna ask a boy for a sanitary napkin or a tampon, that would be crazy…but if you don't know if the person is a male or a female then like you're gonna bleed all over your clothes because that's like gender-specific paraphernalia. Right Eric? But we never finished talking about it because Kimmy said she didn't know the answer because she didn't use sanitary napkins and tampons she didn't have her period yet and Julissa and

I wanted to be early for class because before English Lit if you get there a little early you can watch Mr. Dougherty pick his nose and eat his buggars because he thinks no one is looking. I know Eric it's so gross but it's so funny. Tolstoy! There you are you bad little bear! Eric, Tolstoy was sitting on top of the etymological dictionary. Okay… ragamuffin…r…a…

ERIC: Terisa! Forget about the word.

TERISA: I'll look it up later Eric. I'm so grateful I found you Tolstoy. It was so hard to sleep without you last night. You sit right here on the etymological dictionary until it's time for bed. Eric, I'm going to the basement, I'm gonna get my Knick's jersey from the dryer…it probably…

ERIC: Terisa, sit down with me.

TERISA: Sit down? When are we going to the court?

ERIC: We'll play tomorrow, I promise. Sit with me.

(Terisa dribbles the basketball.)

ERIC: Terisa, stop dribbling the ball.

(Terisa throws the ball into the air and then catches it.)

ERIC: Stop throwing the ball in the house.

(Terisa does basketball-balancing tricks while she is sitting down.)

ERIC: Terisa, throw that ball to me.

TERISA: You told me not to throw the ball in the house.

(Eric takes the ball from Terisa and puts it away.)

TERISA: Something wrong Eric? You're kind of snappy.

ERIC: Terisa, don't you want to dress a little more feminine when we go to church?

TERISA: I'm a female Eric. Female, feminine…it's just a derivative of the same word. How much more feminine can I be…I have a vagina…I don't have a penis… Unless there's something inside me…like an alien…with two biological systems…I think I'd feel something…(Play-acts that she has an alien inside her body) No Eric…as far as I know I'm not an alien or a hermaphrodite. But you know that…I'm thinking about the hairs…

ERIC: Pubic hairs?

TERISA: Arm hair Eric…We were talking about arm hair. Can I see how long your arm hair is? (Pause)You told me you don't shave your pits. I think your arm hair must be pretty long because I noticed in gym class that Jennifer has really really, really long armpit hair. And I said Jennifer, "How come your armpit hair is so long? It looks like you can braid it." And she told me like yeah she can make corn rows and French braids with her armpit hair it just gets a little difficult when she does it herself because she can only use one hand and she said like all the people in her family are really really, really really hairy and they don't believe in cutting their hair because like all the hair on your body is like a gift from God and so I said like Jennifer so how long do you think it's gonna grow and she said she didn't know but her Auntie from the Ukraine was visiting last summer and she was making homemade lemonade with the high speed blender because when you make lemonade in the summer the homemade style with a lot of sugar it's like so the best and she didn't have on a shirt or a blouse with sleeves on it and she turned on the blender without the top on because she forgot to remove some of the seeds out of the lemons and her armpit hair got caught in the blades of the blender…it was…

ERIC: I get the picture…too much of the picture. We're not talking about armpit hair now…

TERISA: You were wondering if I had male and female genitalia?

ERIC: No I wasn't. Terisa, I was asking you about being feminine.

TERISA: You mean more than anatomy?

ERIC: Yes… I mean for example, maybe you can find some fashions you like in one of these magazines.

(Eric spreads the magazines on the coffee table and guides Terisa towards the table to sit next to him.)

ERIC: This is a nice look. And this one is feminine. This girl looks around your age. She looks nice.

TERISA: Nice to whom Eric? I have to be the me I decide to be.

ERIC: Work with me Terisa.

TERISA: I want to work with you on my foul line shots.

ERIC: Terisa!

TERISA: You're yelling Eric.

ERIC: You're talking too much and not listening to me. I'm frustrated. (Pause) Let's look at these magazines together. Let's just find some pictures of fashions you like.

(Eric turns the pages of the magazines trying to get Terisa's attention and interest.)

ERIC: Do you like this look?

TERISA: No.

ERIC: This is a beautiful outfit. I think this is feminine. Do you like this one?

TERISA: No.

ERIC: Do you like any part of what she's wearing?

TERISA: No.

ERIC: TERISA, it would help me if you could provide an explanation of your thinking instead of your "No" and "No" and "No."

TERISA: You just told me you want me to listen and not talk so much.

ERIC: I want you to talk about what I'm talking about when I'm talking to you about it, not about what you want to talk about when you want to talk about it. Oh my God, I'm sounding like you.

TERISA: God has nothing to do with free will choice…isn't that what you tell me Eric?

ERIC: Don't use my words against me Terisa.

(Pause.)

TERISA: Shall we talk about women's fashion undergarments first?

(Terisa reaches under the cushions on the armchair and pulls out several men's magazines with nude and partially nude women.)

TERISA: Thanks for getting these Eric.

ERIC: These aren't for you.

TERISA: Are they for you?

ERIC: They belong to your Uncle Jeffrey. He left them here when he came over to watch the game.

TERISA: That was weeks ago. I'll just call him and tell him they're here. I moved them when I was working on my class project.

ERIC: (Snatching the magazines) No, I'll call him. Class project?

TERISA: The class project for my feminine studies elective class. We had to do a group project on contemporary issues for women in America. And I suggested we do our group presentation on female bondage expressed through foundation garments and everybody was like how are we gonna do that because we have to have primary resources for references and Mr. Willie on the corner stand would never sell us the magazines we needed because of some ridiculous rule that you have to be twenty one years old for adult literature and I was like Mr. Willie this is for a class project and he didn't believe me and so we were like what are we going to do and Stephanie was like we can just present the pros and cons in a debate like real right to life and pro-choice people and I was like no way that is so old school and besides everybody is gonna want to do that for the class project so I said let's think about it and share some ideas at lunch time tomorrow and so when I came home and I was doing my vacuuming chores and I saw the magazines I was like this is soooooooooooooo crazy. All the research materials right in my house and so I told everybody to come over to work on the project at our house because the magazines didn't belong to me and I didn't want to take them out of the house without your permission and besides I had the biggest bedroom and biggest floor space because I was the only one in the group who was an only child and not sharing a room and I didn't think you would mind because it was homework and we were able to finish most of the project in the same afternoon. Remember...when you had your meeting and I thought it was okay but I asked you anyway if my group project team could work at our house and you said it was okay just clean up whatever we messed up. We didn't cut any of the pictures and I put everything back except for the Penelope's Secret catalogue because I wanted to ask you if I could have the fluffy slippers for my birthday.

ERIC: Do the parents of the other girls know how you did your research?

TERISA: No. We took the information but we forgot to make a list of all of the reference materials.

(Terisa goes to the refrigerator and opens the refrigerator door.)

TERISA: Ah! (Scream)

ERIC: What's wrong?

(Terisa stands in front of the refrigerator door holding a piece of old hard pizza and an empty pizza box.)

TERISA: This is the last piece of pepperoni pizza and there's no pepperoni on it. Obviously, we were cheated of our entitled portion of pepperoni because this was an extra-large pie or they didn't evenly distribute the pepperoni on all of the slices, either way, I'm offended.

ERIC: You probably picked the pepperoni off that slice and ate them.

TERISA: Oh yeah. I did.

(Eric takes the pizza and the pizza box and throws it into the garbage.)

TERISA: I'm starving. Can we order the pizza now?

ERIC: We're not having pizza tonight.

TERISA: We have to have pizza tonight its Friday.

ERIC: One of the ladies from the church is coming over for dinner. (Pause) She's bringing the dinner.

TERISA: Bait and hook…Which one is coming?

ERIC: Ms. Clarise.

TERISA: Crazy…she can bang some pots. I had some of her coconut pie. And she makes key lime pie, and lemon meringue pie, and—

ERIC: How do you know she makes pies?

TERISA: She makes pies for snacks for kids in after school programs. Maybe we can go to the movies after she drops off the pie? What do you want to see Eric?

ERIC: She's bringing dinner…not only pie.

TERISA: Crazy. We can take the food to the movies with us. Do you think she's bringing fried chicken? She makes this spicy fried chicken that's so hot it burns your tongue but in a good way.

ERIC: She's not just dropping off dinner. She's staying for dinner.

TERISA: Because?

ERIC: Because she's going to help you…help us with a couple of things…(Pause) Help me…(Pause) I need, you need some, I don't know too much about…because your mother was in charge of those things with you and now that she's gone and you're older and I'm not sure how to talk to you about some things and I want to help and I need to get it right…I need to get it right and…

TERISA: Eric, does this have something to do with the ragamuffin comments?

ERIC: It's all of it…two years makes a difference. When your mother passed you were twelve and you weren't…

TERISA: Stacked? Menstruating? In advanced placement classes?

ERIC: Developed.

TERISA: You want me to wear a bra.

ERIC: Not just that. But yes, maybe you should?

TERISA: There're steroids in the soda Eric. Makes girl breasts big and perky.

(Eric opens the refrigerator and removes all of the soda. He leaves the beer.)

TERISA: Aren't you being a little extreme Eric ? You can't remove all the steroids out of the frig. There'd be nothing left to eat. (Picks up a package of vegan hot dogs) There're steroids in the processed vegan food. It's not public knowledge.

(Eric takes the hot dogs.)

TERISA: And the cold cuts, and the bread…

(Eric empties all the food from the refrigerator.)

TERISA: The only safe food is pizza. Can we order now? (Pause) Eric, you didn't ask about the conclusions of my group project.

ERIC: What does that have to do with brassieres?

TERISA: You're yelling Eric. Remember, you have to provide me with models of good communication during emotionally tense situations.

ERIC: Group project?

TERISA: The group project for my elective women's studies class…Uncle Jeffrey's magazines…

ERIC: I'm missing the connection Terisa.

TERISA: We concluded that brassieres were forms of contemporary bondage devices designed to prevent women from acceptance of their natural, un-airbrushed bodies… Men aren't pressured to wear bras no matter how big their man boobs get. I think Mom would have fully supported my decision to keep myself free of bondage. *Free at last, free at last, thank God almighty we are free at last.* That's my favorite Martin Luther King Jr. speech. I think it applies to so many things Eric, not just the civil rights movement. Although one could argue that female rights, although usually discussed in other historical contexts, "Go Gloria Steinem" are civil rights.

ERIC: Terisa, don't your…hurt when you play ball without a …

(Terisa moves around the living room demonstrating exaggerated movements of her breasts.)

TERISA: Do you mean, do I jiggle and wiggle like jello so much that's its painful?

ERIC: Yes, isn't it painful?

TERISA: No Eric. Even though, "I'm stacked," I don't have any pain when I play ball. I think it's because my back muscles are in pretty good condition from my training with free weights.

ERIC: Maybe you should do a little less free weight training?

TERISA: You want my breasts to be a little more fragile and delicate Eric? Is that the goal?

ERIC: I think the brassieres are to help dresses fit better.

TERISA: I don't wear dresses Eric.

ERIC: I know…but maybe you should wear dresses…

TERISA: Because?

ERIC: Because young ladies wear dresses and skirts and blouses, and pants, but other kinds of pants not just athletic pants, and sweats…

TERISA: There's no dress code at school or at church so what's my motivation?

ERIC: You could look a little more feminine.

TERISA: Maybe I should just expose my vagina then no one would question if I was feminine.

ERIC: Terisa!

TERISA: Vagina isn't a "bad" word. I've been saying "vagina" since I was two. It was definitely one of my first twenty words. Child development research indicates that a child's first twenty words is a very important milestone. I wonder if I can reconstruct my first twenty words. Definitely "dad," "mother," I remember saying mother and I remember neighbors commenting that a little kid would say mother instead of "ma" or "mama" or "mommy" but I distinctly remember saying "mother" and enjoying how good it felt to stick my tongue between my teeth for the middle part of the word…"th," "th," "th," and I remember, "ball," "car," "pizza"…

ERIC: Terisa!

TERISA: Sorry Eric. I wanted to immerse myself in that recollection. I get it. The ragamuffin and the feminine story are the same story…gossip and propaganda from the bait and hook church ladies.

ERIC: Don't call them that Terisa. They are just trying to be helpful.

TERISA: They're trying to get in your pants Eric.

ERIC: Ms. Clarise…

TERISA: MS. Clarise… This was her idea…

ERIC: It wasn't her idea. We need…I need a little help…

(Terisa gets the Penelope's Secrets catalogue that was placed on the coffee table with the magazines.)

TERISA: We don't need Ms. Clarise.

(Terisa pages through the magazines and stops at one page.)

TERISA: Here…this one… This underwire bondage will prop my girls up to stand at attention. That should get the boys looking at my nipples…

(Eric closes the magazine.)

TERISA: I still want the fuzzy slippers.

ERIC: When you see the other young ladies come to church and they have the designer handbags and the trendy clothes, and they have on makeup and have fancy hairstyles don't you think about dressing up a little bit more?

TERISA: No.

ERIC: Don't you think they look nice?

TERISA: Nice for them, not for me.

ERIC: Maybe you need to spend more time with a social circle of girl friends. Maybe you'll want to experiment with dressing up…you like to experiment…Mary Margaret, Bernadette, Francis…those are nice girls…you were in the same classes with them since second grade, you had play dates together, you hung out, and then all of a sudden it stopped when your Mom died.

TERISA: It had nothing to do with Mom. I didn't want to hang around with them anymore.

ERIC: Why not? They're nice girls.

TERISA: Yes, they are nice girls. We're crazy. But I don't want to hang out with them outside of school. I didn't want to go on the playdates anymore. It wasn't fun. I wanted to play B-Ball.

ERIC: I think you should start going on playdates, I mean girl dates again.

TERISA: Do I have to do it with them? (Pause) Eric, do you know what happens on a playdate when you're fourteen?

ERIC: I know it's not Barbie dolls…video games, monopoly, talking about boys…

TERISA: We play with each other. It's for the other kind of play…touching.

ERIC: Touching what?

TERISA: It's not a big deal Eric. It's always in a group so no one feels left out. But it was like feeling left out because after the first time my vajayjay was licked I was like okay but now what…and it's kind of wet and messy afterwards even when we used this plastic thing like a plastic bag you know Eric safety first…it like keeps those bad STDs away but like I was bored and I was like there must be another part to this are you sure because I would rather play ball but like Mary Margaret and Bernadette were always just happy to be together in a cuddly way because they didn't have to come out and say they were lezzies because everyone knew how close they were since second grade it's just that in second grade I guess you don't know what to call it and Francis is bisexual and she was satisfied to just watch and masturbate. They're nice girls…they dress up…they fix their hair…I could hang out with them again if that would make you feel better. But it's boring. I'd rather play ball.

ERIC: Second grade. You had your…second grade… Did your mother know?

TERISA: I didn't say second grade.

ERIC: You said second grade. How old were you seven? Oh, my God.

TERISA: God has nothing to do with free will Eric. Do you know you raised your voice? Are you upset? I said Mary Margaret and Bernadette were in second grade when they were out you know what I mean don't you Eric it's like when you're a little kid you are like so sensory driven you just know what feels good and what doesn't feel good like Mary Margaret and Bernadette I always thought they were lucky like they knew they loved each other and wanted to be together forever since second grade I wonder if like they will ever like officially go somewhere and get married like they would look so cute you know dresses aren't my thing but I can totally see them wearing like wedding gowns together I mean like if they really had a wedding ceremony I wonder what I would wear cause you know we are still good friends even though we don't like hang together like maybe I would wear the NBA team jersey for whatever state they were married in so then I hope they could get married in LA because I so like my LA Lakers jersey but by that time cause I'm sure it would be after college I would have a new jersey I guess anyway Eric I was in sixth grade when I was licked and sucked I guess I was a late experimenter and yeah Mom knew we totally talked about everything it was when you were on sabbatical.

ERIC: Don't change the subject Terisa. I was never on sabbatical from the university.

(Terisa throws the basketball to Eric. They volley the ball back and forth as they volley their words.)

TERISA: Yes, you were.

ERIC: No, I wasn't.

TERISA: Yes, you were.

ERIC: No, I wasn't.

TERISA: You were.

ERIC: I wasn't.

TERISA: Were.

ERIC: Wasn't.

TERISA: You were.

ERIC: Stop! I would know if I had taken a sabbatical!

TERISA: Are you okay Eric? I think anger management classes are overrated. You could just try breathing deep and counting to ten. Sabbatical…it's the word Mom told me to use when you left us. Mom was a very typical good parent. When you left us she gave me a word to say so if someone asked why you weren't around I had a fall back word that would help me feel comfortable in the moment and then I could wait until school was over and cry at home with Tolstoy. When I said sabbatical kids from the academic like parents could totally get it and the corporate parents offspring just assumed sabbatical was some corporate project that kept you away from home but it was so disappointing Eric because I was always prepared to talk about what you were doing on your sabbatical like

I borrowed from Jane Goodall and the chimp research and said you were studying some mutant primate in the remote mountains of Kenya and couldn't be reached and I had to connect it to your real work in English literature so I was going to tell them that you had a research grant to teach poetry through sign language to these very advanced mutant primates but I never got to do that because once I said you were on sabbatical the conversation stopped which is probably the way it should have worked out because Mom told me lies are never justified and saying you were on sabbatical was okay because we were just extending the meaning of the word for you because you were taking a rest from us and that maybe one day you would come back and want us again and then when you came back after Mom died I didn't have to think of it like you came back because Mom died and I had no family to live with I could just think your sabbatical was over and then I didn't feel so bad that maybe you were with me because of guilt.

ERIC: Terisa!

TERISA: It's so old and so okay Eric. I'm resilient.

ERIC: Terisa, are you taking drugs?

TERISA: You can't ask me that Eric.

ERIC: I'm worried about you and I can ask you because I'm your father.

TERISA: Didn't you get some counseling after Mom died about reconstructed families before you became my resident father? I'm sure a counselor would have talked to you about trust. I know you feel entitled to ask me anything because that's the way they do it in the made for TV movies even when the father is like "Wow it's a crisis, the other parent person is dead. Now I have to like really be the father not just like the child support part."

ERIC: Terisa, I...

TERISA: Eric, there's no need. I'm like so over that now. You're my father for real again and I accept that and I know I could have a whole other personal scenario like Crissy from my advanced placement English class who had the worse ultimate bad fortune when both her parents died on a small plane flying over Guatemala but the bodies were never found and Crissy still believes that one day they will like miraculously turn up emerging from being saved by some Indigenous people in the mountains but in the meantime while she's holding on to a little optimism she ended up tragically in the hands of some distant unknown relative persons and the one parent like individual who she really knows and loves the live-in housekeeper Lily is cut out of the picture totally. You did get some counseling before you stepped back into my life right?

ERIC: No.

TERISA: Okay…let me help you…I see the trust issue may be a little out of your reach…and we aren't making too much progress with the female image thingys so let's talk about the list.

ERIC: List?

TERISA: You asked me if I was on drugs but I haven't shown signs of anything on the list.

ERIC: Again Terisa, you're distracting me away from the things I want to talk about with irrelevant information.

(Terisa looks into her backpack.)

TERISA: I didn't think you needed this. It's so basic but I guess I was wrong.

(Terisa hands ERIC an envelope.)

ERIC: This envelope is opened.

TERISA: Of course.

ERIC: This envelope is addressed, "To the parents of Terisa Maria Smith." And you opened it.

TERISA: I open everything addressed to "the parent" and I give you the correspondence that's relevant totally legitimate actions since I don't have a Mom and I consider myself to be one member of a single parent and self-parented adolescent duo or you can consider our situation a parent and child who are co-parents…there are different configurations of families Eric…a mom and a dad; two moms, two dads; a dad and a grandma; a mom and an aunt; a grandma and a grandpa; a mom, stepmom, dad, and stepdad…

ERIC: No more Terisa.

TERISA: Just one more…a nanny, ex-nanny, mom, and cable TV.

ERIC: Are you taking drugs Terisa?

TERISA: Just making light of what's become a tense conversation for you. Let me help you.

(Terisa takes the envelope back from Eric. She reaches into her backpack and takes out a clipboard and pen. She begins to write on the paper.)

ERIC: That's my commemorative Jackie Robinson pen.

(Terisa plays with the pen.)

TERISA: I love the way the baseball moves up and down in the floaty part when you shake it really hard and the thingy at the bottom lights up.

ERIC: You didn't ask me if you could borrow the pen. It's my favorite pen…I've been looking for it.

TERISA: When I'm in study hall it's a great way to trance out because I can watch the baseball float up and down up and down up and down.

ERIC: TERISA, Are you taking drugs?

TERISA: Oh. Right. I'm supposed to be helping with this drug conversation. So this is a list from Mrs. Shatz, the health and wellness teacher…remember I'm taking some elective classes because I took accelerated math so I wouldn't have to take a whole year well anyway (Reads from a list and writes) I'll just make a few changes here that will help with a more personalized understanding of this what seems to be a very important issue for you so let's see "Could your father be heading down a dangerous path? Is your father on drugs? Warning signs: Number One Isolates from the family and the usual family activities. That would be yes. You refused to continue our usual family Friday night activities pizza and basketball. Score one point.

ERIC: This is not about me.

TERISA: Number two: extreme shifts in mood…tense…edgy… Score two points… You're not doing so well Eric.

(Eric goes to the refrigerator and takes out a bottle of beer, opens it and begins to drink.)

TERISA: Alcohol abuse. Can I have a sip?

(Eric puts the bottle back in the refrigerator.)

TERISA: Score three points. The daughter is usually the first to know. Can a person co-parent herself and her parent? Inquiring minds want to know. Number four: truancy. How many sick days did you take last month Eric?

ERIC: That's none of your concern Terisa.

TERISA: I remember you being home a few days but I don't remember you being sick. I'm giving you a point for that. Truancy from employment.

ERIC: Adults are permitted to have mental health days off from work; it's part of the entitlement that comes with being an adult.

TERISA: You left your golf clubs in the living room. Score. Eric plays golf with his buddies instead of going to work. Terisa has perfect school attendance I should skip school and play basketball outside all day but I make the adult choice and go to school. Crazy. This list is actually quite helpful. You get points for every issue on the rest of the list Eric: sudden influence of a new crowd, secretiveness, poor communication. You've been secretly comingling with those schemers, snobs, frenemies bait and hook church ladies that want to change me you cancel our evening without telling me and you don't recognize that I'm suffering from issues of abandonment. Crazy. Eric is on drugs!

ERIC: TERISA, Are you on drugs?

TERISA: No I'm not taking drugs I'm starving I'm hypoglycemic. I need pizza! I need pizza! You have so like ruined all of your trust credits Eric in one evening. You should know I'm not remotely interested in drugs because I wouldn't do anything to jeopardize my game I have to be sharp on the court besides if I wanted drugs I could get them no problem anything anywhere even in here without you noticing and I'll show you.

(Terisa picks up the telephone, dials and waits for an answer while texting on her cell phone.)

It's unfortunate Eric that I have to use such extreme demonstrations… Hello Quincy…yes I know this is your business line…Quincy is my math buddy…he is like so gifted… Oh I was talking to Eric my dad I'm calling on business…I know I never call on business you know how I feel about…but I'm calling for Eric…he's been a little tense lately…edgy…argumentative…suspicious…unable to fulfill his employment responsibilities…he may need something to help him relax…and no synthetic stuff…he's a natural kind of guy…yeah…my thoughts exactly…a little weed…the best you have…he'd prefer domestic grown if you have it…money is not a problem…yes I understand… definitely same day delivery he doesn't care about additional delivery fees…it's an emergency. He needs some calm down support…I'll let him know…it won't be a problem…Eric he has to run your credit card before he can place your order…four ounce minimum Master Card, VISA, Discover… He doesn't accept American Express payments anymore Quincy says the charges to vendors are too much.

ERIC: Hang up the phone.

TERISA: I know you did the extra credit assignment. You are like so amazing.

ERIC: Hang up the phone.

TERISA: I'm really stuck on problem eight. I don't want you to tell me the solution.

(Eric grabs the house phone while Terisa screams to be heard by Quincy and puts away her cell phone.)

ERIC is going to think about it. (Pause) I wanted the extra credit for math.

(Knock at the door.)

ERIC: Does he know where we live?

TERISA: Pizza! I sent a text message to Gino's.

(Eric goes to the door and looks through the peek hole.)

ERIC: It's Ms. Clarise.

TERISA: Time out. Time out. Game change. She can't come in. Where's the pizza man? She probably assaulted him racing to get to the front door. Bait and hook church ladies. I told you Eric they're after you. She's the ringleader.

ERIC: I'm opening the front door Terisa.

TERISA: You can't. You can't. This is my home too. I say, "No, No. Can't come in here." Maybe they're all here. The whole Bait and Hook Sorority for Desperate Single Women. Yes and they're going to propagandize you, convince you to bring one of their members into our home to fix me. This is one big crazy mess, disaster, catastrophe. They must be hiding in the bushes. If you open the door they're planning to pounce on you like desperate man-eating predators. Get their hooks into you and reel you in. Block the door. I need to block the door before they break it down.

(Terisa pushes the sofa against the door, which also pushes Eric out of the way. She piles pillows, and everything she can find to block the door.)

TERISA: Tolstoy. Tolstoy.

(She finds her teddy Tolstoy and cuddles it. She sits on top of the piles on the sofa.)

No surrender.

(Terisa stands on the sofa holding Tolstoy.)

Let us pray. In this, my time of need, I humbly beg thee for protection against my enemy my father's frenemy.

MS. CLARISE: Hello… It's Ms. Clarise. I've brought dinner. Is everything all right?

TERISA: I've attempted to endure my fate in honor and humility but alas I'm overwhelmed and outnumbered by my father, a misguided soul, and a woman who temps him.

MS. CLARISE: Did you remember we had dinner planned Eric? I saw a pizza deliveryman; I told him he must have the wrong house.

TERISA: Ah! (Scream) In my hour of most grave need don't abandon me and leave me in solitude with my earthly agonies. Bless me. Give me courage. Keep me from harm.

ERIC: Move away from the door Terisa.

TERISA: No!

MS. CLARISE: I brought some of your favorite foods Terisa. I made eggplant rollotini. I used Mrs. Mancuso's recipe. I made fried chicken…spicy buttermilk batter….

TERISA: Did you bring pie?

MS. CLARISE: Yes dear, samples of the mini pies that I make for the after school program: key lime pie, sweet and sour apple, cherry…

TERISA: You never brought cherry pie to the after school program.

MS. CLARISE: A new recipe…I thought you might like it.

TERISA: Help me to prevail in my young life over evil and temptation…

MS. CLARISE: I brought you some homemade pizza…I make my own dough.

TERISA: Thick or thin crust?

MS. CLARISE: Both. I didn't know what you preferred. It's still hot. I made a mini pan of both kinds. I'll pass them through the door.

TERISA: I'm leaving the chain on. No tricks. (Eating a mini pie) This is crazy good. Neglected, threatened, and starved… Alas I feel myself pulled by the forces of evil. Put some samples through the door.

MS. CLARISE: I thought perhaps we could play some ball after dinner.

TERISA: You play basketball?

MS. CLARISE: I was captain of the women's basketball team for two years in college.

TERISA: Hear my petition and my heartfelt plea for I am doomed. Amen.

ERIC: I'm opening the door now Terisa. Amen.

(Lights Out)

End of ACT ONE.

ACT TWO: SPRING 2007

SCENE ONE—EVENING

Setting:

Living room. There are two boxes on the coffee table, one with the name "ERIC" written in large letters, the other with the name "TERISA" written in large letters. Eric looks through both boxes.

(Lights Rise)

ERIC: Ten DVDs for Terisa. (Closes the box and opens the box marked Eric) Okay.

One DVD for me. (Picks up a photograph) I remember this. Spring break in Mexico, when things were simple. That cottage was great…pink, lime green, and sky blue with an indoor courtyard…not a home design for the Bronx… easy going…easy living. (Picks up a loud colored tie) You were so silly Kat. I can't believe you kept this tie. Did you ever believe I would wear something like this? I remember secretly putting this tie in a bag for clothing donations.

(Eric turns on the television. He loads, stops, and then reloads the DVD player several times. He loads the DVD a final time and then sits on a chair in front of the television. Kat appears inside the television sitting on a chair. She stares at Eric. Eric checks the volume control and the equipment connections. There's no sound. Eric sits down and watches Kat sitting without movement and without voice.)

ERIC: I suppose this is a still image.

KAT: No it's not.

(Eric jumps up, startled by the life like Kat. He turns the television off. The image disappears. Eric paces back and forth. He loads, stops, and then reloads the DVD.)

KAT: How long did you wait? I'm thinking about five minutes of pacing.

(Eric jumps up startled.)

KAT: Relax Eric. I'm not a ghost. I know you. I simply knew you or rather most of you before I died.

ERIC: You manage to torment me Kat despite your death.

KAT: Could be weeks, days, hours from now. You can't imagine Eric what it's like when a person knows death is coming to collect them inevitably. What day? What hour?

(Eric gets up to shut off the television. He shuts it off, paces and then turns the television on again.)

KAT: Thank you for turning the television back on. Thank you for being here. I'm believing as I make this video that you came back for our child. Jeffrey is recording for me. Wave to Eric in front of the camera Jeffrey.

(Jeffrey waves.)

Thank you for that Eric. I believed you would come. Thought it would be sooner.

Didn't think I'd have to be dead before you returned to be Terisa's father.

ERIC: This is ridiculous. I'm not sitting through a video recording tirade of my failures as a husband.

KAT: I'm sorry Eric. There's not much time. I want to concentrate on Terisa. We have so much unresolved between us. There should have been time.... Being Catholic we don't have the privilege of believing we'll work our relationship out through reincarnation. I'd wish for a purgatory between heaven and hell just for couples and former couples to face each other with their last words attempting reconciliation. Then I'd want you to go straight to hell for what you put me through.

ERIC: Kat, give me a reason to leave on this recording.

KAT: Terisa Maria Smith. This recording, our daughter, Terisa Maria Smith. I'm so grateful you're here for our child…our creation…our blessing. An inconvenient pregnancy you called her. I forgave you… Those words were before she arrived with her spunk and her beautiful combination of you and me…before you could accept her as a real, living person. I take responsibility for my own beliefs…my old-fashioned rulebook of doctrines from the Catholic Church. An abortion was never an option for me. You're not the only person to pick and choose among the Catholic teachings to follow so I don't blame you. (Pause) Eric… we were such great friends. Sex destroyed us. We forgot we liked each other as people. We were great together when our relationship was about supporting each other's scholarship, aspirations, careers…and fun… Sex forced us to be serious in a way we didn't anticipate. And then I got trapped…I fell in love…you stayed in fun mode…and you weren't feeling love for me and I couldn't make you and then Terisa. What would life have been without her? You would get tenure and then accept an option at an Ivy League or big ten university…I'd go to Russia…finish my dissertation…then a post doctorate somewhere. We would have stayed in touch…connecting for fun and good times once in a while…with no obligations. (Pause) We created someone together to love… She didn't ask to be here but she is…and she is deserving of all that's good in life…I know you'll do your best to make that happen. Here is my advice Eric. Be patient, not with Terisa, with yourself. You'll know how to love and care for her as you go. You'll make mistakes, you'll be frustrated, don't give up, let Terisa show you how to love her.

ERIC: Free spirited, new wave hippy, hands off child rearing Kat?

KAT: We never could agree on much. I'm imagining you sitting there shaking your head, dismissing my "irresponsible" parenting. Let your pride go Eric. I never left Terisa, you did. Consider that I might have the advantage on understanding our daughter simply because I've been around and I've had my own trials and errors and more practice with trying to get it right. Terisa won't need help with ordinary things from you. I've taken care of that. I know you looked through her box.

ERIC: (Pushing Terisa's box out of view) I only looked.

KAT: Those tapes are for my conversations with our darling girl. Those conversations that I wanted to have but time has slipped away and those opportunities are gone. Let me know I can keep those private conversations with her… I promise you there is only "girl talk" and then "woman talk." (Pause) When you get these tapes I'll be a dead person, and obviously I can't control anything you do…or can I? Boo! Just kidding. I'll never know what you do, but I'm going to believe that you let Terisa and I continue our mother/daughter time. She'll miss me Eric. These tapes will be a small comfort to her.

(Pause)

ERIC: How am I going to do this?

KAT: You can do this Eric. Allow yourself time to know her. She's not the same little girl she was when you left. Accept her for who she is now and create a space for her to feel free to express herself. Like it or not…this is the way I tried to raise her. Realistically, if you don't create the space for her to be free, she will create the space herself. That's the kind of person she is: "No way, make a way."

ERIC: I can see us bumping heads already.

KAT: You'll bump heads… I have my beautiful bruises from Terisa that I lovingly take to the grave. So I'll tell you what I learned.

(Pause)

KAT: All the years you stayed away, I knew you loved her. We got in the way of who we needed to be together for our daughter. I know you love her now. I want to die with the comfort that you'll care for Terisa with the best of intentions. Mistakes will happen. Accept her, accept who she is, then allow yourself to know her. And when you know her, continue to love her. My final advice is to listen to her more than you talk. (Pause) You're all she has. Jeffrey can barely take care of himself, let alone a teenage girl.

JEFFREY: (Picking his nose) No offense taken.

ERIC: I loved you Kat.

KAT: You didn't love me Eric. I accepted that eventually. Fun is fun and love is love. You grew fond of me… Love should make people better. We weren't better people together. Terisa, our darling daughter, is the better of our not better together. No expressions of guilt needed. We agree we love Terisa and we always had Leo Tolstoy, the greatest realistic fiction novelist of all time. We could agree about our love for Tolstoy.

(Eric ejects the DVD, places it in its case, and puts it on the bookshelf. He turns off the television and sits on the sofa clutching photographs from the box.)

(End of Scene)

(Lights Out)

SCENE TWO—NIGHT

Setting:

Upstairs. Terisa's bedroom. A table lamp is on with dim lighting. The music of Michael Jackson is playing. Terisa is sleeping on her bed without a blanket holding Tolstoy. Enter Eric with the box marked Terisa. Eric turns off the music, straightens out the blankets, puts Tolstoy at the end of the bed and sits on the bed next to Terisa.

(Lights Rise)

ERIC: Terisa? Are you awake Terisa?

TERISA: (Groan)

ERIC: Are you awake Terisa?

TERISA: (Loud groans) What?

ERIC: I want to talk to you for a few minutes. Your Uncle Jeffrey brought a box over for you. Your mother left it.

TERISA: "Вот мой вам совет: не женись, пока вы не можете сказать себе, что вы сделали все, что могли, и, пока вы не разлюбил женщин: Вы выбрали, пока не увидите ее четко, в противном случае вы будете жестоко и непоправимо ошибаются. Жениться, когда ты стар и никуда не годится...В противном случае все, что хорошо, а высокие в вас будут потеряны."[1]

ERIC: Are you speaking Russian?

TERISA: (Groan) Yes.

ERIC: I suspect you're reciting some esoteric passage from *War and Peace*. Only your mother would read a child *War and Peace* as a bedtime story.

(Terisa speaks with a very poor Russian accent.)

TERISA: "Here's my advice to you: don't marry until you can tell yourself that you've done all you could, and until you've stopped loving the women you've chosen, until you see her clearly, otherwise you'll be cruelly and irremediably mistaken. Marry when you're old and good for nothing… Otherwise all that's good and lofty in you will be lost."

ERIC: And of course Terisa you would remember a passage that would torment me.

TERISA: (Pushes around Eric, gets out of bed, sings and performs in a sleep state) Because I'm Bad, I'm Bad. Come on. You know I'm Bad, I'm Bad, And the whole world has to answer right now. Come on.[2]

(After she completes the song and routine, Terisa lies on the floor, asleep. Eric picks Terisa up from the floor, places her in bed, and tucks her in with Tolstoy under her arm.)

TERISA: (Groans)

(Eric picks up the box and walks towards the door. He turns around and returns placing the box next to Terisa's bed.)

(End of Scene)

(Lights Out)

SCENE THREE—DEEP NIGHT

(Lights Rise)

Setting:

Upstairs. Terisa's bedroom. Terisa lies on the bed in a semi-sleep state. Tolstoy puts on Michael Jackson music and dances. Tolstoy dances downstairs to the living room and takes Eric's DVD from the bookshelf. After the dance, Tolstoy removes his bear head revealing he is Uncle Jeffrey.

(Lights Out)

(Lights Rise)

(Terisa sits up in bed. Tolstoy, the typical size stuffed teddy bear is sitting on the bed. Terisa takes a box of DVD tapes from the box left by her mother. She browses through the tapes, separating the ones of interest to her. She reads the labels on the individual tapes.)

TERISA: Menstruation, contraception, sex and childbirth…, um interesting eight SEX, nine SEX, ten SEX… Let's start with these Tolstoy.

(Terisa places a "SEX" tape in the DVD player and turns on the television. Kat appears on the screen.)

KAT: TERISA MARIA, take out this tape and put in tape number one. And watch the tapes in order or they will self-destruct. No, they won't self-destruct. Please place your curiosity on time out and view the tapes in order my darling.

TERISA: You won't know Mother.

KAT: I won't know…but I'll know…and you know what I mean…

(Terisa replaces the sex tape with the appropriate tape.)

TERISA: Yes Mother.

(Kat appears on the television screen. She is walking back and forth carrying books and papers. There are piles all around her. She arranges the papers, then sits down, opens books and then closes them.)

KAT: This isn't going so well my darling girl. I want to tell you so much and I want to tell you so little…find a way to be of comfort to you my darling during a time when neither of us is comfortable. Pancreatic Cancer is like a thief that's come to visit in the night that isn't afraid to show itself. The doctor told me this was the cancer and in the same breath told me I was going to die.

(Terisa gets up from being seated and reaches to turn off the television.)

KAT: I need you to be brave my darling girl… Don't turn off the television. This is Mom…not a ghost… Uncle Jeffrey's here. Wave to Terisa, Jeffrey.

UNCLE JEFFREY: Hey Risa Pisa.

TERISA: I hate when you call me that. Hello Uncle Jeffrey.

KAT: We're doing this together. I know you don't understand right now, trust me.

Get your terry cloth bathrobe, the one that matches mine. We're going to get comfortable in our discomfort. I want you to put the DVD on pause and surround yourself with us. Close your eyes. Take a breath. Count to five then you'll know what else to get.

(Terisa puts the DVD on pause. She collects items from different areas of her bedroom.)

TERISA: Picture box, *War and Peace*, silver handle hairbrush, Lakers jersey, Mother smells…

(Terisa chooses the final item.)

Honeysuckle.

(Terisa disables the pause control.)

KAT: Ready my darling?

TERISA: Ready Mother.

KAT: Do you have the honeysuckle fragrance?

TERISA: Yes Mother.

KAT: Put on a little behind your ears.

(Terisa puts on the honeysuckle fragrance.)

KAT: I want you to feel as though I'm there beside you. (Pause)

I bought all of this…took notes, summarized articles. This mess looks like the piles I made when I was writing my dissertation. Watch this my darling.

(Kat throws the papers into a garbage basket.)

The ultimate file.

(Kat picks up one remaining book on the floor.)

And then there's this piece of trash…

The Complete Guide to Living Like a Lady for the Twenty-first Century.

The ultimate trash…at least for us. I never used any guidebooks for raising you Terisa…just loved you…I was afraid I would miss something…thought perhaps I needed some expert to tell me the most important things my daughter needed to help her live a healthy, happy, and well-adjusted life… The truth is…there's no guidebook for a near dead woman and her daughter. Who the hell can figure this out? (Pause) Stop the tape now Jeffrey. Stop the tape.

(Terisa removes the tape and replaces it with tape two. Kat is sitting on a chair with a guitar. She sings her rendition of "Happy Birthday" while playing the guitar.)

That's all there is for this one my darling. That's why I call this DVD, the birthday. Play it for your birthdays. I wish you many…

(Terisa removes the DVD and reads the label.)

TERISA: (Terisa picks up and reads the label on the next tape) Essentials about Dad.

(Terisa loads the tape.)

KAT: Everyone deserves a second chance. Give your father his. I know he loves you TERISA. He stayed away because of me…not because of you… Give him a chance to share his love for you again. Now here is the difficult part. The feeling of love is easy when you surrender to it, but love is complicated because of stuff…life's stuff…

(Pause)

Love is what people are created for…we're born to love. But then right after a person is born suffering takes over.

Then everyday of existence is an effort to be happy. I'm sounding very Buddhist not Catholic. I'm trying to say... the stuff in life can screw love up my darling girl. I'm trying to tell you Terisa that giving your father a second chance to love you means accepting that he's going to make mistakes with the life stuff. He's going to have to learn YOU. He's going to mess up. He's going to make a big hot mess, and I won't be there to clean it up. The thing about love my darling is that if you believe that love is the most important treasure we have on earth, and I do, then you accept that clean and neat is something you can make a walk in closet, not the stuff around and about love. Your father and I couldn't work through our life stuff, but that doesn't mean you and your father can't. I know this is so much to burden you with my darling. You have to be brave about so many things now. I put you lovingly in the hands of angels. You are loved. You will always be loved. Most of all you must love yourself. Accept your ME. I guarantee you there will be days in your life when "LOVE ME" is going to be so hard, unthinkable, unspeakable... when people around you will try to shape you into their attainable understanding of who you are because it helps them feel more comfortable. Resist my darling. Your life is your own. Your ME is for YOU to decide. The only safety for your happiness is loving the ME your decide to Be. My darling girl, become a sanctuary of self-love. And when you need a champion, I'm here to remind you: BE THE ME I CHOOSE TO BE.

TERISA: Be the me I choose to be.

ACT THREE: SPRING 2009-2013

SCENE ONE—JUNE 2009

In darkness

[Sound Effect: High School Graduation, Pomp and Circumstance played by high school orchestra.]

ANNOUNCEMENT (VOICE OVER): And addressing our graduates, the valedictorian of the class of the class of 2009 Terisa Marie Smith.

[Sound Effect: Applause.]

SCENE TWO—LATE AUGUST 2009

Living Room

(Lights Rise)

ERIC: Almost finished Terisa? I want to miss the commuter traffic. I hope you aren't bringing any more boxes. The U-Haul can't possibly fit another thing.

TERISA: No more boxes. I'm looking for Tolstoy.

ERIC: I put him in the washing machine. I'll send him to you. Just remind me.

TERISA: Okay! (Pause) Mother Tapes. (Takes the Mother tapes out of the box and places them in her backpack) There in a minute.

(Lights Out)

SCENE THREE—JUNE 2013

Living room, ERIC and CLARISE's home. ERIC is dressed in a shirt, tie, and casual pants. CLARISE is dressed in athletic clothing. CLARISE is in the kitchen cooking. Eric is in the living room wandering doing various physical activities including pacing, sitting, standing, and arranging papers. His movements are repetitive, without apparent meaning, and redundant.

(Lights Rise)

CLARISE: Eric, stop pacing. The carpet is already thread bare.

(Eric stops pacing and walks into the kitchen opens the refrigerator door, looks, closes it, then opens it again…and continues with the ritual.)

CLARISE: Never mind. Keep pacing.

ERIC: She's coming home.

CLARISE: You're getting worked up and becoming anxious instead of simply feeling happy that Terisa is coming home. Feel grateful. Feel thankful. Feel joyful.

ERIC: I'm too busy to feel joyful Clarise. She's coming home. Terisa is coming home, it's been four years Clarise, four years…she graduates high school…leaves…the school breaks…she doesn't come home…always an excuse… I know what the academic calendar is…you know what the academic calendar is…we know what the academic calendar is…she knows we know what the academic calendar is…you know we know what the academic calendar is…winter break…intersession…spring break… summer break…it's not different…the academic calendar hasn't changed in four years Clarise…it's an academic calendar…it doesn't change Clarise…she knows we know it doesn't change Clarise…one of the few things we can depend on in this world…an academic calendar…it doesn't change…we like it…she could have come home four spring breaks in four years…two intercessions every year… eight intersessions…four summer breaks in four years… but I know what you're thinking…Clarise…I know what you're thinking… Terisa wasn't taking breaks, she's been taking courses…then what about spring break…no one takes courses for spring break…she still has had breaks… and the question is Clarise…what has Terisa been doing on her breaks. She's hasn't been coming home!

CLARISE: Maintaining good grades so she could keep her full scholarship perhaps. I need more seasoned salt.

ERIC: Ah ha! And that's the point…I know she was in school… she didn't drop out…she graduated but I don't know what else she's been doing. Why Clarise? Why don't I know Clarise? Why Clarise? Tell me why. I want to know. You must know, so tell me if you know. I want to know why. Why Clarise? I'll tell you why Clarise? Do you want me to tell you why Clarise. I can tell you why. Yes, I can answer that puzzle. Let me tell you why? Shall I tell you why? Don't you want to know Clarise? Clarise? Clarise?

CLARISE: Tell me Eric.

ERIC: Because our daughter is too smart. She wins a full scholarship with grants and stipends. I don't have to pay tuition. She doesn't need my money.

CLARISE: And you've been devastated by that…I know…such injustice. An intelligent young lady who carves her own destiny and doesn't need her father's money.

ERIC: It was my right to go into debt from paying her college tuition.

CLARISE: Every parent's hope and dream. I'll do without the salt. We should be cutting down anyway. Although you can increase your high blood pressure on your own.

ERIC: With the money comes entitlement. If I paid her tuition for four years, the bills would come to me… I could have kept tabs on what she was doing. I could have dangled that tuition payment in front of Terisa. Paying the tuition… buying the books, the meal plans, furnishing the dorm room, the student fees, the monthly allowance that bring father's into debt, getting second mortgages on the family home, putting off vacations, borrowing against their retirement accounts…the financial ruin that brings power… Our ancestors struggled for the right to become ruined through debt. Equality for financial ruin.

CLARISE: And Terisa spared you from all that.

ERIC: Injustice disguised. Terisa doesn't need my money so she doesn't come home. The university doesn't need my money so they don't contact me with threats because of late, unpaid bills. The student affairs department won't speak to me. She's an adult. Her life at the university is private. I'm her father…she has no privacy unless I say so.

CLARISE: Terisa is twenty-one years old.

ERIC: I haven't said so yet. And now I have "retro said so" because I've been denied my paternal rights for four years.

CLARISE: "Retro said so," a fake turn of phrase if I ever heard one.

ERIC: It's not fake. Language is dynamic. I'm simply reconstructing "I told you so" and "I said so" to form an expression that suitably fits my experience.

CLARISE: Terisa loved words in a charming, almost romantic way when she was a teenager. I wonder if she still cherishes words outside of their academic value?

ERIC: This is not about Terisa. This is about me.

CLARISE: Yes Eric, all about you…how unfortunate for us. Our teenager has become an independent and accomplished young woman. We'll have precious moments to observe how she's blossomed…but this is all about you.

ERIC: You aren't listening to me Clarise. Terisa had to be brilliant…and it has been the demise of my existence since she was a little girl. Don't talk to me about joy Clarise. *Be grateful Eric. Be happy Eric. Be joyful Eric.* Tell me about joy when in four years I've never had an opportunity to enjoy the joy. Does that make sense? Enjoy the joy? Joy enjoy… Let's examine this Clarise. *Alumni awards, presidential fellowships, "Who's Who of American College Students, Fulbright, Rhodes, Forbes–Thirty under Thirty Young People to Watch, Young Women of Promise for 2013.* Where is my joy Clarise?

CLARISE: You can't be saying you're not proud of Terisa?

ERIC: Proud? Proud?

CLARISE: Will you set the table? She's going to be hungry and ready to eat when she arrives. Some things about children don't change. I'm sure she's a sophisticated foodie now. But then again…she's always been a sophisticated foodie.

ERIC: Proud? Proud? I'm the proudest father on the planet Clarise.

CLARISE: I can see that.

ERIC: She stole the father pride opportunities from me. She's graduated. Not one invitation to awards ceremonies, award dinners, honor society pinning… I read about my daughter in the press like everyone else. Did I get a complimentary copy of *Young Vogue* when she was featured and interviewed? Did I Clarise? Did I Clarise? Did I Clarise? DID…

CLARISE: I guess you didn't. I'll get you a subscription.

ERIC: I don't want a subscription to *Young Vogue*.

CLARISE: All right dear. Do you want a subscription to *Gentleman's Quarterly*? I found the last issue in the crevice of the sofa.

ERIC: That belongs to Jeffery. He left it here when he came over to watch the game.

CLARISE: I watched the last game with you and Jeffrey, remember?

ERIC: Oh, Clarise, you're distracting me. Terisa graduates and she's invited to give the keynote address…my daughter…

CLARISE: Our daughter Eric.

(Pause)

ERIC: Our daughter…

(Pause)

ERIC: Our daughter graduates. And how do I know she was invited to give the keynote address and she turned down the invitation to give the keynote address at the graduation before her peers, alumni, parents, invited guests, our congressman? I find out when I read it in the alumni news because our daughter hasn't called me, hasn't written me, hasn't emailed me, hasn't texted me…

CLARISE: Terisa has never been concerned much about ceremonies. It's still an honor to be asked. She's done the work.

ERIC: This was my time to be proud. To sit in front of the dais, watch our daughter walk down the aisle with her college gown, her cap, her college tassel, her honor colors…This was my time to be proud in front of all those people… What happened Clarise?

CLARISE: I know what happened.

ERIC: I know what happened.

CLARISE: You asked me what happened.

ERIC: I know what happened. I don't know what happened. I know what happened. I don't know what happened.

CLARISE: Are you finished?

ERIC: I need to know why Terisa is coming home now?

CLARISE: I think…

ERIC: I'll tell you what I think…I'll tell you what I think…I think…I don't know what to think… I saw the list… the list published in the alumni quarterly report. She has choices. She has offers…graduate schools, fellowships, externships… She has more offers than any of the graduates in her department. She is one of the most sought after talents at the university. She doesn't need my money. She doesn't need me. Where is she going? What is she going to do? I'll tell you what she's going to do. I'll tell you what she's going to do. I'll tell you what she's going to do. I'll tell you what she is going to do. To do… To do… I don't know what she's going to do. She hasn't told me. And the list…the published list that I saw when everyone else saw it doesn't tell what she's going to do only what her offers are… I shouldn't know her plans when everyone else knows. I should know before everyone. I'm her father.

CLARISE: I know what she's going to do. (Holds up a food tray) Eggplant?

ERIC: What? What is she going to do?

CLARISE: She's going to come home. She's going to see her Mom and Dad. She'll be hungry and ready to eat. Relax Eric.

ERIC: There's a plot somewhere. Terisa has tormented me since she was a kid. Always talking too fast, switching subjects, never answering a direct question, confusing me, talking circles around me.

CLARISE: And now you can verbally maneuver pretty well for yourself.

ERIC: If she told me her plans I probably wouldn't know what she told me because when she's told me anything in the past it's not like telling me…but it is telling me…but telling me in a way that's not telling me because she never gets to the point, and when Terisa is telling something and never getting to the point the communication is never satisfying or effective because I'm entrapped…entrapped to listen always listening attentively because I believed some way somehow the key words that hold the important information would emerge if I could just focus and be patient and hold on for my life, but no man should be expected to focus and be patient when the irrelevant words completely surround the relevant words like an ambush and an attack on whatever sense of meaning and value I believed I extracted from the conversation if it was a conversation because when there's one person dominating all of the turns as a speaker and overloading your ears and every bit of cognitive capacity you have is struggling to keep you alive as a thinking, feeling person, then you have to retreat to the only means of survival left which is to pretend you understand the explanation and say, "Okay."

CLARISE: Okay. We've been given a gift Eric. Terisa is coming home. She doesn't have to for reasons that might be obvious. She's been managing quite well without us… at least academically. She's coming here now because she wants to see us. She wants home. Do us both the favor. Accept the gift, the gift of Terisa coming home. When she walks through the door, don't start attacking her with whys and what ifs and couldn't you have…just let her be our daughter…our daughter who has come home.

ERIC: You're right. What have I been thinking?

CLARISE: You haven't been.

ERIC: She should walk through the door and feel comfortable… accepted…welcomed…not interrogated.

CLARISE: I've been doing my part. Her old room is freshened up. She'll be comfortable in there.

ERIC: Comfortable…she should feel comfortable…I'll congratulate her on all the awards, the accolades…no she won't want that she'll feel I'm prying…no interrogations, no questions…no accusations…just happy to see her.

Comfort…Tolstoy…she left Tolstoy here…Where is that bear?

(Eric looks around the house for Tolstoy the bear.)

CLARISE: You think she'll want her childhood teddy bear?

ERIC: She loved that bear. Where is Tolstoy? Where would she have put him?

CLARISE: I don't know…wasn't in her room.

ERIC: I'll go out and buy another teddy bear, one that looks like Tolstoy.

CLARISE: A twenty-one-year-old bear? Good luck with that.

ERIC: You're right. Impossible. Maybe she'll be upset. She goes away to school and we lose her treasured possessions. Where is that dam bear?

CLARISE: Eric?

ERIC: Are you sure it's not in her room?

CLARISE: Eric?

ERIC: Did you make pizza? No, we need to order pizza. What was the name of that pizza parlor she liked? I don't remember. Why can't I remember the name of her favorite pizza parlor? What kind of father am I?

CLARISE: I made homemade mini pizzas.

ERIC: Maybe we should invite the girls she liked from grade school. Mary Margaret, Bernadette, and Francis? (Pause) Mary Margaret, Bernadette, and Francis… Oh… Oh… No judgment, welcome her, let her know I've missed her… Thank you for coming home… But no thanks for staying away, for ignoring me , for depriving me of all those things parents of college students pray for like a hooded sweatshirt with the name of the university on it.

CLARISE: Any one can purchase clothing from the university bookstore.

ERIC: It's not the same. She was supposed to buy me a hooded sweatshirt with the name of her university and give it to me on Father's Day or my birthday, or Hanukah!

CLARISE: We're Catholic. Would Hanukah work for you?

ERIC: I can't do this... I'm angry... I did everything I could for Terisa... How long did we wait Clarise? ... Wait to get married after we decided to date.

CLARISE: Two years, three months, five days, and seventeen minutes.

ERIC: We waited long enough for Terisa to feel comfortable with us as a couple and to accept the possibility of another mother.

CLARISE: Terisa called me Mom Clarise the first month we were dating.

ERIC: Maybe that's not the best example of putting her needs first... I'll think of a good example... I know there is a good example... I know there is at least one... I'm thinking...thinking...just one...all I need is one... Can I get back to you on this?

We have one child Clarise.

CLARISE: Yes we do.

ERIC: We...I have to do everything I can to make sure we stay a family. This may be the chance. (Pause) Basketball. (Runs to the window to look outside) The hoop is still out there...sort of... Where's my basketball? (Runs to the closet and throws items out onto the floor) Where's my basketball?

CLARISE: When was the last time you played basketball Eric? I invite you to go to the court with me at least once a week and you never come.

(Clarise pinches Eric's love handles around his middle. Eric continues to throw things out of the closet. The living room is a mess. He finally pulls a dirty basketball out of the closet.)

ERIC: Thank God. My ball.

(Eric attempts to bounce the ball; it doesn't bounce but lies motionless on the floor. Eric looks at his clothing.)

ERIC: Clarise, how could you let me dress this way?

CLARISE: You're dressed in your casual Saturday button down shirt, tie, and khaki's.

[Sound Effect: Doorbell ringing]

CLARISE: That's probably…

(Eric pulls off his pants, shirt, and tie.)

ERIC: That can't be TERISA, she has a key.

(Clarise stares at Eric's partially clothed body.)

CLARISE: It's been a long time ERIC…she probably lost her key or maybe she wants to feel respectful of our privacy…

[Sound Effect: Doorbell ringing]

ERIC: Maybe I ordered pizza? (Pause) Gino…Gino's Pizza Palace… That's the pizza she likes. I must have ordered it. Lots of pepperoni on every slice. I'm a good father.

CLARISE: I told you I made mini pizzas.

ERIC: Where are my basketball shorts Clarise?

(Doorbell rings. Terisa waits outside for the door to be answered. Clarise walks towards the door. Eric blocks the door.)

I need my basketball shorts and a team jersey.

(Eric pushes the sofa against the front door.)

[Sound Effect: Doorbell ringing]

TERISA: Is everything all right in there?

(Eric and Clarise struggle in a tug of war like battle moving the sofa towards the door and away from the door.)

CLARISE: I probably put them in a donation box somewhere.

ERIC: Sweatpants. I have sweatpants. Clarise, help me I need my pants. I can wear sweatpants and a tee-shirt. I'll look relaxed, welcoming, and ready to break the ice with a friendly game of one on one.

(Sound Effect: Doorbell ringing)

TERISA: Is everything okay? Can I help you with something?

ERIC: Yes…I can wear sweatpants…but will they be the sweatpants I wanted…the sweatpants I deserve Clarise… no…because my sweatpants don't have a university name on them. I don't have sweatpants with a hooded sweatshirt to match that my daughter gave me on a Father's Day as I deserved.

(Clarise pushes the sofa away from the front door pushing Eric to the floor while wearing only his boxer shorts and tee-shirt surrounded by the items he threw out of the closet.)

[Sound Effect: Sound of a key opening the door.]

CLARISE: You're incredible. Don't you dare question her or judge her Eric or you'll have to deal with me.

(Door opens. Terisa enters. She is pregnant and has some difficulty navigating in the space.)

TERISA: I didn't want to use my key…I heard strange noises…is everything okay?

(Clarise and Terisa hug and kiss.)

CLARISE: Welcome home Terisa.

TERISA: It's been a long time Mom Clarise. It's good to see you. Hello Dad.

(Eric stares at Terisa's pregnant body, avoiding looking at her face, while scrambling to locate his pants, shirt, and tie.)

ERIC: Hello Terisa. Welcome home.

(Eric looks at Clarise. Clarise indicates with non-verbal communication that Eric should follow her last instruction.)

Well…you look…you look…you…you…welcome home Terisa…excuse me while I put on my clothes.

(ERIC manages to put on his shirt and tie in an awkward way.)

Your Mom Clarise and I were just about to play some basketball before you arrived.

(Terisa looks out of the window.)

TERISA: I can see my old hoop has been frequently used since I've been at school.

(Terisa picks up the basketball and attempts to dribble. The ball lays flat on the floor.)

TERISA: Or maybe not.

(Eric picks up the basketball while staring at Terisa's belly.)

TERISA: Playing basketball without dribbling Dad?

ERIC: This is an old ball. There's a new baby…bbb all around this house somewhere.

CLARISE: We can sit…

ERIC: Want to play some baby…ball…basketball?

TERISA: Maybe later Dad. Right now, I'm starving. What's cooking Mom Clarise?

CLARISE: (Exits to the kitchen) I'll bring out some appetizers.

TERISA: Do you still play ball Mom Clarise?

CLARISE: In the park, every chance I get. I still have high hopes that your father will join me. (Picks up Eric's pants from the floor and tosses them to Eric) Let's start with homemade mini pizzas.

TERISA: Pepperoni?

CLARISE: On the side.

TERISA: You are so thoughtful Mom Clarise. I'm not eating much processed meat.

ERIC: Gino's Pizza Palace. You like Gino's Pizza Palace.

TERISA: That's right Dad. I'm impressed that you remember my favorite pizza. Dad and I had Gino's Pizza every Friday until the first Friday you came over. How old was I?

CLARISE: Fourteen going on forty. Eric dear, perhaps you should go to the bathroom and freshen up. Splash a little water on your face and put on your pants. Remember to zip up.

ERIC: Sounds like a good idea. Excuse me Terisa. I'll be back shortly. (Stands up to exit while holding his pants. Walks towards the bathroom and stops) Um…Terisa…It's good to see you.

TERISA: Good to see you too Dad.

ERIC: Gino's Pizza Palace…. It took me a while…but I remembered…Gino's Pizza Palace. (Exits to the bathroom)

TERISA: You didn't tell him I was pregnant.

CLARISE: You know I keep my promises…and this one about you being pregnant…despite my better judgment. Four years of keeping a secret that we're in touch is one thing… but I've given you more than enough time to work things out with your father Terisa. Keep your promise to me now. Do your part to repair your relationship with him. You need this situation resolved and so does your baby—it is just one baby, right?

TERISA: Right on both.

CLARISE: I believe love and time can heal all hurt.

TERISA: Just let me have a little more fun before everything gets serious.

CLARISE: You saw him Terisa. He's in shock. I told him to be nice and not judge you. He doesn't know what to say or do.

TERISA: A little more time…please Mom Clarise.

CLARISE: Be gentle and I won't interfere.

(Enter Eric from the bathroom fully dressed.)

ERIC: I'm fine. Fine. Fine. Fine. So very fine. You were completely right Clarise, little water splashed on my face…I'm a new man…. Here I am with the two most important women in my life…my daughter and my wife…I'm thankful…I'm happy…I'm joyful. A cold beer will be just perfect now.

(Clarise and Terisa bring the appetizers to the living room. ERIC goes to the refrigerator and opens the refrigerator door.)

TERISA: Bring me a cold one please Dad?

ERIC: Beer? You can't have beer?

TERISA: Lighten up Dad. I'm twenty-one now, I can drink in public so I can drink at home.

ERIC: Yes, but beer is bad…so very bad for you.

TERISA: Bad for me but not for you Dad?

ERIC: That's because, that's because…you're…fat. That's right… you're fat…

CLARISE: Eric!

TERISA: You've put on a few yourself since I last saw you. A few pounds over but you still look great. Don't I look great Dad?

ERIC: You look great.

TERISA: (Poses in various positions that accentuate the size of her belly) You're not just saying that, are you?

ERIC: You look great.

TERISA: Not a little bit overweight…maybe around the middle…

ERIC: You look great.

TERISA: Thanks Dad. You know they say that after the initial freshman fifteen, college women continue to gain weight year after year.

(Terisa plops herself on the sofa between Clarise and Eric. She places a tray of hors d'oeuvres on her protruding belly.)

TERISA: Mini pizza Dad?

ERIC: No thanks.

TERISA: (Stuffs her mouth with several mini pizzas) Fantastic.

CLARISE: Save room for dinner.

TERISA: What's for dinner?

CLARISE: A little antipasto, garlic bread and spaghetti.

TERISA: What kind of gravy?

CLARISE: Puntanesca sauce.

TERISA: Did you use Mrs. Mancuso's recipe?

CLARISE: Of course.

TERISA: When I was in high school, Mrs. Mancuso told me the history of Punttanesca sauce. She said prostitutes created it. The sauce had a little bit of this and a little bit of that, all thrown together.

TERISA: (Shaking her hips and belly) I didn't get it then but I do now. *Punta little over here and punta little over there.* I was also thinking that it's interesting that the word *puny*, the most common urban slang for vagina seems to be a derived word from *punttanesca*. But it is a bit confusing because if *puny* is a synonym for *clitoris* then the derivation of the words doesn't make sense. What do you think Dad?

ERIC: CLARISE, do we have anything else for dinner?

CLARISE: No dear.

ERIC: I'll have my spaghetti plain.

TERISA: Mom Clarise I'm starving. I can eat a whole loaf of garlic bread myself.

(Terisa grabs the garlic bread and rips through it wildly with her teeth, stroking the sides of her mouth with the bread and using it as a phallic object. She makes soft, sensual orgasmic sounds. She looks at the bookshelf.)

TERISA: Tolstoy! Oh my God, my first and only teddy bear. Right where he belongs, on top of my favorite etymological dictionary and next to...Mom's special edition of *War and Peace.* (Picks up *War and Peace*; flips through it and then returns it gently to the shelf)

War and Peace...You save everything Dad. (Squeezing herself between Eric and Clarise on the sofa)

TERISA: I stopped in town before I came here. I met some of the girls at Gino's Pizza. Gino has grandkids that work in the pizzeria. I couldn't believe it. Sure made me feel old. Do you remember Mary Margaret and Bernadette? They're still together. I wish I could have gone to their wedding. They had a destination wedding...Thailand. Mary Margaret had the most amazing reconstructive surgery there. You should see her penis Dad.

ERIC: No, I shouldn't.

TERISA: I mean...she showed me her constructed penis. It looked so natural...a work of art. It looked better than some of the penises I've seen...and I've seen quite a few. (Scream) Ah.

ERIC: What's the matter? What happened?

TERISA: We've been eating and we didn't say grace. (Embraces the hands of Eric and Clarise) Mom Clarise, I want to say the blessing. Isn't this nice. saying grace together? A big happy family?

TERISA: Let us pray. Lord...thank you for the food we have received and are about to receive. Thank you for touching Mom Clarise's hands so she could make Puntanesca sauce with perfection the way it was meant to be prepared in the tradition of whores and prostitutes. And thank you for the garlic bread. We are eternally grateful for all long things, living and non-living, that we can place in our mouth and enjoy the sensuous experience of licking and chewing and stroking. We are grateful for the joy of using our bodies for the glory of your good name. And Lord, we humbly thank you for family; our special family that knows love not judgment provides the bond that keeps people together. Despite our desires and our temptations to do the work of the devil and criticize and question and ridicule and blame and interrogate...we are forever grateful that you have sparred us...LORD...we thank you for the glory of this family reunited. Say Amen Dad.

ERIC: Amen.

TERISA: Lord, we thank you for guiding us with love and acceptance so that we can relish in the joy of being together. Say Amen Dad.

ERIC: Amen.

TERISA: We're flawed and evil in our earthly ways. Those ways of the devil that encourage us to question our family members and sit in judgment of them. Say Amen Dad.

ERIC: Amen.

TERISA: We know that it is only when we come to our salvation in heaven that we will be judged and on earth no father should judge a daughter. Say Amen Dad.

ERIC: Amen.

TERISA: We understand that our life in the family must be that of unconditional love and for that we say…

ERIC: Amen. Amen. A…men. Amen! You're pregnant. You're pregnant!

TERISA: Yes, I am Dad.

ERIC: Four years…it's been four years…and you finally decide you show up to see your parents and you're pregnant. What could you have been thinking or not thinking? Did I miss something? Did I miss the conversation about contraceptives…birth control pills, condoms…safe sex… you knew about oral sex when you were in grade school… did I forget to tell you what happens when you have sex without a mouth? …It's your fault Clarise.

CLARISE: My fault?

ERIC: You were supposed to be my back up. Fill in. Say what I forgot to say or wanted to say or tried to say or forgot to say or felt too uncomfortable to say or didn't think to say or said the wrong way. That's what parents do. Fill in each other's blanks. How did this happen TERISA? I don't mean how did this happen? I refuse to let you confuse me. Why did you allow this to happen?

CLARISE: Eric. Terisa.

ERIC: Came home to see us…came home to see us…and I'm seeing a lot of you…and then some…I'm seeing that you're pregnant.

TERISA: I'm ready for dinner Mom Clarise.

ERIC: Look at her Clarise.

CLARISE: Yes, I'm looking at her. She looks beautiful.

ERIC: It makes sense now…no calls…no visits…you don't come home…you're doing a little more at school than hitting the books…you're screwing around and getting knocked up.

CLARISE: Listen to yourself. That's enough Eric.

TERISA: I'm so hungry, but I'm losing my appetite.

CLARISE: I knew Terisa was pregnant.

ERIC: You knew?

CLARISE: I knew and I promised Terisa I would let her tell you herself.

ERIC: A little late for telling Clarise. I'd say she's showing. How long have you known Clarise?

CLARISE: Terisa and I never stopped communicating while she was in school. It wasn't to deceive you Eric.

ERIC: I'm hearing deceit. I'm seeing foolishness. (Pause) Everything makes sense now. Why you didn't attend your graduation… Why you didn't accept the opportunity to give an address at the ceremony. I suppose I should thank you. I didn't have to explain why my unmarried daughter with the top shelf education, with the numerous opportunities for further scholarship, with extensive offers to help propel her career, allowed herself to get knocked up like some kid from the projects with a round the block public school education…I would have given you money for an abortion.

CLARISE: That's enough Eric.

TERISA: The way you knocked up Mom and wanted to give her money to abort me?

ERIC: Your mother never told you that.

TERISA: She didn't, but we both know the truth, don't we Dad?

CLARISE: Is this true Eric?

ERIC: Clarise…

TERISA: Title: Two Forbidden Lovers, Synopsis: White college student gets knocked up by Black college professor. Black college professor offers money to white woman for an abortion. She refuses. She has the baby. Black professor does the right thing…after all…he loves her…she's not some black ho from the projects. Shot-gun wedding. Move to an unassuming neighborhood in the Bronx. Part Two: Not so simple. A few years in…Dr. Eric Smith goes on sabbatical…or what Mom told me my Dad did when he left our family. (Hands Eric a compact disk) The Mom tapes. This one was yours.

ERIC: You always had an annoying habit of opening things that didn't belong to you.
Clarise…

CLARISE: Secrets for the greater good? I'll be upstairs. I'll leave you and Terisa to catch up on old times. (Exits)

TERISA: It was in the box Mom left for you. I put it in my box.

ERIC: Your mother and I loved each other. We were both starting out in our careers. Your mother was offered a fellowship to continue her research on Leo Tolstoy at the University of Moscow. It was a once in a lifetime opportunity. There was a position open in my department…everyone liked me… respected me… I was on the short list…they were holding the position open so I could apply after my dissertation defense.

The whole situation…the timing was unfortunate… It was not the right time to have a baby…

TERISA: And yet here I am. The almost dead baby all grown up.

ERIC: There's no way to reconstruct our history Terisa. You're angry. I understand.

TERISA: You understand?

ERIC: I understand that you're wondering what might have been. You stayed away…

TERISA: I've been trying to separate the truth and the lies about us. I've been trying to deconstruct all of the events we shared as a family…all the events we didn't share because you weren't there. Truth, lie, or illusion. Will I ever know?

ERIC: You came into the world despite my objections and I loved you. Once you were here I couldn't imagine my life without our precious baby girl. There's a whole world between being a boyfriend and being a husband… Being a good father was lost in my separation from your mother. But you… Terisa. I don't know what to say about…

TERISA: My baby?

ERIC: Are you replaying some misguided interpretation of your mother's scenario? How can this kind of expression of your anger be worth it…in any way? I can't see you as someone who would simply be stupid and forget to use contraception. (Pause) I didn't mean stupid.

TERISA: You meant stupid. Would you like to question me about late term abortion now?

ERIC: Your mother was an exceptional student. Like you… She had an opportunity to be an exceptional scholar…like you… We planned that she would finish graduate school once you were…we didn't get there… I can't say anything that will make this feel right for either of us.

TERISA: Rape. I was raped on campus. I was knocked up Dad, from a rape. Assault isn't discriminatory.

ERIC: How…? What?

TERISA: I reached out to Mom Clarise. She was there for me.

ERIC: You could have reached out to me? Oh…not too much confidence for trying that I suppose.

TERISA: An old friend was there for my day-to-day challenges… Remember Quincy?

QUINCY: Your high school drug dealer friend?

TERISA: He's a financial analysis now. Doing very well. Living in midtown. (Pause)

When I was afraid to stay alone Quincy was kind and thoughtful. He allowed me to be and feel whatever I needed to be and feel in each moment. This baby is my now. He…

ERIC: He?

TERISA: A boy…ultrasound confirmed…and healthy… (Pause)

He didn't choose when to come or how to come but he's here and that's all that matters. I made a decision for me. I couldn't control how my baby was created, but he'll be born to a mother who loves him and who will not give him up because of inconvenience. My decision is not political, it's not religious. This is my life, my body, and my life. The right thing for me. I plan to accept an offer from a firm in New York. I'm reviewing the conditions to make sure I can have flexible hours for my Mommy work. I'll need help. I need family.

What about for you Dad? Are you willing? Will you be Grandpa?

ERIC: I've made mistakes.

TERISA: I've made mistakes. This is about the now. How will we construct our lives now?

ERIC: One moment at a time is probably best. I've missed you Terisa. If you'll have me I want to be Grand Da. Not Grandpa. And I want to be Dad. (Pause)You…want to live upstairs…in your old room?

TERISA: Just for a few months after the baby is born so Mom Clarise can help me adjust. Then Quincy and I are moving in together.

ERIC: Are you a couple?

TERISA: We're friends. Good friends. That's where it starts.

ERIC: Yes, with parents and grown up children too.

TERISA: I think so.

(Terisa's water breaks. Eric screams towards the upstairs.)

ERIC: (Shouting towards upstairs) Clarise, you're going to be a grandma, or a grandmother or a nana…our child is having a child…a boy child…a grandson…a boy in the family…

(Terisa begins cleansing breaths for natural childbirth.)

CLARISE: (Shouting to Eric downstairs) Yes, I know Eric. Should be soon.

TERISA: Sooner than you think…

ERIC: (Shouting towards upstairs) I know you and Terisa have been talking… I understand but I don't understand but I do understand that the understanding is not so important. We probably cannot understand. We're different people… we perceived the same events with different eyes. I mean different interpretations…

CLARISE: Everything all right down there?

ERIC: Terisa and I are beginning over in a new way, with moments…

TERISA: And this is an important moment.

CLARISE: Sounds wise.

ERIC: We want to understand what we don't understand but wish we could understand because if we could understand it we think we might not make the same mistakes we made in the past but that can't be true because we understand events through our own lens of experience and we make decisions based on our beliefs about our experiences…I'm not sure I'm sure…

TERISA: I'm sure.

CLARISE: I found a bassinet at a thrift store. I'm cleaning it up for Terisa's room.

ERIC: What do you think Clarise? Would people make the same decisions if their understanding of events were altered?

CLARISE: I thought you and Terisa decided to live and love in the now…

TERISA: (Scream) Now. The baby's coming now. Now.

CLARISE: (Runs down the staircase) You're not due for two weeks.

TERISA: My doctor estimated the time. I didn't go to graduation because I was having back labor.

ERIC: Hospital…ambulance…no drive…where are my keys… Should I call Quincy?

TERISA: No hospital…

ERIC: No hospital?

CLARISE: You have to call her nurse mid-wife.

TERISA: Quincy's returning from a conference in London. He'll be at JFK airport tonight. Will you pick him up Dad and talk to him? And don't ask him about drugs. I told you he doesn't do that anymore, except the legal ones…and call Mary Margaret, Bernadette, and Francis. Everyone's phone number is in contact list on my cell phone. But don't call Francis…. It's better to send her a text…

ERIC: Where are you having the baby?

CLARISE & TERISA: Upstairs.

ERIC: Upstairs? You can't have a baby upstairs.

TERISA: You said I could live here with my baby.

ERIC: You always twist what I say Terisa. I didn't mean from the moment of birth.

(Clarise helps Terisa stand up. They walk towards the staircase.)

CLARISE: I could use your help here Eric.

ERIC: Where are you going?

(Terisa's child birthing sounds become more intense. Eric imitates them.)

CLARISE: Eric, you are not the one having the baby.

TERISA: Ah (Scream)

ERIC: What's wrong?

TERISA: I want Tolstoy…and Mom's *War and Peace* special edition.

ERIC: Are you going to read *War and Peace* while you're delivering the baby.

TERISA: I want to have Mom close to me when I deliver. And Dad…I'm enrolled in a combined MD/PhD program for next fall. The focus is on research not clinical work. I'll need your help…(Scream) Help me.

CLARISE: Breathe Terisa. Concentrate on using your breath to soothe the pain. You'll need all of your strength to bring Little Eric into the world.

(Eric collapses to the floor. Clarise and Terisa continue upstairs.)

TERISA: (Shout from upstairs) I love you Dad.

ERIC: (Quietly, while seated on the floor) I love you Terisa. Thank you Kat.

KAT: (Enters from the bookcase. Holds Tolstoy and her *War and Peace* novel. Walks up the stairs and looks back towards Eric) You're welcome Eric.

(Doorbell rings several times.)

VOICE OF DELIVERY MAN: Gino's Pizza Palace. Pizza delivery.

(Lights Out)

End of Play

Endnotes

1 Lev Nikolayevich Tolstoy (1828-1910), also known as Leo Tolstoy, was an internationally known Russian writer of novels, short stories, and plays. He wrote *War and Peace* in 1869. It is considered to be one of the greatest novels of all time.

Russian Pronunciation Key

Vot moy vam sovet: ne zhenis', poka vy ne mozhete skazat' sebe, chto vy sdelali vse, chto mogli , i , poka vy ne razlyubil zhenshchin: Vy vybrali , poka ne uvidite yeye chetko., v protivnom sluchaye vy budete zhestoko i nepopravimo oshibayutsya. Zhenit'sya , kogda ty star i nikuda ne goditsya... V protivnom sluchaye vse, chto khorosho, a vysokiye v vas budut poteryany.

2 Adapted from Bad (Epic Records 1987). Written and performed by Michael Joseph Jackson (1958-2009), singer-songwriter, the "King of Pop."

Tidy Black Green Simians

Skin Kin

Writer's Notes:

Beginning with the mandates of Walter Cromwell in England, there were efforts to remove the "disposable" Irish Catholic minority from England to the island of Barbados. The sugar cane industry needed able bodies to harvest and process this white gold. Black people kidnapped from West Africa entangled in the transatlantic slave trade were inhumanely forced to work in this institutionalized system of servitude. Irish came as slaves with different circumstances. They were political prisoners, poor, and indentured workers. All were subjected to the cruelties of the sugar cane plantation. Even those with written contracts for work were schemed into situations that usually led to death rather than salary and freedom.

Kate and Sade were two women who found themselves amidst the evil, having met on the Kingsley plantation. The play begins in the hiding place after their recent escape.

Characters:

Kate: A young Irish woman

Sade: A young Nigerian woman

Setting:

Barbados, circa 1650

The inside of a cave on a mountaintop.

(Lights Rise)

(Kate is standing. Sade is sitting on a large bolder watching Kate as she tells a story with great animation.)

KATE: He had a strong jaw and piercing eyes. Folk say sinners burst into flame when he stared at them.

SADE: Then he was a magician?

KATE: I suppose you could say so Sade… Where was I? And he was a tall man like no other. But when he went into battle against good and evil he could grow taller than the tallest tree.

SADE: Kate, do you mean as tall as a mango tree?

KATE: I wouldn't quite say that Sade. We don't have mango trees in Ireland.

SADE: As tall as a palm tree then?

KATE: Sade, I would like to finish my story. Do you suppose you could hold off your interruptions? Your questions are terrible for my concentration.

SADE: I can appreciate the story better if I can understand the details and make connections to things I know.

KATE: We don't have palm trees in Ireland.

SADE: A coconut tree then?

KATE: The size of the tree doesn't matter to the point of the story. The important fact is that a man could make himself grow tall if he so desired.

SADE: Tall like your tall story tale.

KATE: Do you want to hear the story of St. Patrick or not?

SADE: (Gesturing yes)

KATE: Tall…tree…yes. When he walked, the earth would shake. Sinners who heard him coming down the road would run for their lives. He carried a staff of different colors. It glistened in the sun and absorbed the light.

SADE: (Looks away. Hums an indigenous rhythm to herself)

KATE: What's wrong now?

SADE: Nothing.

KATE: Something is wrong. I don't have your attention and you've disrupted my creative process.

SADE: I can't forget it.

KATE: Can't forget it?

SADE: How can you expect me to enjoy a story when some of the basic information is unclear?

KATE: Like what?

SADE: Like, what is Ireland?

KATE: We've talked about Ireland. My home, my love, the born place of my people, my nation.

SADE: I get all that. The land of your tribe. But…

KATE: But what?

SADE: I can't get a picture in my head of what Ireland looks like. If you want the story to engage me, I need to know more.

KATE: I'll save the story of St. Patrick for another time.

SADE: You told me it's an island.

KATE: It is.

SADE: If you lay your head on a pillow at night in Ireland and then open your eyes in the morning, what do you see?

KATE: Forty shades of green.

SADE: That's a lot.

KATE: I believe we have more expressions of green than any other land.

SADE: The colors. Is that, are that what makes you want to go home? You miss the colors.

KATE: I miss the life I imagined in Ireland. When I left, my people were in terrible times. But when times were good…

they were very good. A hard life is better together with people you love.

SADE: But…

KATE: Night is falling. We'll be able to spend a wee bit of time in the open air. Will be splendid.

SADE: We need to gather some provisions from the forest. We'll have to stay on the mountaintop though. You wandered too far last time. No more risks Kate.

KATE: Just investigating our territory.

SADE: Our territory? You say that as if we owned this place instead of borrowing it for hiding.

KATE: As for now. It's our temporary home. We staked our claim.

SADE: And won't be too much longer. What is your plan?

KATE: We can talk about that soon. Why don't you tell me a story?

SADE: Are you avoiding telling me the plan? I'm thinking it will be a wonderful surprise like the leprechauns you mentioned on the travel up the mountains will rescue us. The ones with the pot of gold at the end of a rainbow.

KATE: You remember about the leprechauns, eh?

SADE: And the gold. Will be enough for both of us to leave the island and start a new life.

KATE: …what about that story you were going to tell.

SADE: A woman called Iyodeli traded some cloth for yams at the market. She came home, cooked them, pounded them, and gave them to her husband for dinner.

KATE: And?

SADE: And he enjoyed them. End of story.

KATE: That's not a good story. That's not a good story. It should have characters, a setting, and a plot. It should have events that are exciting and make you eager for more.

SADE: She also made a large bowl of millet.

KATE: Your brevity is disappointing.

SADE: You do you and your stories. I told you a story that was fine.

KATE: Selfish.

SADE: You're culturally insensitive.

KATE: And how is that?

SADE: In my village, "Storyteller" is a job passed down through a family. Storytellers protect our oral tradition. They help the people remember our life and our ancestor's wisdom. My family line was bronze artisans.

KATE: Can you pretend?

SADE: Pretend?

KATE: Imagine.

SADE: No.

KATE: And why not?

SADE: If I'm going to spend my time imagining something, it will be imagining myself free and away from the island of Barbados.

KATE: Stories pass the time.

SADE: Then you can have that job. You can be the official storyteller of this mountaintop until we are ready to leave. And when will that be Kate?

KATE: Not quite sure.

SADE: What is the plan for escape from the island?

KATE: Not quite sure.

SADE: Do you have a plan Kate?

KATE: It's in the development phase.

SADE: I planned our entire escape from the plantation. All you had to do was show up at the right time, in the right place. I packed the provisions. I found the route. I vetted the freemen to trust. I was the scout getting us through the forest and up to the top of this damn mountain. You were in charge of the island escape plan. That's what we agreed.

KATE: And I much appreciate everything you've done Sade.

SADE: I don't want your appreciation. I want to leave Barbados.

KATE: Will you please consider that I volunteered for the more difficult task of the island escape?

SADE: I trusted you.

KATE: And I trusted you. You need to have faith that a plan will unfold.

SADE: Faith? I think it's time to get those leprechauns.

KATE: You're not encouraging me Sade. I'm stressed. When I'm emotionally vulnerable, I can't have a free flow of ideas that will lead to a solution.

SADE: You want me to step lightly around your feelings?

KATE: I want you to believe in me and trust me. I believe and trust you.

SADE: I've demonstrated that I can be trusted. I got us here.

KATE: You need to have faith in me.

SADE: I put my faith in the Orisha.

KATE: What is that?

SADE: The Gods.

KATE: You mean God.

SADE: I said what I mean. Gods. Ellegba, Shango, Yemaya…

KATE: Is that like the father, son, and Holy Ghost? (Makes the sign of the cross)

SADE: Stop it Kate. You're not going to distract me with your fake interest in my…

KATE: No, no not fake. I'm Catholic. I've felt the persecution of the Protestants. Sade, no one should interfere with your right to practice worship of God…or Gods…

SADE: If you have rituals, you better start using them before I have to summon the Orisha who sits on my head.

KATE: Rituals? You must mean church… There's no church here of course but I can pray.

(Folding her hands for prayer.)

"Dear God the Father,"
Have mercy on us. Lord have mercy. Christ have mercy. Lord have mercy. Christ have mercy."

SADE: (Picks up cutlass from the provisions and dances as she sings and chants; Indigenous language)

KATE: (Looking on) That was very interesting. Was that a ritual?

SADE: For Shango, the warrior God, fearless.

KATE: Well then. As I mentioned, religious rights are essential. Will you put the cutlass away now?

(Sade returns to a calm disposition as she puts the cutlass away.)

KATE: You haven't told me much about your kidnap to Barbados.

SADE: If I wanted to tell you I would have.

KATE: (Pulls up her skirt, revealing her legs and petticoat) I've been marking the time I've been on this island on my petticoat. It's March 17th, the day we celebrate St. Patrick.

SADE: St. Patrick, your Orisha. Is he going to liberate us from Barbados?

KATE: (Pulling down her skirt) The day's not finished.

SADE: Your skin is two colors.

KATE: I'm one color, white.

SADE: Red.

KATE: No, I'm just fully cooked from the sun. I'm burned. The color on my thighs is my true color.

SADE: You're the same color as the enslavers.

KATE: It's more than skin color that makes people accept other people as their own. In the eyes of the British, I'll never be more than a monkey.

SADE: They call Black people monkeys.

KATE: Are you? Part monkey?

SADE: Are you?

KATE: Prove that you're not part monkey.

SADE: (Watching Kate) You first.

KATE: (Back to the audience. Pulls up her dress and shows her backside) See no tail.

Now you.

SADE: No.

KATE: Then you have a tail.

SADE: Are you afraid of monkeys Kate?

KATE: Maybe.

SADE: Then I'm a monkey with a big long tail ready to kick your skinny white ass if you don't get us off this island.

KATE: You have a tail.

SADE: I left the Kingsley plantation without permission but with intention. I have a price on my head. I'm not cutting sugar cane again.

KATE: You have a tail.

(Sade pulls up her skirt, revealing her backside to Kate.)

SADE: "Ashes fly back into the face of she who throws them."[1]

KATE: You have a beautiful rump you know.

SADE: Something else I should know about you?

KATE: Something else? I said you had a beautiful rump. I didn't say I wanted to pluck you.

SADE: And you have nice legs.

KATE: Really?

SADE: Really. Skinny, but shapely.

KATE: And the shape of your rump is outstanding.

SADE: I always felt it was too round and too big.

KATE: Not at all. It fills up your skirt nicely. No bustle needed.

SADE: Let's go out into the evening air. Watch the sun come down.

KATE: Suits me fine.

(They step outside the cave and sit.)

KATE: Those moves you did inside the cave when you were calling Shango, scary but beautiful. Like a dance.

SADE: Passed down for generations.

KATE: We have dances at home. Passed down as well. On a day like today, after church, the folk would celebrate St. Patrick with drink and dance.

SADE: Show me what the dance looks like.

KATE: I can't.

SADE: Selfish.

KATE: No, I really can't. We need lots of people. Men and women. We make partners. And there's a caller. He tells us the steps to make and the ways to move. Side to side. Together and apart. In a shape, like a circle.

SADE: I don't see a God coming down to earth from that.

KATE: Only the God of Drink my dear. Only the God of Drink.

SADE: Teach me some.

KATE: Can't.

SADE: Is it a secret?

KATE: (Kate takes Sade's hands) Okay… Come on… We need music. Like a fiddle, and a pipe. Let's try. We only have each other so you'll need to follow me. I'm the leader.

(Sade drops her hands.)

KATE: Leader in the sense that I make the decision where we should go on the dance floor.

(Kate guides Sade through a reconstructed Irish folk dance. There is improvisation of language to support the movement as instructed. Kate and Sade dance until they move into frenzy, falling to the ground.)

SADE: And I have rum.

KATE: As do I.

(They each dig up bottles of rum buried in the dirt near the cave entrance. They stand up then trade bottles.)

KATE & SADE: Cheers.

(They hold up the bottles but don't drink.)

KATE & SADE: I don't drink.

KATE: I've seen many a good Irishman including my Pa destroyed and perished by drink. It numbs the pain for a moment. You forget your sorrow for a moment. It changes no circumstances.

SADE: Sugar cane. The enslavers' white gold. My people make the rum that keeps us working like beasts. The blood of my people makes this drink.

KATE: Why did you bring that bottle?

SADE: To remind me what going back to the plantation means. Why did you bring that bottle?

KATE: For bribes.

SADE: So you did have some ideas for escape.

KATE: Evolving.

SADE: (Sitting down) I like sitting here watching the sun disappear. It reminds me of the peace I felt with my family near the River Niger before…

The men were hunting. We were doing chores together. Gathering water. Washing cloth. They must have been watching us for a while. They knew exactly when to raid. That was the day my world became unrecognizable. All gone. My mother. My sisters. Two aunts. Between the death marches and the sea passage. All dead. When my last friend, Efeundele, passed to the other side from exhaustion at Kingsley's, I knew I needed to leave.

KATE: Did you have a husband and children at home?

SADE: Not yet. But it was coming soon. There were suitors, but my father hadn't decided. I had so many dreams of womanhood. I was of age. It was my time.

KATE: I had a Beau. His name was Blackie.

SADE: He was Black?

KATE: No, folks called him Blackie. I don't know why.

SADE: Doesn't make sense to me to call someone Black when they're not. The enslavers don't call my people Whitey.

KATE: May I tell you about my Blackie please?

(Sade indicates that Kate should continue.)

KATE: He was my one true love. In my dream mind, he was the man I would marry in the village church. We would have a beautiful farm together in the countryside. We'd have a house filled with ten children. Bliss. Kate and Blackie, his given name was Michael, and their lovely brood.

SADE: A life come and gone…like mine.

KATE: Michael was a rebel. Fighting for the rights stolen from us by Cromwell and the Protestants. They were our enslavers in Ireland. Not like Barbados. A cleansing of sorts. Control and destroy. Keep Ireland pure for the protestant minority. Taking our land, food…making work impossible. Families without the smallest morsels to feed their young. When the land he'd inherited was stolen, it was the last brutality my Michael could bear.

(Pause)

I could speak the Queen's English and pass for Protestant. So it wasn't a problem getting a job as a housemaid for the local magistrate. I watched him like a hawk until I saw where he kept his lock boxes. I finished my day early while the magistrate traveled to a meeting. I left the back door open and slipped the keys to Michael. The plan was simple. Michael would open the boxes and find his deed. Slip me the key back before the next morning. The magistrate returned home early. That was the day my life changed forever.

KATE: They told me the hanging was quick. His neck snapped in one piece. It's awful when the people are tortured and linger because of a faulty noose.

(Pause)

So you see, I can make a plan. Whether I can make good plans is the question.

SADE: I believe your Blackie was a warrior. He made a choice as a free man. He knew "you must be willing to die in order to live."[2] I was kidnapped. My choice is to live free. If I meet the fate of a noose I'll die and become an ancestor.

KATE: And here I am, Barbadosed with other disposable Irish women. Found guilty of being an accomplice. Before I left Ireland, they had their schoolboy fun. The magistrate paraded me on to the auction block and traded me to the captain of the good ship Elvira for a hog. I was to be untouched and safely delivered to Kingsley, the magistrates brother. Property for the exclusive whims of his sexual perversions. Tidy. Let's gather some fallen mangos before the birds and the real monkeys eat them.

SADE: I thought you had servant papers.

KATE: You mean indentured servant papers? No, not me. But plenty of the women on the ship had them. Some of them with stars in their eyes, actually believing they would earn wages and be free to return to Ireland after time was served. Slavery by another name. I suspect their contracts will be bought and sold a number of times and they will be dead before the contract is finished. Another tidy way for these vicious men to get work in these fields without pay. We suffer in the fields with a label on our heads, monkey. Black and White is a blur.

SADE: A blur for you. In the fields you're Red. When you have your chance to be White again, when you're free, will you remember the Blacks cutting cane next to you in the fields?

KATE & SADE: (Pause; stare)

SADE: Suppertime. Want some candy? Found a way to make good from the bad.

KATE: Scrumptious. Want biscuits?

SADE: (Preparing to dine) Will be wonderful to eat food fit for a meal.

KATE: We will have a proper meal my dear. (Laying out a picnic) Let's see. We have some meat stew, some rice, some spinach, and some potatoes. I lifted plenty from the kitchen. I shared with the other kitchen help so they wouldn't be telling about my shopping.

SADE: We should eat the food cold. A fire could attract some attention.

KATE: All the fragrant spices in the food make eating a pleasure whether the food is hot or cold. We don't have seasonings like this in Ireland. Maybe a little salt and pepper is all.

SADE: We love to cook with spice at home. "Hot Hot" is my favorite.

KATE: I take it "Hot Hot" means what its name says?

SADE: Burns your tongue. Makes the whole inside of your mouth swell and itch. You'll want water but the water will only excite the burn. Delicious.

KATE: Lovely eh?

SADE: You don't think Kinsley will be missing his supper?

KATE: Not at all. He's preoccupied.

SADE: With what?

KATE: (Eating) Being Kingsley's whore had its privileges. He plucked me with a sugar cane stalk and then his shrunken dick. That needed to be the last time he took me. So I found a way to drug him. I gaged his mouth with tobacco leaves and then cut off his balls. Oh, and I chopped the balls up and put them in a stew.

(Sade spits out her food.)

KATE: Not that stew lass. Slop for the hogs. I hope the swine don't get sick from the swine. Sade, I'd say my last day of work has been done. The plan I have is never go back.

[Sound Effect: Talking drum.]

SADE: (Listening to the drum) Then we agree. Leaving the island is the only way to survive.

KATE: (Gestures in agreement)

SADE: You hear that? I've been following the messages from the drums since we left. The talking drums have gotten louder and stronger. One message from the east. One message from the west. An insurrection is coming in the east. Calm water and calm air good for travel is coming to the northern shore. Good calm water for those who can get to the ocean near St. Lucy.

KATE: I'd enjoy going back and burning the fields with the others. Make a mess.

SADE: My revenge will be my freedom and a good life for myself.

KATE: The ship that brought me here docked near St. Lucy. I remember seeing smaller boats stored in a bay. We'd need more than rum to bribe for a boat.

We have more. We have the courage of St. Patrick. With his staff he chased the snakes out of Ireland. We have the strength and resistance of your Shango.

SADE: (Shows gold from a sack) We have gold. I'm like the leprechaun with the pot of gold in your story.

KATE: This is Kingsley's. How did you get it?

SADE: Our wages. (Dividing the gold) I'll give you half. When he plucked me, I made it my business to find out. Equal pay for our suffering.

KATE: I don't know what to say.

SADE: My people say, "Thank you." Take it. I know, "What I give, I'll get ten times over."[3] (Pause) I have a watchful eye Kate. I understand that, "A cheetah doesn't show her spots until after she snatches the chickens."

KATE: I have the luck of the Irish.

(Lights Out)

End of Play.

Endnotes

1, 2, and 3 Nigerian proverbs of unknown origin

Filthy Black Neighbors

Enuf

Characters:

Clayton (Clay): Husband (White, middle-aged)

Gretchen: Female Black Bear (adult)

Bystander: African American adult woman

Naomi: Wife (White, middle-aged)

Junior: Unseen bear cub

*Writer's Note: the same actor plays Gretchen and the Bystander Gretchen wears a costume piece that is black (e.g., T-shirt, or simple dress). The item is removed before the Bystander appears on stage.

Setting:

Present Day. A cottage in the woods. Midday through evening.

(Lights Rise)

(Clayton stands with his back to the audience. He's in front of the kitchen stove. He holds a spoon and stirs ingredients in a cooking pot while talking interspersed with singing opera with music playing in the background. He sings poorly with joy.)

CLAYTON: (Sung) La Donne` Mobile qual piumaalvento. (Spoken) You're like a changeable woman, risotto. But today, I conquer you. (Sung) Muta d`ac cento e dipensiero. (Spoken) Today, you are totally mine, perfection. Just the right amount of rice, broth, seasoning. Perfection. I love you my darling. I know the secret. Slow stir. Low flame.

(Enter Naomi. She turns off the music.)

CLAYTON: I need the music. I'm creating a culinary masterpiece here. (Sung) La Donnae` Mobile!

NAOMI: Clayton—

CLAYTON: I'm not turning around Naomi. I have to watch and stir.

NAOMI: Clayton. (Holding up two photographs in her hand) I need you to look at this now.

CLAYTON: Are you bleeding? If not, then it can wait.

NAOMI: It can't wait. We have a problem.

CLAYTON: I'm going to have a problem if I don't finish this risotto in time for my Men's Poetry Shout Out.

NAOMI: How are you making risotto without cheese?

CLAYTON: Cheese! I forgot the cheese. (Searching the refrigerator) Relax Clayton. I can still add cheese if I do it now before the second boil.

NAOMI: (Still holding up the photographs) There's no cheese.

(Clayton stops looking.)

NAOMI: I had a grilled cheese sandwich for lunch. I was in a mood.

CLAYTON: (Throwing the pot and spoon in the sink) That cheese was imported from Italy and thirty dollars a pound. What am I supposed to do now Naomi?

NAOMI: Bring pizza, wings, and beer. You know, food most men eat at a normal men's club. We have a bigger problem than your failed rice dish. Blacks.

CLAYTON: Blacks?

NAOMI: (Putting a photograph close to Clayton's face) Blacks!

CLAYTON: (Looking at the photograph) Whoa. That's a big Black Mutha…

NAOMI: (Holding up another photograph) Look at this one.

CLAYTON: How many does she have?

NAOMI: At least two little, not so little crumb snatchers.

CLAYTON: Where did you get these photographs?

NAOMI: Alice had been telling me there was something suspicious happening near the neighbor's property. The blue house near the apple grove.

CLAYTON: That place has been abandoned for years. It's a wreck. Filthy.

NAOMI: And now there're filthy blacks there.

CLAYTON: There has to be an explanation.

NAOMI: Alice.

CLAYTON: Crazy, paranoid Alice.

NAOMI: Alice has a high-speed surveillance dual telescope camera on her second floor deck. The camera has a timer. They come out of the house and sneak around at night.

CLAYTON: Maybe just passing through.

NAOMI: They've settled in. I know it. A family of squatters.

CLAYTON: Then leave them alone.

NAOMI: You can't be serious Clayton. What's going to keep them from crossing over our property line?

CLAYTON: (Looking through the kitchen cabinets for more cooking ingredients) And if they do, maybe we'll have to do something, or not.

NAOMI: You aren't seriously thinking that it's okay for Blacks to be our neighbors, are you?

CLAYTON: Don't make trouble where there's none.

NAOMI: I'm talking about Blacks, Clayton. Trouble follows them. They steal. They're aggressive. They're filthy. They live like animals. And if there's one family now, that's only the beginning. Soon, they'll be more families. And then soon, they'll be more of them than us. We'll be outnumbered and we'll be the minority. They'll push us out.

CLAYTON: Don't be ridiculous Naomi. Nothing has happened.

NAOMI: Nothing has happened yet, but it will.

CLAYTON: Why can't we just get along Naomi?

NAOMI: Because they're Blacks. They will always want what we have, and they don't deserve it.

CLAYTON: Having a home is a basic right.

NAOMI: Then let them get a home with their own kind, somewhere else.

CLAYTON: If that mother is really living in that abandoned house, unfit for any family, maybe it's because—

NAOMI: Sounds like you're more concerned about her, then me.

CLAYTON: You sound like some hillbilly red neck.

NAOMI: Is that how you see me Clayton?

CLAYTON: No. But that's how you're behaving. Fearful. Unjustified fearful.

NAOMI: I'm not going to apologize for how I feel or for who I am. And by the way, your below the Mason Dixon line self is more redneck than I could ever be. (Pause) We've worked hard for everything we have, and we have a right to privacy, and safety.

CLAYTON: Inheritance equates to entitlement, not hard work.

NAOMI: Are you saying my grandfather didn't work hard for this land?

CLAYTON: Let's not go there Naomi.

NAOMI: Spit it out Clayton. I know what you really believe anyway.

CLAYTON: (Attempting to walk away) You inherited your grandfather's entitlement and his temper.

NAOMI: (Throwing an object at Clayton) My people can trace ancestry in these mountains into the seventeen hundreds.

CLAYTON: And?

NAOMI: I deserve to live free, comfortable, and with my own kind.

CLAYTON: And crazy Alice, whom you wanted nothing to do with until she discovered Blacks in the neighborhood is your kind?

NAOMI: Yes, under the current circumstances, she's one of us.

CLAYTON: (Slamming the kitchen cabinet) We don't have any more Arborio rice.

NAOMI: After everything I've told you, you're more concerned with a rice dish for a "foo foo" men's poetry group than—

CLAYTON: Thank you for letting me know how you really feel about my poetry group.

NAOMI: Yeah, I'd prefer to tell my friends that you're at the shooting range or watching a game on a Sunday afternoon. Normal stuff for a straight, married white man.

CLAYTON: I'm going to ignore what you've said Naomi because I think you're scared, and lashing out. It's natural to feel anxiety, some fear when you're experiencing something new. We've been indoctrinated to be fearful of Blacks since we were kids, for reasons that never made sense.

NAOMI: They're aggressive. They're killers. Every day on the news there's some incident.

CLAYTON: Don't take those incidents out of context. I think they may attack first because they feel they have to protect themselves.

NAOMI: You're useless Clayton. (Pause) Where is my grandfather's shotgun?

CLAYTON: In the lockbox in the basement where it belongs.

NAOMI: (Looking through drawers) You moved the key. I need it.

CLAYTON: Need it for what?

NAOMI: I need to be ready to defend us because my pacifist husband will probably try some verbal de-escalation crap if those Blacks come over here to attack us.

CLAYTON: Nothing has happened. Nothing will probably happen.

NAOMI: And when it does, I'll be ready. If she comes on our property, I have the right to shoot and defend.

CLAYTON: (Picking up keys and wallet) I'm going into town.

NAOMI: Now? Forty-two miles away?

CLAYTON: I'm going to pick up more ingredients. I'm not showing up to the poetry meet up without a homemade dish.

NAOMI: What about me?

CLAYTON: What about you?

NAOMI: Give me the key.

CLAYTON: In your state? No.

NAOMI: And what do you think is "my state of mind," Clayton?

CLAYTON: (Brief stare) That lock box is filled with mementos. Those civil war weapons from my family's Virginia on the wrong side of history are in that box too. Every time I watch a white supremacist march on television, or read about innocent White people murdered by other White people for their beliefs and opinions I think about my inherited Civil War weapons. I convince myself that generations of my family were simply misguided by pride and a convoluted belief that they were protecting their rights.

NAOMI: I want the key, Clayton. This has nothing to do with racism, or your ambivalence about your family. I know and understand my family. My father and all of my uncles kept a rifle by their side at the kitchen table when they ate family meals. Why? Because, they could. And they felt it was necessary. I'm telling you I need to keep a gun out because I need to feel safe, and because now it's necessary.

CLAYTON: *New York Times*, page…three. White woman shoots unarmed Black in Catskill Mountains. When questioned by the sheriff she explains, "I wasn't attacked but I feared for my life."

NAOMI: I can't be here without access to a gun.

CLAYTON: You can't go shoot a Black because you're afraid. You're better than that.

NAOMI: My father, and my uncles never threatened Blacks or anybody. They were just ready. It's important to be ready.

CLAYTON: Ready? When you keep a firearm at "readiness," you've convinced yourself that a gun is the first line of defense. You're telling yourself that the best solution to any conflict is going to be firing your weapon. And if you fire your weapon, the outcome is likely to be death. No second chance to evaluate the situation differently, or try alternative solutions. You fire your weapon, and you better be right, because there's no second chance. There's no "do over."

NAOMI: You're my husband. You should understand.

CLAYTON: I'm your husband...and your friend. And as your friend, I'm telling you that your family turned you into someone that the Naomi I love wouldn't like.

NAOMI: Blacks should be confined. Locked up. They're like children that need to be monitored, and supervised at all times.

CLAYTON: Confined without cause?

NAOMI: With cause. We know who they are. They've proven it. We need to believe it.

CLAYTON: You're profiling all Blacks as if they were the same.

NAOMI: I DON'T WANT TO LIVE NEAR BLACKS! I don't have to explain it, or justify it. It's how I feel. This isn't about social policy. I'm not running for political office. I don't care what happens in other neighborhoods. This is about our filthy Black neighbors.

CLAYTON: I'm leaving you in the comfort of your irrational fears.

NAOMI: (Pacing) Don't leave me Clayton.

CLAYTON: Keep the doors locked.

NAOMI: That's not enough.

CLAYTON: I'll walk around the house and check the fences before I go.

(Clayton puts on a light jacket. Exit Clayton. Naomi looks through Clayton's coat pockets for his keys. Exit Naomi to the basement. Enter Clayton. He takes the key to the lockbox out of a cookie jar in the kitchen. He removes a floorboard in the kitchen, and takes out a metal box. He checks a handgun in the box and places it back. He places the keys in the box. Clayton exits. Enter Naomi. She places Clayton's keys in his heavy jacket. Enter Clayton.)

CLAYTON: I walked around the house. I checked the fences. There's no opening.

NAOMI: (Offering Clayton the heavy jacket) Take your lined jacket. The weather looks threatening.

CLAYTON: (Checking heavy jacket for keys) You'll be fine Naomi.

NAOMI: If they don't have what you need at Sheffler's Market just come home. Don't drive further north, please.

CLAYTON: Chances are— she's frightened of us. If she comes by, you don't have to let her in our house but you could welcome her into the neighborhood. Blacks can't all be the stereotypes we know. Believing they are is dangerous. Try being friends. Keep it simple. Be a good neighbor.

(Exit Clayton. Exit Naomi.)

GRETCHEN: (From off stage) Carry as many of the apples as you can into the house Junior. Stay away from the roads. Mama will be back soon. Big black bear hug and a kiss. (Kissing sounds)

(Gretchen enters the house. She smells. She looks around. She removes a handgun from underneath the floorboards and places it on the kitchen counter. She turns on the opera music Clayton had been playing before he left the house and moves to the music. She picks up the pot with the burned risotto and inspects it.)

GRETCHEN: Oh Clayton. How did your burn the risotto this time? A waste of good food… A little more water next time. No cheese? A fail proof recipe…that's what you need.

NAOMI: (Enters kitchen) Clayton, did you…

GRETCHEN: (Turns around; aims hand gun at Naomi) Hello. Don't be alarmed. I'm your neighbor. Have a seat on the sofa. (Picking up handgun higher and aiming it at Naomi's head) Have a seat.

(Naomi sits on the sofa.)

GRETCHEN: I finally figured out that you don't cook. Whenever there's delicious smells coming from your home, it's because Clayton is cooking.

NAOMI: You've smelled around our home?

GRETCHEN: I've been having multisensory experiences with you, and your house. I smell your husband's cooking of course. I've peek-a-booed you and Clayton in your bedroom.

(Gesture) Your mating is uninteresting. I taste the food you waste and throw away into the garbage. I hear everything Clayton sings. I know he has a fondness for Italian operas. Urinated all around the house. Needed to mark my territory from the other bears.

NAOMI: Urinated on the house?

GRETCHEN: My urine smells sweet as the mountain breeze. I'm not surprised you didn't notice any unusual aroma.

NAOMI: That's disgusting.

GRETCHEN: It's all in one's perspective Naomi. You urinate in the outhouse by the lake, hiding in a vertical box. Your urine christens the ground just like mine. Embarrassed by your skinny buns? I'd be. (Looking at her own rear) Black bears are so fortunate to have ample, round, and luscious hind parts. Is Clayton a butt man?

NAOMI: Clayton is coming back soon. He's gonna…

GRETCHEN: You're dumber than I thought. I've stood outside your basement door and listened to you talk. I always say to myself, "Naomi can't be that stupid." Now that I've met you in person, this encounter is good evidence of your limited mental capacity.

(Naomi gets up and tries to run to the door. Gretchen stands in front of the door.)

GRETCHEN: You know where you belong. (Pointing) Over there.

NAOMI: What do you want?

GRETCHEN: You're not in a position to rush me. Besides, Clayton won't be back for quite a long time. Sheffler's market closed at noon today. Arnie Sheffler went to the hospital to check in on his sister Katie. She's expecting twins, runs in the family. Katie's husband Mark is away. Did you know Katie and Mark are thinking of moving back into the city? He has an offer with a startup. They're both tired of the country life. Also, probably thinking about educational options for their kids. (Pause) I digress. So anyway Clayton will try to drive into town. He won't get the message that his poetry group meeting is cancelled because you guys have such poor cell phone reception in these mountains. He'll probably get struck in the snow. He should have put money into all-weather tires, or snow chains. Clayton's only flaw: Penny wise, and pound-foolish. By the way, you can be more supportive of his poetry. (Singing) *Teddy bear turn around. Teddy bear, teddy bear touch the ground, teddy bear—*

NAOMI: It's not going to snow.

GRETCHEN: Trust me. I have an instinctual sense about the weather.

NAOMI: You're an intellectual Black then.

GRETCHEN: And you're a dumb Brunette.

NAOMI: I need a glass of water.

GRETCHEN: I can do that. I'm sorta a "Care Bear."

(Gretchen goes to retrieve the glass of water. Naomi attempts to exit. Gretchen stares down Naomi, and blocks her.)

GRETCHEN: I can outrun you. I'm physically stronger than you. And you already have proof that I have superior vision, hearing, and smell. Hum… What about taste?

NAOMI: (Running to the sofa) If you're going to eat me, just do it. Get it over with. No, wait, let me overdose first. I won't feel any pain. I need OxyContin, Xanax, Vicodin, Valium, and I'm going to need Adderall. And a fifth of whiskey. Have mercy.

GRETCHEN: Don't flatter yourself. I prefer salmon, but really trout. Seasonal, wild caught trout from the Panashaw River is exquisite. Another thing I have in common with your husband. We're both "foodies."

NAOMI: Don't talk about my husband anymore.

GRETCHEN: Jealous that another female finds him desirable? Nothing to worry. I don't interbreed. Mixing a Black and a Brunette would degrade the quality of my species.

NAOMI: You know about us. Our habits. Our neighbor's lives. How is that possible?

GRETCHEN: We have a sophisticated system of knowing on trees in code, stomping on top of boulders, and beats. Talking Bear code. (Demonstrating hip hop like beats and sounds)

NAOMI: What else do you do?

GRETCHEN: Have you read, *The Bear Who Sat by the Door.*

NAOMI: (Starring) No.

GRETCHEN: *Invisible Bear? Black Bear Revolution? A Cultural Analysis of Black Bears in North America?*

NAOMI: Black Bears were mentioned when I was a kid in high school but we never studied Black Bear history. Brunettes in my community always lived separately from Blacks so I never had first-hand knowledge about—

GRETCHEN: Blacks have always had to know everything possible about Brunettes simply to survive. Hunting seasons, poaching, enslavement, gentrification... Need more?

NAOMI: Eat me.

GRETCHEN: I may have to reconsider my one-day a week vegetarian diet.

NAOMI: What do you want?

GRETCHEN: I'll get to that. But first we're going to play games. I want to enjoy myself. Remember, Clayton said, "Be a good neighbor. Try to be friends."

NAOMI: I should be a friend with someone who's entrapped me and threatens me?

GRETCHEN: I think the problem between Blacks and Brunettes is that we don't live together as equals. We don't have leisure time together. Our relationship becomes drowned in negativity. If you tried to know, and understand us, like we've been forced to know, and understand you, we might be able to coexist. (Pause) You have responsibility here Naomi. We're going to play together now. My rules. We have plenty of time, it hasn't started to snow. Give me a minute to check on my cub. (Opening up the front door, looking out, and speaking to junior) Good work Junior. Keep moving those apples. Don't pick up the rotten ones on the ground. Leave those for Clayton, and Naomi. (Looking at Naomi) We have to be kind. Winter affects everyone. (Pause) What's that? (Pause) No Junior, you cannot touch her Brunette hair. That wouldn't be culturally appropriate. (Coming inside the house and closing the door) My Junior is a good cub. Looks like his father, I think. Most Black male bears look alike. (Going back to the door, opening it and talking to Junior) Love you. Love you back. Love you more. Big bear hug, and a kiss. I'll be finished soon. (Pause) No, she's not interesting. (Closes the door)

NAOMI: All you do is insult me. Want me to apologize for being Brunette?

GRETCHEN: (Looking at the books. Pull out one book) *The Three Bears...*

NAOMI: Be careful with that. It's a special edition copy.

GRETCHEN: Are you a teacher?

NAOMI: For adults. I'm teaching a course on images of girls in children's literature and that relationship to adult women's equity, and equality issues.

GRETCHEN: None of my business really, but do you think you know enough about this female character to make generalizations about all female people animals.

NAOMI: Goldilocks was a Blonde but all female people face the same struggles to be equal in societal positions of power, and have the same access to acquire material wealth.

GRETCHEN: Blondes and Brunettes hate each other.

NAOMI: We're sisters in the struggle on every issue except hair care products.

GRETCHEN: I'm not a people animal but even I know that Blondes are preferred in your society.

NAOMI: That's changing. We—

GRETCHEN: I don't care. (Pause) What I care about is that books like these indoctrinate children from as early as preschool with notions of superiority to Blacks.

NAOMI: We are superior.

GRETCHEN: (Throwing the book at Naomi) Read.

NAOMI: (Opening the book reluctantly) Once upon a time, there were three bears.

GRETCHEN: Go on.

NAOMI: There was a Papa Bear.

GRETCHEN: No single parent household? No out of wedlock bear? No deadbeat Black bear dad?

NAOMI: What do you want me to say?

GRETCHEN: Keep reading.

NAOMI: A Mama Bear, and a Baby Bear. One day Mama Bear made some hot porridge.

GRETCHEN: Stop. Skip to the part where they leave the cottage.

NAOMI: I have to read a little bit more about the porridge for that part to make sense.

GRETCHEN: Do it.

NAOMI: The porridge was very hot. So the three bears went for a walk until it got cool.

GRETCHEN: I've heard enough. (Pulling down books from shelves and throwing them) Did you read anything about who owned the cottage?

NAOMI: No, it's assumed.

GRETCHEN: What's assumed?

NAOMI: I don't want to say things that will get you angry. I'm not responsible for this story.

GRETCHEN: What's assumed?

NAOMI: That the bear family lives in government subsidized public housing.

(Gretchen snatches the book and rips it up.)

NAOMI: Hey. That book can't be replaced.

GRETCHEN: The bears owned their own home. Papa Bear worked for years with a European traveling circus until he had enough people dollars to buy the cottage free and clear. Because (Indicating that Naomi should finish the sentence)

NAOMI: Because the interest rates were too high?

GRETCHEN: You dumb Brunette.

NAOMI: Because he couldn't decide between a fifteen year rate adjustable mortgage with a balloon payment in the end or a thirty-year fixed? (Pause) Maybe his income wasn't enough to qualify him for a loan?

GRETCHEN: Because, Blacks couldn't get mortgages. They were redlined.

GRETCHEN: Papa Bear and Mama Bear had a tradition of walking through the forest before dinner. It was one of the activities they treasured as a family before winter hibernation. While they were gone, a Blonde broke into their home. She ate all Baby Bear's food. She broke Baby Bear's chair. She slept in Baby Bear's bed. When the bears returned home, they discovered Goldilocks in the bedroom. She woke up, ran out of the cottage, and into the town. She told everyone she was fearful for her life. Fearful that Papa Bear was going to rape her. The Blondes and the Brunettes banded together with torches. They burned a bear effigy on the front lawn. They set the cottage on fire. They lynched Papa Bear, and skinned him alive. Mama Bear, and Baby Bear became separated as they ran through the forest. Mama Bear died from starvation. Exotic animal pet owners eventually enslaved baby Bear.

NAOMI: You can't change history because you don't like it.

GRETCHEN: All about perspective Naomi. *The Three Bears* was written in a way that serves Blonde and Brunette animals. This way the atrocities don't have to be acknowledged. And by the way, the Mama Bear was making risotto. They were descendants from bears in the Italian Swiss Alps.

NAOMI: If your story retelling is true, I'm sorry. But it has nothing to do with me. I'm not responsible for actions that weren't mine.

GRETCHEN: You shouldn't be blamed, right?

NAOMI: Right. Has nothing to do with me.

GRETCHEN: Being a Brunette, walking through the woods, surrounds you with entitlement. You didn't earn it. You inherited it from your ancestors who were only concerned about themselves.

NAOMI: I'm not responsible and I refuse to bow down to you or any Black and grovel because I'm Brunette. I'm not ashamed of who I am. I'm not ashamed of being Brunette.

GRETCHEN: Your silence makes you filled with blame. Your silent refusal to acknowledge that being the person you are automatically gives you privileges whether you choose to use them deliberately of not. (Pause) You can't imagine my life Naomi. You'll never have the opportunity to walk in my paws. Since you can't, try to do something for yourself, and for me. Step out of your comfort zone and watch the world like a movie. Who's on top? Who rules? Who do you want to be? You don't want to be Black. Who hurts? Who dies with despair?

NAOMI: I contribute to the World Wild Life Fund, The Catskill Mountain Nature Society, The Bronx Zoo (Pause) Maybe I'll rethink that donation. Clayton and I aren't here to bother you. You are bothering us.

GRETCHEN: Do you want to know my name?

NAOMI: You're my captor. You're holding me against my will. I don't need to know your name.

GRETCHEN: If you don't know my name, you don't have to acknowledge that we are both animals. If you don't acknowledge that I'm an animal you don't have to consider that I have the same needs, the same emotions, the same suffering as you. (Pause) My name is Gretchen.

NAOMI: I would like to say, "Nice to meet you." But it's not.

GRETCHEN: I know. I heard you. "I DON'T WANT TO LIVE NEAR BLACKS."

NAOMI: That statement was spoken to my husband and it was private.

GRETCHEN: Speciesism in private is okay?

NAOMI: I'm not a speciest. I was only expressing my preference. I want to live with my own kind. I have that right.

GRETCHEN: There's no pleasure in my tormenting you.

NAOMI: Yes, there is.

GRETCHEN: Maybe a little. (Pause) How does it feel to be dominated, without control over your own life? (Pause) Segregation worked for most Blacks historically. Everyone wants to own their own life. Pursue one's own happiness. That house on the hill is filthy. It's full of garbage, and old bathroom fixtures. It stinks. I wouldn't be surprised if there are dead bodies cemented in the walls that are still standing.

NAOMI: The sheriff only found one of the bodies from the Catskills serial killer.

GRETCHEN: Stay on topic Naomi. Blacks in this region are desperately looking for places to hibernate. All of our dens were collapsed or bulldozed over when the construction for the Glamour Spa Camps started.

NAOMI: I'm so sorry.

GRETCHEN: You voted for rezoning and against maintaining sanctuary land.

NAOMI: For the lower taxes.

GRETCHEN: Only concerned about consequences for yourself.

NAOMI: I don't think so. (Pause) Maybe. Maybe not.

GRETCHEN: Save it for the believers in liberals.

NAOMI: (Looking at the snow) Alice showed me a photograph of your cubs. Will you tell me about them?

GRETCHEN: Junior was gathering apples for our food binge before hibernation.

NAOMI: My apple… (Pause) Never mind.

GRETCHEN: Junior is a sweet, hard-working cub. Sally, she was the feisty one in the litter.

She's dead. The hunting season was expanded to reduce our population. Sally was caught up in it. The sheriff has sent her fur for processing by now.

NAOMI: I was pregnant once. Clayton and I didn't think it was the right time for a family. I was working on tenure. He was frequently traveling.

GRETCHEN: I don't want to hear your entitled female Brunette hard luck stories. How would you like to live without choice? It's the season, June or July. Mate. Get pregnant. Give birth. I was three years old when I was pregnant. Elliot claimed me. Copulation. And then he was off chasing as many females as he could before he got caught preying on underage females. If I had a choice, I would have waited until I was five years old. I was healthy, active, and able to climb the tallest pine trees. I would have chosen to wait. If a Black is healthy and able to avoid people predators, there could be a good life, up to eighteen years old. That was my plan. You're almost eighteen years old, right?

NAOMI: Yeah, close to.

GRETCHEN: I'm tired of these games. You're boring me with your ignorance, with your fake liberal concern. We'll play the real game now: Black Roulette. (Loads the gun with one bullet and then revolves the chamber)

NAOMI: Maybe I can help you. No one is going to look in that abandoned house. It's been that way for years. Alice is crazy. No one will listen to her rambling about you and your family.

GRETCHEN: You did.

NAOMI: You said yourself that I was a dumb Brunette. (Pause) We have plenty of food. I can give you packages of instant porridge.

GRETCHEN: Haven't you been listening? We eat risotto! (Pause) (Examining handgun) Recognize this gun?

NAOMI: You're scaring me. Please stop.

GRETCHEN: Of course you don't recognize it. Your husband, whom I have some respect for, has been keeping this hidden from you. He never thought he would have to use it. So easy for me to take it and return it when I was finished.

NAOMI: You were terrorizing other neighbors.

GRETCHEN: I had the trigger customized to accommodate my paw grip. (Pause) Ask me?

NAOMI: I don't know how to answer you. Everything is confused when you talk.

GRETCHEN: Ask me what I want?

NAOMI: What do you want?

GRETCHEN: Speak to me like I'm an animal like you who deserves kindness and consideration, and respect.

NAOMI: What do you want from me, Gretchen?

GRETCHEN: I want you to be a good neighbor. I'm going to stay here and torment you until you convince me that you can be. And my second amendment rights are helping me do that.

NAOMI: Second amendment? The constitution has to do with people.

GRETCHEN: Your founding fathers got it wrong. They got the words right but they couldn't interpret the constitution without a speciest perspective. That placed them on the wrong side of history with all except the second amendment. Their interpretation of the constitution with an unwritten lens of prejudice and discrimination on the basis of species helped them build their glory on the backs of others. Except the second amendment, bear arms.

NAOMI: Bear arms has to do with people and guns.

GRETCHEN: Bears have to right to carry guns. And I've never had to exercise that right Naomi. I've never been an aggressor. I kill for food. I avoid mixing. Comingling…well frankly I don't like your kind.

(Revolving the gun chamber.)

But I'm crazy Black now. I can't live with the constant threat of losing my home, offspring, and my own life. (Revolving the gun chamber) One of us has to die. (Revolving the gun chamber)

NAOMI: I can't change anything that's happened.

(Gretchen revolves the gun chamber.)

You don't want to die Gretchen. What about Junior?

GRETCHEN: I won't wait passively for my only cub to be killed. A cub should never die before his mother. (Revolving the gun chamber) It's going to happen. They're killing unarmed Blacks for sport. I wake up each morning wondering if, "This will be the day that I'm killed, or…" (Revolving the gun chamber) Is it crazy to want to live my own life and be free? (Revolving the gun chamber)

NAOMI: I can't change people animals.

GRETCHEN: (Revolving the gun chamber) Ask me what I want.

NAOMI: Please leave me alone.

GRETCHEN: Ask me what I want.

NAOMI: What do you want, Gretchen?

GRETCHEN: I want you to be a good neighbor.

NAOMI: I'll do anything.

GRETCHEN: (Putting the revolver down) I don't want you to do anything. I want you to be a good neighbor. (Grabbing and holding Naomi so she is unable to move) I don't like guns. I like to fight real female style if I have to. I maul my enemy to death. You're close enough for me to crush your limbs and make tracks in your face so Clayton won't recognize you. Maybe he would recognize your hind parts.

NAOMI: Don't do it, please. I want to live.

GRETCHEN: How does it feel to beg for your life? Wasn't it Robert Frost who said, "Fences make good neighbors?" We have a fence that separates us. My cub and I will stay on our side of the fence in the filthy house. You stay on your side. We'll have a good place to hibernate. It's identified Native American sacred ground. Hunters will go elsewhere.

NAOMI: I understand.

GRETCHEN: Alice is certifiably crazy. If you tell her the house is haunted, maybe... Just take care of it. Can you do that Naomi?

NAOMI: Yes.

GRETCHEN: (Releasing Naomi's arms) Good. I feel better. For some reason, I believe you. (Pause) One concession. We agree to share the apple tree. Blacks believe the gifts of the land are for sharing. The food on the land is getting sparser. It's very hard to find good patches of wild berries. We can't roam far anymore. Share the apples with us. Agree that we're not stealing.

NAOMI: Yes. I'm sorry about all of this.

GRETCHEN: I don't need you to be sorry. I need you to be real. I don't need you to like Blacks. Make this personal. About your family and my family. Don't hide behind a banner. Accept being neighbors. Peaceful coexistence. (Hands the gun to Naomi) Needs to go back under the floorboards before Clayton comes home. Our secret.

NAOMI: (Places the gun on a table near the door) I want to give you packets of instant porridge.

GRETCHEN: That's nice of you, considering I was about to slash your face. (Pause) In times like these, I'm not turning down food. Thank you. I'll check on Junior, and I'll be back.

(Exit Gretchen. Naomi looks for instant porridge. Enter Bystander.)

BYSTANDER: Hello.

(Enter Clayton. He picks up the gun and shoots the Bystander in the back.)

BYSTANDER: (Collapsing) I needed directions to town.

CLAYTON: (Dropping gun) I saw a BEAR.

(Lights Out)

End of Play

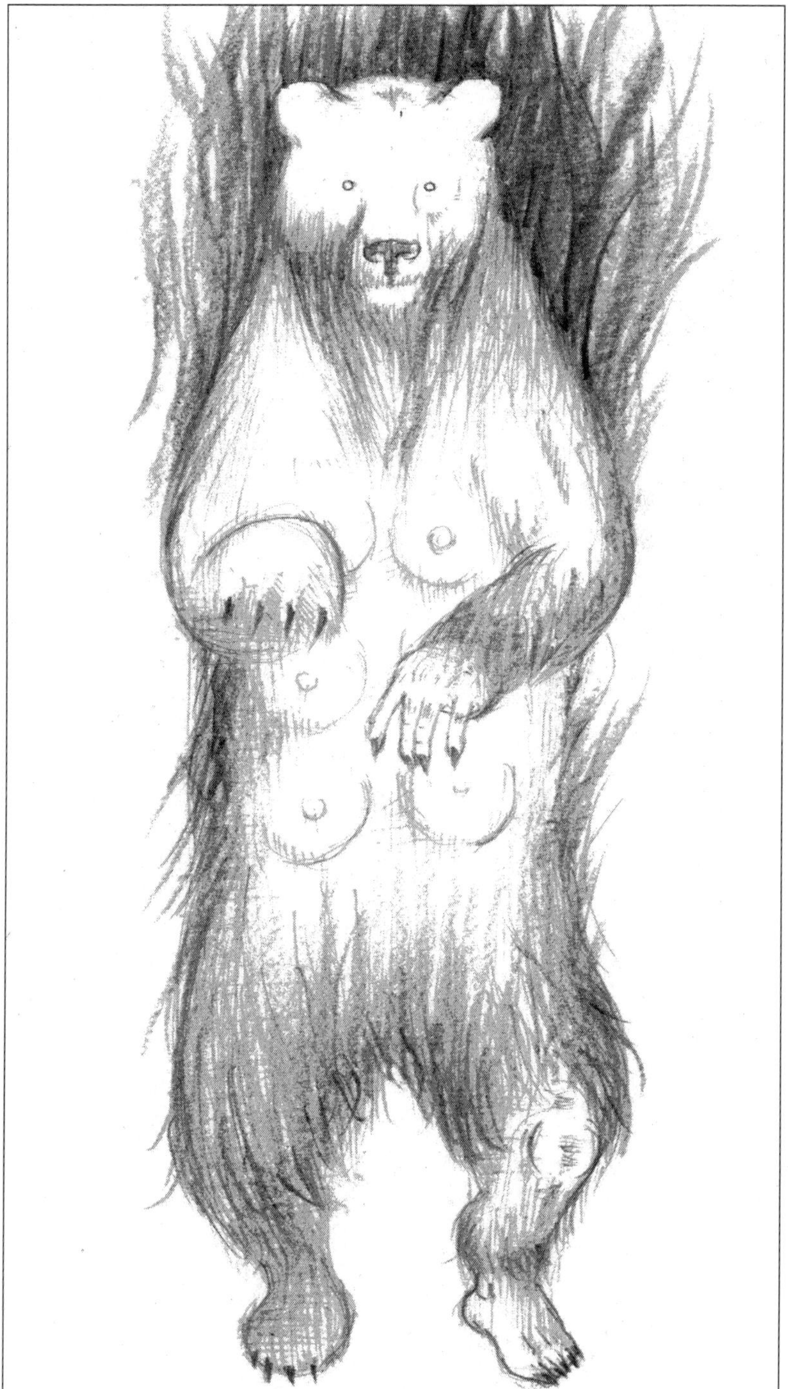

May the dead and the undead rest in peace.

White Epilogue

Playwright Cesi Davidson's epigraph, which appears after the last play in her new anthology, reads "May the dead and the undead rest in peace." Poignant. Why does she use the word "undead" and not the "living"? Who is she speaking about when she uses the words "dead" and "undead"? Why should the undead rest in peace? Central to her anthology of plays is systemic racism and how it manifests within Black lives. Davidson's brilliant stories are powerful in that the Black characters, while riddled within a world of racist ideologies, are powerful, resilient, and even joyful in navigating the world on the shoulders of their ancestors.

If we identify as White in American society, we must acknowledge that our privileged experiences have been infused with our own racism. And as long as White racist systems of oppression exist, we will never be liberated from a system that harms Black Americans. Since racism steals and destroys our humanity, those of us still living are all members of the "undead." Humanity can't rest in peace until racist systems, institutions, and individual discrimination are dismantled. Humanity must do more to become antiracist. We must want to live in a world liberated from racism. We must want to live in a world where Black Americans are embraced and live in their full humanity. Davidson's work challenges the undead to rest in peace through actively and unapologetically engaging in the liberation of humanity.

Examples of human liberation and dignity abound in her storytelling. In her play *Shut the Door*, we witness doors that won't open, and the gatekeepers who keep them shut; yet we also read about her empowered characters: "We're the pauses between words. We're the uncluttered, uncomplicated thoughts that connect one earth dweller to another." Davidson's play *Sambomammiejockey* provides powerful examples of the ways in which racism systemically spews its poison in every aspect of American life: criminal justice, higher education, employment, and housing. In addition, racism infiltrates intersecting social identities of race, class, socioeconomic status, and sexual orientation. Davidson's character Malcolm X, warns, "America won't even admit that the wound is there." If White America doesn't admit the wound is there are we the "undead" Davidson calls out in her epigraph? We certainly can't rest in peace unless we admit the wounds of racism are real and restorative justice begins to heal those we have harmed.

In her play *Adagio*, a young Black protagonist Natasha rises up in voice and intention by insisting that her White teacher listen and not impose her worldview. In *Beullah Rising*, through role reversal, Black and White characters learn empathy and humility through experiences with the use and abuse of power. The question of what will you do with your Whiteness, your privilege and power, is centered in Davidson's *Tidy Black Green Simians*. The weaponizing of Whiteness on unarmed Black men resonates in Davidson's final play *Filthy Black Neighbors*.

In bringing about transformative change we must immerse ourselves in the experiences of those who are prevented from living their full humanity, open the doors, intentionally practice humility and empathy, use our White privilege to be the best neighbors we can be—only then may we all rest in peace on earth and beyond.

Tobie S. Stein, PhD
Professor Emerita, Brooklyn College
Author: Racial and Ethnic Diversity in the Performing Arts Workforce (Routledge 2020); Leadership in the Performing Arts (Allworth 2016)

Black Epilogue

Without inner change, there can be no outer change;
without collective change, no change matters.
Rev. Angel Kyodo Williams

Cesi Davidson's compelling, challenging collection of stories in *America Acirema* is at once an indictment of the messy generational progeny of America's original sin of slavery and a call-to-action for remedy. She does so with a wickedly vivid imagination and smart, bodacious theatricality. With a nod to Shakespeare's *Hamlet*, these stories are unapologetic, rub-your-nose-in-it, audacious "abstract and brief chronicles of our time." Beware, the faint of heart and thin-skinned, "here be dragons."

Davidson's canvas excavates explosive stereotypes and radioactive hot button "isms" (*Whizz* and *Pretty*). She reveals what Black trauma looks, feels, and sounds like underneath the knee of white supremacist behavior on its neck, what it is to resist, cope with, internalize, and adapt to life without control, with truncated choices. Her language and imagery, at times graphic and difficult to take (*Pee*), extends from the rough, distorting treatment Black people have encountered historically in New World America and is thus aptly flavored with surreal, absurdist, satiric, wryly humorous, and anarchic flourishes. This is life through a Black looking glass.

She investigates America's Gordian knot of racial and relational history with a sensitive ear for authentic Black speech (*Hole*), authentic contemporary youthful babble (*Eric and Terisa: Deconstructed*), and inventive theatrical daring anthropomorphized bears in *Filthy Black Neighbors* ; dream/memory-scapes in *brother & sister Chronicles;* live bodies walking out of televised DVDs in *Eric and Terisa: Deconstructed.*

Her Afrocentric-rooted lens captures recognizable universalities: sibling tensions in *brother & sister Chronicles*, the ache of missed opportunities in the fable-like *Hole*, love's many faces and facets and the pulse of trending social-psychological phenomena in *Eric and Terisa: Deconstructed.* All visitors are welcome to this world-view.

Plays are meant to be staged, but *America Acirema* is also a great read as dramatic literature. Some of the stories would make pithy short films. Davidson's perceptive understanding of life's dicey realities urges courageous truth-seekers, most particularly White people willing to lean into disruptive discomfort, to do the work of alchemizing their inner vision as a first, essential step to becoming a "good neighbor" (*Filthy Black Neighbors*) and by extension, a good citizen in a re-constructed "now" where broken people can be healed.

Such a rebirth requires the naming of and killing off of the root causes of the malaise. Some things need to die in order to create a void into which new life, new energies, new paradigms of living can be poured. Half measures of gradualism, finding common ground, meeting in the middle will not suffice. These stories are thrown gauntlets that summon us to effect inner revolutions of thinking, of believing, of doing. Davidson demands the kind of agency that Marcel Proust wrote in 1923 was "the only true voyage of discovery" in *La Prisonnière*, volume five of his *Remembrance of Things Past* (or *In Search of Lost Time*): "to possess other eyes, to behold the universe through the eyes of another, of a hundred others, to behold the hundred universes that each of them beholds, that each of them is."

And with new eyes, do better.

How fitting, then, that Davidson is a dramatist, for the ancient Greek root word for theater is theatron: the seeing place.

Benny Sato Ambush
Professional Theatrical Stage Director, Educator, Producer
November 2020

Afterword

Dwennimmen

The Adinkra symbol borrowed from the Akan people of West Africa is pictured in the headers of this book.

It illustrates humility and strength with its
representation of two rams butting heads.

America cannot separate itself from its history.

How can Americans learn from our history and position ourselves in the world with a global sensibility?

We are flawed.

We don't always share.

We need continued truth and reconciliation.

We are capable of expressing love.

We are capable of change.

With humility, we can recognize our ability to change for the better.

Here lies our strength.

Acknowledgments

I followed my ancestors to Harlem, New York City. It was in this community that I experienced the collective voices that evolved into the characters of the plays in this book. New York City Public Library managers Victor Simmons (Countee Cullen Library) and Junelle Carter Bowman (George Bruce Library) provided the public spaces for theatrical readings of the work. *Eric and Terisa: Deconstructed* appeared at the prestigious National Black Theatre as part of their Keep Soul Alive program.

Ideacoil, Jacob Restaurant, Mozel Watson Wines, and Sister's Uptown Bookstore, cornerstones of community support in Harlem, generously contributed to artist and audience support. Talented artists helped me lift the work from page to stage. Actors who were members of Actors Equity Association appeared courtesy of that organization. This book wouldn't have been possible without the guidance of Celeste Rita Baker. Kath Wilham worked tirelessly on the editing of this book. Without her dedicated efforts this work wouldn't have been possible. Daniel Sklar and Zachary Sklar, my friends and mentors provided feedback on the manuscript. Tom and Timmi Duchamp of Aqueduct Press provided guidance and encouragement as I entered the world of independent publishing. To all, I'm grateful.

The Artists

Miriam Agwai, Lauren Annunziata, Marie Barrientos, Gregory Bastien, Lucia Bellini, Sara Berg, Collin Biddle, Husani Blaze, Paul Bolger, Cate Bottiglione, Amara Brady, Sadrina Burney, Trevania Campbell, Amanda Cannon, Elaine Davis, Charles Duke, Ariel Dupas, Pierre Edouard, Charles Everett, Jose Febus, Michael Flood, Xavier Galva, Hope Garland, Tristan Halstead, Lorna Haughton, Denise Allesandra Hurd, Kene Holliday, Mateo Hurtado, Mary Hodges, Ralph Emerson John, Sandra Kazan, Sarah Kiefer, Ariel

Kim, Starr Kirkland, Justin Lord, Rachel Lu, Shereen Macklin, Isreal Mc Kinney Scott, Bruce Miller, Marie Elena O'Brien, Caitlin Perez, Reynaldo Piniella, Alex Purcel, Doris Koya Prester, Joanna Rhinehart, Melissa Riker, Clea Rivera, Judith Roberts, Nzingtha Smith, Illana Stein, Martha Steketee, LeVera Sutton, Rosita Timm, and Jak Watson.

My family inspires me, and elevates my voice.

Author Biography

Cesi Davidson is an American playwright. Her sensibility as a writer grows from a feminine life with African heritage. After earning a doctoral degree in the Speech, Language, Hearing Sciences and a flourishing career as a speech language pathologist, she expanded her reach into dramatic writing. She reimagined her experiences to create compelling stories that give voice to her witness of human suffering and triumphs. Periods of spiritual introspection resulted in the writing of hundreds of plays that demonstrate a broad range, fearless creativity, and cultural responsiveness. The core of her science and art is communication. She writes to encourage thoughtful reflection, understanding, and compassionate conversation from a moral focus that we are one human family. Her plays are created for entertaining reads and vibrant theatrical events for the stage. America Acirema is a love song. This fourth collection of stage plays provides glimpses into the complexities of American life through realistic fictitious characters. Dr. Davidson's books are available through Aqueduct Press and Articulation NY LLC. When she isn't writing and producing plays Cesi enjoys the company of family, friends, and nature.